at t
time
ated his words. "In my dreams it is perfect between
us. You are perfect in my dreams." He gave her another soft wet kiss.

"Want me to describe what I see?" he whispered,
his lips nibbling at hers.

She nodded, unable to speak.

"I see you, a long stretch of smooth golden brown
skin attached to a body that I'd just finished exploring completely. Your hair is wild around your head,
and those strong legs of yours are wrapped around
me. I love your legs," he said, taking her lips in another wet, open-mouthed kiss. "I see your arms holding me in place…your head is always thrown back
in my dreams, my name always on your lips, encouraging, then demanding, showing me just how you
like it, how you…like…me," he said slowly, tying
her mind up in knots with his image of her, her body
pure fluid now.

He took her lips again, this time in a bruising
kiss, mouth open as her tongue welcomed him in.
He pulled back, watched her from beneath lowered
lashes, his breath a pant, as she tried to catch her
breath.

—◠—

"I want you," he whispered, her skin tingling
the sound of his words. "I've seen us a thousand
times." A shift of his hips inward into hers punctu

Lights Out

Ruthie Robinson

Genesis Press, Inc.

INDIGO LOVE SPECTRUM

An imprint of Genesis Press, Inc.
Publishing Company

Genesis Press, Inc.
P.O. Box 101
Columbus, MS 39703

All characters in this book have no existence outside the imagination of the author and have no relation whatsoever to anyone bearing the same name or names. They are not even distantly inspired by any individual known or unknown to the author and all incidents are pure invention.

ISBN-13: 978-1-58571445-2
ISBN-10: 1-58571-445-3
Manufactured in the United States of America

First Edition

Visit us at www.genesis-press.com
or call at 1-888-Indigo-1-4-0

Dedication

To my family: Ronnie, my first husband of 23 glorious years. My daughter, Kennedy, who reminds me all too often that I'm not as important as I think I am. And to my son, Miles, who cringes at the start of yet another book. Love you all!

Acknowledgements

Continuous thanks to Lisa, Andrea, Gwendy Gail, Linda, Cassie, and Kathy Lesko, for your unwavering support and encouragement. A special thank-you to Earline and Telisa for your emergency response, experience and expertise.

Chapter 1

Joe pulled into the parking lot of Lights Out Coffee in search of his morning cup of *get your ass in gear*. He stopped for coffee most mornings with no preference for any place in particular; they were all interchangeable to him. Yesterday had been his first time here. It was conveniently close to both his home and his nephew's school, and he could work from almost anywhere.

He entered the shop. The line was long, as it had been yesterday. This must be a popular place. He walked over to take his place at the end of the line, giving a nod to the guy who stood in front of him—some type of rent-a-cop.

He scanned the shop while he waited. It was new, and had been open about a month, maybe. He couldn't remember exactly how long, but remembered passing a huge sign advertising the grand opening. He sort of liked the look of it, large and roomy with an abundance of tables and soft, cushiony chairs; he hated the hard kind. It offered Wi-Fi and a plethora of outlets near most of the tables.

He even liked the obnoxious color scheme of purple, blue, and apple green, mixed in somehow with a boxing theme. Go figure how they'd come up with that pairing. Posters of boxing greats adorned the walls

along with famous pieces of boxing memorabilia encased in glass. He didn't know if they were the real
thing or fakes, but they were tastefully done, at any
rate. Small boxing gloves in the same loud colors
adorned the black polo shirts and aprons of the employees.

He'd worked from here yesterday morning. The
music was not too loud—he'd been able to hear himself think. His eyes roamed over the employees on
duty today. There were two of them this morning: the
same older woman he'd seen yesterday making the
drinks and a tall African-American woman with light
brown skin and lots of curly hair, like the afros of old.
Hers was a little curlier, framing her face, a headband
holding it back from her eyes.

She was average in looks, nothing to write home
about, a six on a ten-point scale, but scoring higher
when she smiled. She was laughing now. Her full lips
glistened. Her eyes sparkled. Her body was her best
asset hands down, at least what he could see of it. She
appeared athletic, always his preference, and tall.

—∿—

Piper Renee Knight knew how to work her customers, male or female, and get them in and out quickly.
She knew which questions to ask to find that sweet
spot where intake met up with desire and need. Knew
what it took to get you off to a good start in the morning, feeling oh so good and energized; if you needed
an afternoon quickie or a late night snack, she was

ready and more than able to provide assistance there, too. She could even get you to talk and smile during the experience…the coffee experience, that was. She'd been serving her customers successfully at her first Lights Out Coffee location, her baby, for the last two years.

It was seven in the a.m. and her shop was filled with people, all standing in line waiting their turn in their rush to get the fuel that made their engines purr. They had places to go, people to see, jobs to get to, and she was a vital aid in their quest. Sometimes it was easy-peesy, and other times as difficult as herding cats. Today, it was working like a dream.

"White chocolate mocha," Piper said to the woman who'd stood now in front of the line. She hadn't learned all of the regulars by name at this location yet, just knew them by their drink orders, but it would only be a matter of time before she did. White chocolate mocha was a plump sista with long flowing locks. She was a regular in that she came in at least once a week, maybe twice.

Piper plucked a cup from her stack and wrote WC on it, passing it off to the barista, fancy name for mixer of coffee-like drinks, responsible this morning for preparing the complicated drinks orders while she ran the register, handed out pastries, and poured the more simple drinks.

This morning she was joined on the stage by hardworking and dependable barista Estelle, not her usual college student employee. Estelle was in her mid forties with kids in high school, and working at Lights

Out Coffee supplied her with fun money, coffee, and entertainment.

Standing behind WC was low fat latte with two sweeteners, normal order for red-headed Elle of the WMW (watch my weight club). She plucked another cup from her stack, noted the order, took Elle's card, ran it through the register, and handed her the slip for a signature. Piper felt satisfied as she watched the woman move on down the line.

Next on deck was "Give it to me black" Hugo, a short, white, slightly balding guy who worked nights. If he was pulling a double, it was "Give it to me black with three shots of espresso."

"Getting off from work?" she asked, giving him the once-over, taking in his rumpled security guard uniform, fake gun in the holster by his side.

"Nope, gotta get back. Someone called in sick," he said, grimacing.

"So it's tall, black, and potent?" she asked, drawing out the word potent, smiling at him.

"You got it," he said, handing a five-dollar bill over to her. "So you've been keeping yourself busy, with the two shops and all?"

"Yep, it's been wicked crazy since this one opened, but I'm managing. I've been alternating daily between the two," she said, handing him his change.

"I miss not seeing you every day," he said, giving her a wink.

"Not as much as I miss you," she said, winking right back and adding an air kiss. He smiled, used to this over-the-top flirting from her.

Hugo was one of her die-hard regulars, had been coming in for coffee since her first shop opened two years ago. When she'd opened this second location, he'd switched—said it was closer to his job. She could set her watch by him. She took his travel cup, which was twice the size of any of the cups she offered. Since he was a very good customer she filled it full to the brim, added three shots of espresso, screwed the lid on, and handed it over to him.

"See you around."

"You bet," he said, walking away.

Joe stood before her now and he watched her take him in. She seemed startled for a second, a reaction not uncommon for him. He watched her eyes quickly scan his body, her perusal smooth and slick.

Her smile widened, her eyes gleamed. "You can have whatever you want this morning," she said, drawing out her words, invitation in her eyes. He wasn't sure if she was serious or not.

"I'd like a bagel and a large coffee, black," he replied.

"I'm disappointed in you," she said, pointing her finger at him, her full, shiny lips turned downward. "Here I had you pegged for the oatmeal kind of man. It's a shame really, 'cause the oatmeal here is extraordinary, especially when heated, sweet…filling…all that melted brown sugar sliding over your tongue…and so good for you," she offered, leaning toward him, in the old black and white movie vamp way.

5

He chuckled, "All that, huh? Hard to pass up, but probably more than I could handle," he said, smiling now. She was not at all what he'd expected.

"I know, right? Guess you'd better stick with your bagel and coffee. There's safety there."

He smiled, taking in the flush on her face, the smattering of freckles resting on her cheeks, lips glossy and parted as she leaned into him, with her finger crooked and beckoning him closer. He leaned in. Just because. Her finger pushed the strands of hair that blocked his ear from her view, tucking them behind it, before she put her mouth near his lobe, like she'd known him forever. His eyes moved to the v of her polo shirt, taking in two pert breasts, while breathing in her fresh floral scent.

"Bet you…like…it…. warm," she whispered, eyes peeking at him beneath slightly lowered lashes, when he'd turned his face to hers, like they were the only ones in the shop.

"Excuse me?" he replied, at a loss for words.

"The bagel, you wanted it warmed, right?" The eyes staring into his were fiendish now, and full of humor as she pulled back from him, turned her back, and stuck a coffee cup under the dispenser. He caught her laughter.

He chuckled in surprise, looking around, hoping he didn't have too many witnesses to being caught that far off his game. He caught the older woman making drinks smiling at him, as if saying "she put one over on you." He smiled back sheepishly.

"Here's your coffee. I'll bring the bagel over to you in a sec," Piper said, giving him a wink. He took his change from her hand and put a dollar into the tip jar.

"Thanks," she said, following him as he walked away. God, he was a beauty, patting herself on the back—commending herself for her excellent display of confidence. She'd played it off well. He hadn't a clue what a shock to her system he'd been. Her eyes followed him to a table near the front.

Eye candy, indeed. A too-pretty face, this shy of being a girl; his teeth were a little bit crooked; his hair long and blond; steely grey eyes; and a body that was meant to be treasured, worshipped, loved. Lucky the female who had the rights to it. Piper glanced over at Estelle, who'd caught her eye and fanned her face, causing Piper to laugh.

She sighed, her eyes darting back over to him again as he'd taken a seat, now looking over his BlackBerry. Middleweight, the nickname she'd internally given him just then, was one fine man. He was about six feet to her five feet, six inches, and about 160 pounds of firm flesh. Nice guns sat snug and visible in the short sleeves of his shirt. Trim upper body, slim waist, and a firm and fine ass.

She'd spent enough time in her dad's boxing gyms growing up, so she had a working knowledge of weight, anatomy, and physiology and how it came together to lovingly create the perfect male specimen for the sweet science that was boxing.

"I don't know what I want," were the words that spilled from her next customer's mouth, pulling her from her thoughts. This was her least favorite request. It put a halt to a moving line faster than a speeding bullet.

One collective sigh rose from those in line behind this woman. They, too, knew the type well. One customer rolled her eyes and checked her watch. No worries today, Piper wanted to tell them, they had her in charge, kicking ass and moving the line. They would not be delayed, not on her watch.

"I'm watching my weight," the woman continued.

"Yes," Piper said. Of course she was, weren't they all. "I'd bet you'd like a low-fat latte. We offer either coffee- or tea-based. They're mostly milk—skim for you, of course—and a shot of coffee, tea, or flavoring if you'd like," Piper said, hoping to be helpful. She knew this little-ole-helpless-me type.

"Okay, I'll try the coffee version."

"Would you like the vanilla or another flavoring— the vanilla can be sugar free?"

"Vanilla will work, I think," she said, twirling her hair around her fingers.

Piper, a smile in place, rang up her order. "Thank you," she said and watched the woman move off to wait for her drink. She smiled at her next customer, another regular. Two shots, iced coffee, room for cream. She was back in her groove.

—⁂—

Joe checked his BlackBerry, mind still at the counter with her, surprised and interested. She'd caught him off-guard. He couldn't remember the last time that had happened to him. He chuckled again, eyes roaming over his list of things to do today.

He'd watched her as he'd waited his turn. She'd been part drill sergeant and part tease. He took another sip from his cup, watching as she'd smoothly moved the girl who'd hadn't known what she wanted forward in line. Inwardly, he smiled at her efficiency before going back to his review of e-mails.

"Here you go," she said, a few minutes later, setting his bagel on the table in front of him. She stood near his shoulder, her smile sexy, hands on very curvy hips, long legs encased in low-riding skinny jeans. He loved low-riding jeans on women. The jeans were tucked into black Ropers.

"Thanks," he said, his eyes finding hers, looking up into her face, roaming over her features—golden brown skin, soft brown eyes, full lips. He loved her hair, soft, curly, and everywhere. His eyes traveled downward, taking in the Lights Out logo on her shirt that covered the two chirpy breasts from earlier. He liked those two tremendously.

"So, Middleweight, is this your first time here?" Her words brought his attention back to her face.

"Middleweight?"

"You get the boxing theme, right?" she asked, her eyes moving around the shop, hands doing that Vanna White thing.

"Yep."

"I know the sport a little. What's your weight?"

"Why?"

"Your weight?" she asked again, her head tilted to the side, her hands went to her hips, all sass and strength, her smile put upon..

"About 160 pounds."

She looked him over, walked around his chair, head still tilted to the side, assessing.

"You're what, about six feet?"

"Yes."

"If you were a boxer, middleweight would be your fighting class," she said.

"Is that so?"

"Yes, that's so," she said mimicking him, continuing to walk around his chair, giving him the once-over, same sass, eyes twinkling now.

"You fight a lot?" he asked.

"It depends on what kind of fighting you're talking about," she said, moving her eyebrows up and down. He laughed.

"I'm more of the soccer kind of guy," he said, smiling.

She nodded. "But you could really work some boxers, and not the human kind, either. I bet they're killer on you," she said, looking him over again, before she smiled and then laughed.

He joined in. "We could see for ourselves if you wanted too," he said. His eyes turned smoky.

"Maybe. Without boxers has its possibilities, too," she said, clearly enjoying herself.

"You and your mouth," he said.

"What about it," she said, slowly, drawing out the words, as she leaned over him.

She has this vixen thing down pat, he thought. "Is this you all the time?" he asked.

"What? Charming, sexy, sharp of wit and quick of tongue?"

He laughed again.

"Yes, it's me, most times. Here, anyway," she said, smiling again, stepping away from him. He chuckled, eyes changing again.

"Cut it out," she said.

"Cut what out?"

"Smoldering," she said, pointing to his eyes.

He laughed outright at that. "Smoldering, huh?"

"So back to my original question. Is this your first time here?" she asked.

"Nope, stopped by yesterday, but you weren't here. I would have remembered," he said.

"I'm here every other day," she replied, in case he was interested.

He nodded.

"My line is backing up, and we can't have that," she said, looking toward her counter. "Nice meeting you, Middleweight. Hope to see you again," she said, suddenly shy now.

He was surprised to see it there concealed beneath her words, visible for just a second. She turned and headed back over to the counter.

Really, really nice body, he thought. The back view matched its front—her ass was round, curvy, and firm in those low-riding jeans. He watched as she made her way back to the counter, stopping to pick up a discarded coffee cup from a now-vacant table.

—◊◊◊—

Second week in May

It was late evening. Joe pulled up to the front of a yellow two-story home and parked. Home Away From Home, an after-school and summer care program, started two years ago by Reye Jackson—correction, Reye Stuart now. Why was that so hard to remember?

He was pushing it, behind schedule again. He'd gotten tied up with a customer and was running late to pick up Shane, his nephew. He'd been running late a lot more lately, the result of changes at work earlier this year, a more demanding assignment, and much larger territory. He was still working on how to manage it, along with Shane's schedule.

Shane rushed through the front door, backpack thrown over his shoulder, followed by Reye, who walked up and stood behind Shane. Both were in front of him now, both with smiles on their lips.

"Uncle Joe, Reye and I been working on my shooting. Maybe I can play forward this year for the team," he said.

"Hey, Joe. He's getting to be quite the soccer player," she said, ruffling Shane's hair, before looking at Joe again and smiling.

"He and I have been working at it, too, when we have time. Less so since this new promotion. Sorry I ran late," Joe said, smiling his apology.

"No worries. Did any of those names I gave you work as a back-up plan?" she asked.

"Nope. Called all of them. Most wanted more hours. I just need someone to pick up Shane from school, take him home, make sure he gets his homework, and eats dinner. I'll keep looking," he said.

"Let me know if I can help," she said, her phone ringing. "Let me catch this," she said, giving Joe a smile. "Bye, you guys. See you tomorrow, Shane."

"You ready?" Joe asked, looking down at his nephew.

"Been ready, stay ready, born ready," he said, smiling at his uncle. "I'm hungry," he added, walking down the sidewalk to the car.

"What do you want for dinner?"

"Tacos," he said.

"Sounds good, buddy. We'll pick up something on the way home," Joe said, getting in the car, putting on his seat belt, and waiting for Shane to do the same.

"What did you guys do today?" he asked, pulling away from the curb.

Joe listened as Shane talked, pulling into the drive thru line at the Taco Café, home to their favorite soft tacos, marveling at how far Shane had come since his mother's disappearance almost two years ago.

Joe had sought and gotten temporary custody of Shane, enrolled him in a small private school, and purchased a home for the two of them in the vicinity of the school. He hoped Shane felt loved and safe. He did his best. He'd been giving thought to making the custody arrangement permanent, but that could cre-

13

ate a whole new set of problems, maybe even bring Meghan, Joe's sister and Shane's mother, back into their lives. He'd recently hired a family lawyer after getting the referral from Stephen, Reye's husband. Joe had met with him once, but hadn't gone back.

Shane had settled in well, better than he'd hoped. In the last two years Shane had grown into this confident and carefree child. Joe was very pleased with the transformation; he knew firsthand the havoc that came from the dissolution of one's family. He would do everything within his power to make sure Shane would have a better life.

—⁊⁊⁊—

First week in June

Two weeks later Joe stood in line at Lights Out Coffee; he was a regular now, waiting his turn at her mouth. He inwardly smiled at how odd and X-rated that sounded to him, but he liked her sharp wit and sexy banter. And he liked the coffee here, too. He knew she worked today. He had figured out her schedule, and made a point to stop by when she was on duty, either picking up his coffee to go or ordering a bagel to eat while he worked.

"Another large coffee, black, for Middleweight," she called out to Estelle, her smile and eyes teasing.

"Bagel this morning?" she asked.

"Yes," he said, smiling.

She leaned in close and whispered loudly into his ear for the early morning crowd. "Doesn't the missionary position get a little old?" she asked. He slowly turned his head to face her, surprised that she could surprise him still.

She pulled back. "Bagel always on the bottom, cream cheese always on top. Every day, the same thing," she said, loudly, for the regulars. Most knew of the bantering between her and Joe. She teased everyone, but with him, it seemed different, like she was serious about the sexual part. He was beginning to hope so, anyway.

He grinned. "I don't want to scare you away with too many changes," he said. "For some I have to keep it easy. I'm not sure you're up for all that I bring."

One of the regulars behind him laughed, a few others snickered, and one woman fanned her face.

"You're all that, huh?" she said, captivated.

"And then some," he said, loudly, causing the male regulars behind him to hoot, his eyes still locked with hers.

"Whew," she said, laughing now as she set his coffee on the counter, fanning herself too. She and the woman in line smiled at each other in mutual understanding. He laughed at that and so did she. Was he serious? she asked herself, taking his money from him.

"You handle yourself very well," she said.

"A better question is, can you?" he asked, invitation in his eyes.

Was he for real, she wondered again, and what if he was?

"I'm sure I can," she said, handing over his cup of coffee. "I'll bring your bagel over to you."

"Thanks," he said, handing her cash. "You can put the change in the jar," he added before turning away. She watched him walk to his customary chair in the booth near the front window and pull out his laptop.

—∽∾—

"What kind of work do you do?" she said, standing next to his booth five minutes later. He hadn't looked up at her approach, his head bent over his laptop.

"IT, computer stuff. I'm in the division that supports most of the systems for Ryder Corp."

"Interesting," she said, but her voice indicated otherwise. He chuckled.

"Joe?"

Piper and Joe looked up, looking for the person who'd called his name, and found a very attractive woman walking toward Joe's booth. She wore a cute, flirty dress in a nice muted red, matching shoes, and her red hair flowed down her back. She looked polished and professional.

"Sondra," he said, smiling at the woman while Piper watched the woman's face brighten as she exchanged greetings with Joe. Piper noted the familiarity and recognition of what was between them in the woman's eyes.

"You working?" Sondra asked, eyes only for Joe.

"A little."

"Let me get my coffee," she said, glancing at Piper with expectation in her gaze.

"You have to go to the counter to order," Piper said, sugary sweetness personified, her head tilted to the side, fake smile in place. What was up with her? She didn't do "this," whatever "this" was—marking territory that she didn't own. She turned to find Joe's eyes on her, laughter in them, like he knew what her problem was.

"Sondra, this is…" he said, continuing to look at Piper.

"Piper," she offered.

"Hi," Sondra said, but clearly wasn't interested. She quickly dismissed Piper and moved back to Joe.

Pout those lips, girlfriend, Piper thought uncharitably.

"I'll just be a second," Sondra said to Joe before turning away, her cute, perky butt swinging from side to side as she made her way to the counter.

Piper watched her leave, irritated that she had been made to feel like the help; which she was, but still. She shook her head and turned to find Joe's eyes on her.

"Piper, huh."

"Joe, huh."

"Joe Sandborne," he said, sitting back in his booth now, watching her. She had no idea what he was thinking.

"Piper Knight," she replied.

"Interesting name."

She shrugged. "I yam what I yam," she said, and he chuckled. "Duty calls," she added, reluctant to leave his side. She liked their sparring, and was disconcerted by Sondra's arrival. Why was that, she'd like to know.

17

"I'll see you later," she said.

"Sure," he said, watching her as she turned and headed back to her counter. She was interested, and he suspected it had been underneath her bantering from the beginning. She teased others, but with him it had felt like more; lucky her, he was with her on that.

Was she up for what he wanted? He hoped so. These last few weeks had felt like foreplay to him, and he was ready to move past this stage. He was a little frightened at the chemistry between them, but ready for the heat he suspected they could generate.

Shane had put a damper on his sex life. He tried his best not to mix women with his nephew, and he didn't do long term. He managed to maintain minimal, simple relationships, tending to take one woman on at time and she, he decided, was next on his list.

Chapter 2

First week of June

"Afternoon, Renee," Mr. Harper said a couple of days later as he entered Lights Out late in the afternoon. Like clockwork, regular as the sun. Old Mr. Harper, 82, stopped by at 2 p.m. every day for a cup of black coffee and a slice of lemon cake. Always, forever, amen.

He was one of her favorite customers, even though he refused to call her Piper.

"Hello, Mr. Harper," she said, giving him a smile. "Having your usual?"

"Yes, young lady," he said, watching her pour his customary coffee into a cup before placing it in a saucer for him. She added a piece of lemon cake on a cake plate and a napkin and fork, and followed him to his table. His hands weren't as strong as they used to be.

Piper knew he left for his dessert and coffee during his wife's nap, usually after they finished lunch. She walked over and grabbed today's paper and brought it over to him. "Enjoy," she said.

"Thank you," Mr. Harper said, giving her another smile.

"Let me know if you need anything," she added, turning and walking back to the counter, where a customer waited. The door opened again and she was surprised to see Joe enter. He was usually part of her morning group. But him here now would work, too. She was always up for seeing him, her blood warming at the sight of him. She turned her attention to helping her next customer.

—◊—

Joe headed toward the counter, his eyes following Piper's path as she walked toward the counter and started in with the customer in front of him. Today was the day, time to move this whatever he was feeling towards her along. It had been on his mind, simmering like you wouldn't believe.

Piper watched him as he took his place in line. He'd always teased and flirted with her, but for the last couple of weeks it seemed like he was hinting at more. He had moved up the teasing until she wasn't sure she could keep up with him. Could she keep up with the other, too? Not that he'd asked, but if he did…no way did she think he was relationship- or marriage-minded. It was probably more like he'd wanted to see if her wordplay matched some other kind of play.

She usually blew off most requests for more, but Middleweight was a horse of a different color. She didn't lie to herself; she was attracted to him. Who wouldn't be? He'd been good, his comebacks sharp — excellent even. He gave as good as he got, and the possibilities for that trait were endless.

"Middleweight," she said, when he stepped up to the counter. "Don't usually see you in the afternoon."

"I was hungry for something more," he said.

"Okay," she replied. They were no longer only discussing food. "What would you like?"

"For now I'll take a sandwich and an iced coffee," he said, reaching into his pocket for his wallet and pulling out his card. "Would you bring it over to me? I'd like to talk to you about something," he added.

"Sure," she said, taking his card and running it through the register before handing it back.

"Thanks," he said, walking away, dressed casually today in jeans and a snug t-shirt. She sighed.

She walked over to him five minutes later. He was reading over his BlackBerry. The paper he had picked up sat on the table beside him.

"Easy afternoon?" she asked, eyeing the newspaper, noting the absence of his laptop.

"Not too bad," he said, not elaborating further, not that it was any of her business. She continued to hold his eyes, watching as they changed over to smoky. He was so out of her league. What was she doing here, playing with this?

"So, Piper, are you all talk? Or is there something behind all that teasing you pass out?"

"What do you think?"

"Don't know, could go either way."

"There's enough."

"Enough, huh," he said, taking a sip from his coffee, sitting back in his seat, all relaxed.

"What do you do when you're not working here?" he asked.

"A little bit of this and that," she said, her eyes locked on his. "What do you have in mind?"

"I think it's time for you and I to put all of our energy to a different use, to find out if we're all talk."

Translated that meant if she were all talk.

"You do, huh," she said.

"Yes—I do," he said, reaching for her hand.

She nodded, running her eyes from head to toe and back again while he watched her, no disguise for the lust and desire reflected in those grey peepers of his, leaving little doubt as to what energy he wanted to make use of.

"Like what you see?" he asked.

"It'll do in a pinch," she said and he chuckled.

"Hook up with me then," he said preferring the direct approach, choosing clarity in his requests, straightforward, less room for misunderstandings later.

"Hook up, huh? That's all you want?"

"All I want? That's one way to look at it," he said. His other hand had joined its mate, holding fast to hers. Strong hands, long lean fingers. She swallowed.

"Maybe. I'll think about it," she said, looking around, a little disappointed. What had she expected? A thoughtful, committed, more substantive kind of guy? She chuckled at the lunacy of those thoughts. She'd apparently lost her brain there for a second.

"I promise it will be worth our time, you won't regret it," he said, as if he'd read her mind.

She smiled. "We'll see. I'd better let you get back to work," she said, giving him a wink.

—∞—

Second weekend in June

Late Saturday afternoon Piper opened the back door of the shop for the caterers to enter. She could smell the food and recognized the scent of some of her favorites. Dirty rice, a big black kettle of gumbo, home-baked bread, and it had her mouth watering and her stomach growling something fierce.

"That smells good," she said, trailing along behind the owner and chef, Ms. Nadine.

"It is good," Ms. Nadine replied matter-of-factly. She was always short and to the point, as if words didn't come cheap in this day and age. Piper followed her into the kitchen and watched as she set her pots down on the work table before turning around to head back out to their van.

"Do you need me?" Piper asked.

"Nope, just need you out of the way."

She was used to Mrs. Nadine's gruff, no-nonsense manner and was past being offended by it. Ms. Nadine was the owner of Dirty Rice Catering Company and maker of the best Cajun food this far north of Lake Charles. Piper had liked her from the start and loved her food, so much so that she was willing to do just about anything for it. If staying out of the way was required, she could easily do that.

She left the kitchen and traipsed over to the stage located near the middle of the shop. She'd removed the tables and chairs earlier, her shop now in the final phase of its transformation from coffee bar to juke joint. Austin was known for its live music, and she was a big lover of it.

The second Saturday of every month was reserved for zydeco night at Lights Out Coffee. She started the second month she'd opened at her first shop, found a local band that played zydeco music, hung multicolored lights from the ceilings, and tried to recreate one of the favorite events from her childhood.

She'd grown up listening to zydeco on the radio. It was a combination of rub board, accordion, fiddle, guitars, and drums played by great old timers like Clifton Chenier and newer artists like Cedric Watson and Corey Ledet.

She'd followed her grandparents around to many a church bazaar and hole in the wall, where children and families were always welcome. The men drank beer, talked, and danced with their wives and kids to the sounds of zydeco blasting from the speakers.

Food, always plentiful, had been cooked lovingly by mothers and friends. The large community potluck had always been a competition for the best dirty rice, étouffée, gumbo, and homemade bread.

All with full stomachs, she, her friends, and her cousins would dance around the floor, partnered up with any available boy, or each other if boys were scarce. They'd imitated their parents, moving to the music, steps quick and eager or slow and easy. Those nights were the best of her childhood.

Tonight would be the first time zydeco night would be held at her second location. Unlike her first shop, she'd built this one with size in mind, with a dance floor and a stage. She'd wanted community access, for parties, meetings or small events, poetry readings on Sunday nights—a place for the locals to feel at home.

There was an area available for kids to watch DVDs or play video games on the plasma TV that hung on the wall, as well as crayons and small toys for the kids to play with.

The crowd, a mixture of the old, young adults, and families, had been growing each month, and she hoped the change to this venue would increase its size. She'd been pleased so far with its popularity.

—☙—

Joe was headed over to Lights Out, his blood humming. He was excited. He had seen the flyer advertising tonight's event on the counter a week ago and made plans accordingly. He hoped she'd be working tonight, or, better yet, that she wasn't and was free to leave with him.

He'd found a sitter for Shane, but he was running late because good help was hard to find these days and the sitter had been late to arrive. If he played his cards right, the night would end with them together, and that would be perfect.

He entered the door, surprised by the size of the crowd and the transformation of the room. The coffee shop had been transformed into a dance hall. Bright colored lights hung from the ceilings and people sat around the tables, talking or eating. Some were dancing on the dance floor that had been added just below the stage.

He spotted her at the counter and started in her direction. He could use a beer.

"Would you like to dance?"

He felt someone touch his elbow and turned to find a woman standing really up close and personal, her face a few inches from his. He took a step back.

"Would you like to dance with me?" The words spilled from her mouth in a rush, like it was now or never. A regular wallflower type, brunette, painted-on jeans, way nervous. There was a little hint of I know he's going to turn me down in her eyes, but a bit of challenge, too.

Why not, he thought.

"Sure," he said, taking her hand, leading her to the dance floor, watching the surprise in her eyes that he'd agreed. He smiled at her and hoped she'd relax enough to enjoy herself. He twirled her around the dance floor and her smiled widened, surprised that he could dance. He smiled at his dance partner and she smiled back. He gave himself over to the music, moving them around the floor.

—∞—

Well, would you look at that, Piper thought as she stood behind the counter-turned-bar, watching Middleweight move around the dance floor with a woman, and not the type she figured he'd go for; not the beautiful type, not like Sondra from the other morning. Maybe he'd felt sorry for the unpretty ones; she included herself in that group. Piper had come to terms with her average looks a long time ago, and that was why his hookup request had surprised her—but he hadn't asked to hook up with her looks, just their energy and chemistry. Of course he could move, all grace and sex and totally captivating.

"Could I have a beer?"

"Huh," she said, catching herself. "Sure," she added, bringing her eyes back to the job at hand. She smiled at the man her head still with Joe on the dance floor. She'd watched Middleweight enter her shop alone a few minutes earlier, watched as he'd performed a quick scan around the room, felt a surge in energy when his eyes had collided with hers. She'd thought he'd been headed her way before that girl had stopped him, and she was surprised that he'd agreed to dance.

The next person in line wanted a glass of wine, keeping her from following him. But her gaze returned to him later on as the song ended and he made his way to her line. Should she or shouldn't she take him up on his offer? She'd learned to be wary of the too-good-looking for a reason. They scared her. Was she willing to toss all those hard-won lessons away for a few nights? Are you kidding me, her other self shouted loudly in her head. Hell yeah, she was going to take him up on his offer. She was due for some plain old no-holds-barred sex.

She sighed, turned away from him, and glanced over the shop, taking in the people laughing, dancing, and talking. She was pleased with tonight's outcome so far. She liked the people in this neighborhood. They were her kind of people, friendly, fun and diverse. She was also delighted to find some of her regulars from her other shop here.

"What can I get for you tonight?" she asked, gazing into Joe's eyes. She couldn't help herself, it seemed. Beauty demanded appreciation.

"A Shiner Bock," he said, his eyes roaming over her quickly, taking in her hair, soft and full, framing her face, and her dress softly falling over her body.

"Zydeco night?" he asked.

"Yep, I grew up with the music. I see that you know it, too?"

He nodded in confirmation

"One beer?" she said.

"Yes, one beer, no date tonight. Poor me," he said, but his smile and eyes said otherwise.

"You seem to be doing well so far," she said, turning to retrieve his beer.

"I'm holding out for you," he said, waiting until he had her attention.

"Me?"

"You."

"For….?"

"For whatever," he said, his eyes never leaving hers.

"You sure are confident."

He shrugged, his eyes still locked on hers.

"Think about it," he said, giving her another smile, taking his beer, and walking away.

—∞—

Joe sat back in his booth later on that night, relaxed. He hadn't been this stress-free in a while. He didn't dance anymore, just kept an eye out for Piper, followed her as she worked, hair a halo around her head.

He could see her better now, standing near the stage in a soft yellow dress that stopped mid-thigh. She had a beautiful body. Her long, shapely legs were outfitted in funky tights tonight, and those black Ropers on her feet again. He tracked her as she walked back over to the counter and talked with her fellow employee before grabbing the dolly and heading to the back of the shop.

She was interested, just as he'd thought. He had caught her looking over at him more than a few times tonight. At this moment she was making her way toward the back, pushing an empty dolly. Thinking she might need some help, he followed her.

Piper wasn't in too big of a hurry to get back up front. She opened the door to the larger of the two storage rooms, pushed the dolly in, walked over to the beer and wine supply, and started to stack two cases of beer and one of wine. That was all she needed to restock the fridge up front.

Loaded up to her satisfaction, she leaned her dolly onto its back wheels, preparing to leave, took two steps backward, almost clearing the door, and bumped into something hard. She twisted her head around, seeking the impediment to her progress, and gazed into Joe's soft gray eyes. He was blocking her exit.

His hands went to her waist to prevent her from moving forward. One hand, anyway. The other moved down a little, to her hip.

"Huh, sorry, I wasn't looking where I was going," she said, trying to steady her cargo while moving away from him. She was flustered at being this close to him. He could have helped, but instead he stepped closer, hand still at her hip and waist. Her eyes swung back around to him, giving him a what-are-you-doing look.

"Not a good idea to back out of a room, especially with a load of beer. You never know who you might bump into," he said, laughter in his voice, stepping closer still. Pushing her and her load back into the room, he bent his head to her ear, admiring the softness of her hair.

"Copping a feel?"

He leaned in closer to her. "I'm just helping out a woman in distress. What's wrong with that?" he said, his voice smooth and low.

She shrugged her shoulder, trying to dislodge him from her ear.

"What are you doing?" she asked, it coming out a little more Marilyn Monroe-like than she'd intended as she lifted her shoulder again, hitting her head softly into his this time.

"What do you think?" He'd dodged her head butt somehow, a very smooth move. She was impressed.

"Uh…" she said, feeling his hands move from her hips slowly upward, smoothly over her waist, up to rest just under her breasts. He stepped in closer, pushing her further into the room. She felt all of him at her back now and she swallowed. He chuckled softly. Who knew chuckles could be so sexy? She turned her head to look over her shoulder and met his eyes again. He was serious now and very aroused, staring back at her with steely eyes.

"Come home with me? After you're done here?" he said, quietly, hands moving up just a bit more toward her breasts, his thumbs grazing the underside of them softly. She bit back a moan.

"You get straight to the point, don't you?" she asked, breathless, and set the dolly back on the floor before it fell and she lost her load.

"Yes."

"Why?"

"Why what? Why do I want you to come with me or why do I get straight to the point?" he asked, voice reverberating over her skin as his lips moved, going from her ear to just underneath it. She unconsciously tilted her head to the side to give him better access, and felt the smile on his mouth against her neck at her small acquiesce.

"Why me?"

"I told you, we would be good together," he said, hands still grazing, his thumbs moving tantalizingly slow, back and forth.

"I'd be just sex for you?"

"Not just sex, Piper, but great, probably mind-blowing sex."

"Honesty work for you?"

"All the time," he said, hands completely cupping her breasts now. She laughed. It popped out, and then she moaned at what his hands were doing.

"Great, huh?" Her hands moved up to surround his wrists. What to do now? She didn't want him to stop. Then he grabbed her hands and turned her to face him.

"Great," he repeated, intense now, eyes locked on hers as he took her hands in his, eyes never leaving hers. He watched the desire inhabit them; he had seen it before, but what was on display now was more than he'd anticipated, providing a surge in heat to his blood supply.

He tilted his head, leaned in to touch her lips softly. He appreciated that she was close to him in height. She'd opened her eyes wide, following the descent of his mouth as it moved toward hers, and watched as his lips touched hers. Her eyes closed then and he heard and felt her sigh as he kissed her, slowly, moving his tongue along the seam of her lips. He gently pushed into her mouth and found her tongue waiting for him. He stroked it once and pulled back, not too far, just a mere inch away, head resting on her forehead.

He let go of one hand, and pushed the door behind them closed, not breaking eye contact with her. He walked himself backward to it, pulling her along until his back touched the door; then he turned her so that she rested against it. He took her hands, his fingers entwined with hers, and went in search of another kiss, lifting their hands to rest just beside her shoulders against the door. He continued to kiss her softly, his tongue dueling and dancing with hers.

She groaned and he pushed in closer, pressing his body into hers against the door. She was firm, yet soft in the places he'd wanted her to be. He raised her hands above her head, secured her wrists in one hand while the other hand went back to her breast, back to that slow torturous grazing. He pulled back slightly from her mouth, his lips now at one corner of hers, smoothly moving along her jaw, pushed her hair out of the way with his nose, and found her ear again.

"I want you," he whispered, her skin tingling at the sound of his words. "I've seen us a thousand times." A shift of his hips inward into hers punctuated his words. "In my dreams it is perfect between us. You are perfect in my dreams." He gave her another soft wet kiss.

"Want me to describe what I see?" he whispered, his lips nibbling at hers.

She nodded, unable to speak.

"I see you, a long stretch of smooth golden brown skin attached to a body that I'd just finished exploring completely. Your hair is wild around your head, and those strong legs of yours are wrapped around me. I love your legs," he said, taking her lips in another wet, open-mouthed kiss. "I see your arms holding me in place…your head is always thrown back in my dreams, my name always on your lips, encouraging, then demanding, showing me just how you like it, how you…

like…me," he said slowly, tying her mind up in knots with his image of her, her body pure fluid now.

He took her lips again, this time in a bruising kiss, mouth open as her tongue welcomed him in. He pulled back, watched her from beneath lowered lashes, his breath a pant, as she tried to catch her breath.

"What am I doing in this picture?" he asked against her neck, en route to her ear again. "I'm moving within you, and it feels mind-altering. Can you feel it?" He sighed and pushed his hips into hers. "That would be me, in you, pushing in smoothly before gliding out, as fast or as slow as you'd like." He took her arms from over her head, turning her so that she faced the door now, his hands covering hers, holding her in place as he moved to stand flush behind her before pushing his hips inward."

She moaned and turned her head to the side and looked into grey smoldering eyes, which pulled her in. His mouth went back to her ear; she couldn't see his face, could only feel him at her back. From head to toe, she could feel his hips pushing and she pushed back, her body with a mind of its own.

"Then, we would start all over again," he said, stepping back from her.

She turned to face him, her eyes full of desire, and he smiled.

"Think about it," he said. She nodded, eyes still a little glazed. He leaned in and kissed her softly again before grabbing her dolly. "Open the door, Piper," he said, grinning now, watching as she followed his instructions. She opened the door and stepped to the side to allow him to leave. She stood there for a moment trying to regroup.

Breathe, girl, and get your ass in gear. You can't stand here all day. She ran her hands over her face before following him out and back to the front.

—⚬⚬—

Do these people not have homes to go to? he wondered from his seat near the front window, where he'd continued to watch her work. He'd affected her. He'd given up keeping track of the number of times her eyes had sought his with remnants of their earlier interlude visible in them.

She wanted it, too. He knew that fact like he knew his own name, and, as much as he hated to admit, it wasn't going to happen tonight. He was approaching his glass slipper time, and that fact hurt. She seemed to be the one in charge tonight, all questions went to her. This party was nowhere near finished, which meant she wasn't available for what he wanted. Not tonight, anyway.

He stood up and made his way to the counter and waited in line again until he reached her. She looked up, surprise and thinly veiled want reflected in the eyes that stared back at him.

"I've got to go. Another obligation. It seems like you might be a while," he said.

"Yes…" she replied.

"So another time?" he asked.

"Okay," she said, fully on board now, no use in pretending otherwise.

"I'll see you Monday," he said, satisfied that he would get his opportunity in due time. He pushed back the impulse to lean over the counter and kiss her. He was patient when he wanted something.

Chapter 3

Sunday night and finally Piper had made it to one of her favorite places—her bed—and earlier than she'd expected. It had been one long day today at the shop; throw in Zydeco night the night before and she was more tired than normal. No rest for the weary or the self-employed. She left Saturday night without doing the major cleanup. That she'd done this morning, followed by a full day of work and ending with poetry night.

Her mind moved back to Joe. Joe had been on her mind constantly since their foray into the storage room. Joe's skills had been masterful, and the encounter had replayed in her mind since then.

She hadn't had sex in two years and was close to forgetting what the whole sex experience felt like. But from what she could remember, it could be fun, really good with the right partner, a great reliever of stress and a super cardio workout. And she'd bet good money that sex with Joe would be one for the ages. He was totally in the not-to-be-missed category. Hell, he'd probably been born with that special sex gene, the one given to the gifted at birth to make a joyful noise unto the world.

So he would be a walk back in a direction that hadn't been all that good for her. She'd tried the hookup route before, numerous times, in fact, and it hadn't worked much for her. She wanted the husband, the kids, and the long haul and had stopped pretending otherwise long ago. She was holding out for a younger version of her grandfather. An old-school man, a partner, willing to put family first, who didn't mind working with her to make their life better, to achieve their goals. Did they make that brand of man anymore?

All that aside, her answer was yes. This one time, or two, or however many she could get with him. Yes, she was giving herself permission to indulge. He would be the exception to the self-imposed rule she'd implemented two years ago. She was all in, not if, but when, followed closely with, where?

Her cell rang—her father's ringtone—and she reached for it, wondering why he was up so late.

"Pops," she said by way of greeting.

"Renee, I need to see you tomorrow, early. I'm out of town the rest of the week, maybe the next two," he said.

"Okay." So much for hello, and since when did he start apprising her of his schedule?

"What's up?"

"Don't want to talk about it tonight. I'll see you in the morning, and I'll have your sisters with me."

"Is Christina coming, too?" Piper asked, perking up at the thought of seeing her little sisters. She also liked her dad's third wife, Christina.

"No, just me and the girls."

"Well, I'm usually at the shop by 6:30. Tomorrow I'll be at the new location until noon. What time will you be there?"

"Don't know, just early. Look, I have to go," he said and disconnected.

"Sure," she said into silence, wondering what was up with dear old dad. He usually was cool as a cucumber, but tonight he'd sounded harried and rushed. She'd find out tomorrow. She turned off the light next to her bed and went back to pretending Joe was here next to her, whispering in her ear, moving within her.

—⁂—

Third week in June

Mac Knight pulled onto the freeway, and looked at the faces of his youngest girls in the rearview mirror. Taylor, the older of the two, baseball cap on her head, looking like a boy, and Kennedy, the opposite in dress from her sister.

He pulled out his cell and hit the number for his wife, their mother, Christina. No answer. It rolled over to voice mail just as it had the other twenty times he tried it. He was past irritated, really living in the anger zone now.

"Christina, I need you to call me," he said into the phone, his words tight, like stones being thrown against a wall, hard, one stone at a time, each with the full weight of his body behind it, a hard nick of sound.

He disconnected and looked at the girls again. They were both staring back at him.

"Your sister is looking forward to seeing you," he said, adjusting the tone of his voice, reducing its hardness.

They nodded.

Taylor and Kennedy looked at each other in silent agreement. They'd tread easily around their father today. He was angry again this morning, as he'd been all of yesterday. They'd mostly stayed in their room while he walked, paced, stomped around their home, phone in hand, calling around for their mother, who was nowhere to be found. He'd told them this morning, after breakfast, that they'd be going to visit their sister for a while and they should pack up. So here they sat with their two dogs in their cages wedged between them, suitcases in the trunk.

They were looking forward to seeing their sister, too. They didn't know her that well, but anything was better than this, they both thought.

—⁊⁊⁊—

Joe entered Lights Out mid-morning the following Monday, later than normal. He didn't have any appointments until eleven, and he wanted to talk to Piper without the regular early morning crowd—those who'd derived enjoyment from watching them spar.

His eyes quickly scanned the room and found her at the counter, her back to the door, leaning against it, hair wild, curly, and full, apron tied around her trim waist.

She was talking to the black-haired girl that worked there too, whose eyes found his as he walked toward the counter, offering him a smile.

Piper turned to see who had come in. Judging by the interest in Shannon's eyes—they'd kind of glazed over mid-sentence—he must be handsome. Shannon didn't waste her time on the attractiveness-challenged. She turned to find Joe standing before her, smiling, hair framing his face, touching the shoulders of a tight-fitting polo tucked into expensive grey slacks. Grey eyes stared back at her, looking good enough to eat. He smiled and it did things you wouldn't believe to her insides. He lifted his eyebrow in question and she looked away, that shy part again.

"Having your usual this morning?" she asked when he reached the counter.

"Yes," he answered. And then he leaned in close, his mouth to her ear. "So," he whispered, getting right to the heart of the matter.

"I'll bring over your bagel and we can discuss it in private. Let me get your coffee first," she said, shutting down any further discussion in front of Shannon.

Piper turned, reached for a ceramic cup, and sat it under the dispenser as Shannon looked on. Shannon followed Joe's gaze as it moved down to check out Piper's ass. It was covered in a stretchy black skirt, wide, big belt resting loosely at hips that dipped and swayed as she moved. Piper turned back and his eyes returned to hers. He took his coffee from her hand and handed over cash.

"Keep the change," he said.

"Thanks."

He gave her a final smile before turning and walking over to sit at one of the tables near the middle of the shop.

Piper turned to find Shannon's quizzical eyes on her.

"Can you handle the counter for a second?" Piper asked.

"Yes."

Piper placed Joe's warmed bagel on a plate, grabbed a napkin, knife, and cream cheese, and walked around the counter and over to him. He turned as she reached him.

"So, this weekend maybe?" he asked, getting right to the point, again, single-minded in his pursuit.

"When and where?" she asked, her words knocking the wind from his sails. He sat back in his chair, surprised. That was the last thing he'd expected her to say. His blood boiled in anticipation. He loved that she offered no pretense, no games, none whatsoever, knew what she wanted and went for it.

"So Saturday night tentatively...." he started to say, and before he could get her response, someone shouted "Mac!"

Joe and Piper turned, their eyes landing on a tall man who was making his way toward the front door, and in a hurry.

"Hey, Mac," the man shouted again, waving his arms above his head, in case the volume of his voice hadn't gotten everyone's attention the first time. He was overjoyed and apparently excited at seeing the renowned middleweight boxing champion of old, the famous Mac "Lights Out" Knight, enter the shoppe. Joe sat up, equally surprised. What were the chances that he'd get to maybe meet the famed boxer? He was still in fighting form, Joe noted, taking in the two young girls by his side. One looked to be about ten, the other one maybe pre-teen, near his nephew's age. Both were light-brown skinned with almond-shaped eyes.

The autograph seeker, a tall, beaming Hispanic male, paper and pen in hand, met Mac just as he and the girls cleared the door. Joe watched as Mac said a few words to the gentleman, smiled, shook hands quickly and signed the paper, distracted, before walking over to them. Joe remained seated, shocked and awestruck.

"Renee," Mac said, coming to stand next to their table. Joe rose from his chair, then held out his hand.

"I'm a big fan," Joe said, extending his hand for a handshake. Mac stood for a second, his eyes assessing Joe, before accepting Joe's hand in his.

"Hello," he replied, looking between Joe and Piper, who was now smiling at her sisters. "Would you excuse us for a moment, young man?" Mac said to Joe and started toward the back of the shop. He hadn't waited for a response from Joe. Piper rolled her eyes at the astonished expression on Joe's face. She hated when her dad did that.

She smiled at her sisters again, reached for their hands and turned to Joe. "I'll see you later," she said before turning to follow Mac toward the back of the shop, leaving Joe standing there.

He stood for a minute, watching the foursome as they moved off, entering the hall that lead to the office, before he sat down, amazed by what had just transpired.

"Do you need a refill?" The black haired girl appeared at his shoulder, giving him a start. He'd been engrossed in the scene and hadn't heard her approach.

"Thanks," he said, extending his cup to her, watching as she poured.

"That's the great and famous boxer, MacArthur Knight, in case you didn't know," she said.

"I grew up watching him fight."

"Did you know he was Piper's dad?" she asked.

"Piper?" he replied, mind still processing. "No, I didn't," he said, surprised by that, too.

"Yes, Piper, the woman whose ass you were checking out earlier," she said, finding humor and pleasure at being able to address what she'd considered to be a slight against her earlier, not to mention just plain old rude behavior.

He ignored the comment, processing this new information about Piper.

"She owns this shop and another shop over on Fifty-fifth Street, her first. Ever been to it?"

Joe shook his head. "No," he said, another surprise in a string of them today, not that it would have made any difference for what he'd wanted from her.

"Her famous father helped her get started, put up the money for her first shop. Wished I had a dad that helped me. Anyway, he used to co-own it with her, but she bought him out earlier this year."

"Really," he said, soaking up the information.

"You're not one of those guys trying to get to him though her, are you?" Shannon looked over him, speculation in her gaze.

"Nope," he said, more than a little offended. He didn't have to use anyone to get to anybody. He worked hard for what he accomplished in his life.

"You can never be sure. I didn't think you were the type, but like I said, you never know," she said. He didn't respond. She kept right on talking.

"I'd like to own a place like this one day. Been saving up to, almost done with school, one year remaining," she said, looking around the place, desire and aspiration in her gaze.

No response from Joe, who was now looking at his BlackBerry. The bell rang, indicating a customer had entered the shop.

"I better get that," she said.

"Sure, thanks," he said, pointing to his cup. His hands moved to his backpack, removing his laptop from it. Booting it up, he was lost in thought. Piper was the daughter of the famous Mac Knight and owned not one, but two coffee shops. He was impressed. Nice, sexy, and smart. He looked around the shop once again, now understanding the source of the boxing themed decor, and tried to concentrate on work.

—∞—

"What's up, Dad?" Piper said, following him into her office, smiling as she looked over at her sisters.

"Hey, Kennikens," Piper said, using the nickname she'd given to her youngest half-sister long ago and bringing Kennedy into her arms for a hug.

"Hi, you, look at how tall you've gotten. Come give your big sister a kiss," Piper said, standing up and reaching to hug Taylor.

"Too big for hugs, Piper," she said, walking toward her anyway, allowing herself to be pulled into Piper's arms.

"How about you and Kennedy go out to the front and ask the girl at the counter for something to drink or eat while I talk with your sister," Mac said.

"The adults want to talk," Taylor said, walking from the room, Kennedy following behind her. Piper followed them out the door and down the hall and watched as they walked to the counter. She caught Joe watching them, but had no idea what he was thinking.

She turned back to her dad, leading him back to her office. He turned to her as he entered.

"I think Christina has left me."

"What?"

"You heard me. I think Christina has left me. She'd been talking about going home to Vietnam to visit her mother. I knew her mother was sick and I was okay with that, thought she'd take the girls with her, but I woke up yesterday morning and found her gone.

"The note she left me told me that," he said, agitation creeping into his voice. "I've got businesses to run. I can't take care of two children. What was she thinking?" His anger quickly took the handoff from agitation as he walked back out into the hall, looking back toward the front at the girls, apparently waiting for their drinks. Taylor had a muffin in her hand.

He'd spent yesterday doing his best to take care of them, but he wasn't cut out for this day-to-day fatherhood. He'd provided a roof over their heads and money to live. That was enough. The daily care was Christina's responsibility.

"So," Piper said, not sure how to respond. "Did you guys have a fight?"

"I do not fight, Renee, unless it's in the ring, and my boxing days are long behind me," he said, turning his back to her, walking to the end of the hall, and looking out into the main area of the shop. He turned around and walked back, passing her to enter her office again. This walking back and forth was giving her a headache.

"Are you seeing someone else?" she asked.

He gave her a hard look and then turned away. "I think her mother's illness was just an excuse. She's been talking about leaving me, but I just didn't pay much attention to her. She's been screaming and throwing tantrums. I don't have time nor patience for that kind of behavior. She is not three," he said, still looking at her.

No, but she was really young when you married her and she probably didn't know how much you like women, Piper thought.

"I have obligations, responsibilities in other areas of the country. I can't take care of kids. You have to help me," he said, turning to face her. "I was hoping to leave the girls with you."

"With me," she said, eyes wide, taking a step backward.

"It's the only logical solution I could come up with. I don't have any support in San Antonio now that Christina is gone. I have the apartment here, so it makes sense that they remain here with you."

Makes sense to whom? she thought, staring back at him, recognizing that he was indeed asking her to take care of his children.

"You're serious?" she asked.

"Yes, I'm serious," he said.

"When will I have time to take care of two kids?"

"You have more time than I do. I'm needed in San Francisco tomorrow for at least a week, maybe two."

"I can't. Really, Dad, do you know what my schedule looks like? I'd have to hire someone else to fill in for me, and I'm running way lean as it is. When is Christina coming back anyway?" she asked, feeling overwhelmed. "All the kids' stuff is in San Antonio and school is starting up in what, two months? Don't they have to be there?" Piper searched her brain frantically for any and all reasons to say no.

"There are perfectly good schools around here. Your house is more than large enough, and weren't you thinking about renting it out?" he continued, as if it had been decided.

"What about my shops?"

"Speak to my accountant," he said, reaching into his jacket pocket for a card and handing it over to her, Mr. I-have-an-answer-for-everything. "I'll have a checking account opened for you. He will transfer funds to help you with the girls plus extra to help you manage at the shop, to hire additional employees if you need to," he said.

"I just got done paying you back for the first shop," she said.

"This isn't a loan, just my way of helping you while you help me look after your sisters," he said, placing heavy emphasis on the your sisters part. She'd run out of ideas, and he could tell. He could always read her, and knew how to parry and feint, he being the superb boxer and all.

"It will work out. You can handle this, Renee. You can handle anything. We'll make more long-term plans when I return. I can help you. I can try, at least, but not today," he said, pulling her into his arms. "You're my oldest and more like me than you know. You will always do what's necessary." He knew how much family meant to her. "Do this for me, Renee," he said, looking down into her face.

She sighed, her mind still reeling with the thought of what long-term meant.

"It can't be that hard. Besides, don't you plan to have your own children one day?"

"Yes, but not today. I'd hoped to find a husband first."

"Consider it practice for children of your own, which, may I remind you, won't wait forever. Do you even date anymore?"

"Well, I won't have time for men now, will I? You can kiss your chances of having grandchildren good-bye," she said as she placed her arms around him. She gave up the fight, sighing deeply. She began thinking about the changes she'd need to make to her schedule to accommodate her sisters.

"It probably wouldn't hurt to check out the schools here in town for me in case Christina doesn't return soon. There is a private school near here. Call my assistant. She'll give you the name. I've given to them in the past," he added.

She inwardly groaned at the request. "Sure," she said, hoping it wouldn't come to that.

She with children? Not sure that was a good pairing, but she was a lot like her father. She didn't want someone else taking care of family, especially her sisters. Family was, well, family, and priority numero uno.

"The girls' things are in my car. I'll help you bring them in," he said.

"Do you need a moment to talk to them?"

"No, they knew why we were coming here. Christina left detailed instructions, lists for me that I'll pass on to you," he said, walking toward the front of the shop with her beside him.

She looked around the shop. Joe was gone. She walked outside, stopping as she looked down at two dog crates parked near the front door, wondering who they belonged to. She shook her head, looking up to see Taylor walk out into the sunshine, followed by Ken.

"So we're going to stay with you," Taylor said, pretending indifference. Piper knew better. She knew what having new people take you in was like, and the worry that came from that, even if they were your family.

"Yep," she said, taking in Taylor's look of displeasure. "Hey, you'll like me. It'll be fun. Now I won't have to hire more employees. You two will be my new slaves," she said, and Ken laughed. Taylor didn't.

"These two yours?" she asked, pointing to the two dogs, whining to be let out of their cages now that they'd recognized family.

"Yes, this is McKenzie," she said, pointing to the first crate, "and this is Pepper."

Piper sighed internally. Hopefully they would not be here long. Christina would come back on the next flight once she knew her kids were not with their father. That was Piper's wish, or her hope, at least.

"Take them in while I get the rest of your bags. Come back here and check after you put them in my office to make sure I've gotten all of your goods," she said.

"Kay," Taylor said, picking up one cage and heading inside. Ken grabbed the other.

Piper walked over to her dad's fancy car, hit the button to release the trunk, and looked at enough luggage to last for a year. She picked up the two largest duffle bags, hauling them to her car. So much for a short stay, she thought, heading back to grab the two smaller ones. Taylor had come out and picked up one of the remaining bags. "Video games," she said. They loaded up Piper's auto and headed back inside, Taylor leading the way.

Her dad was still hard on the women in his life, she thought, trailing behind Taylor. He had always been a hustler, from a large, loving, but poor family. He'd needed to make his way early, turned to boxing, starting out small, and grew into something big. He knocked out the champion in a fight everyone had expected would be a beat down for him. He had always been about business, always looking for more, never feeling he would ever have enough money. And women. She sighed, hoping he hadn't done what she thought he might have done. She knew that about him, too, but she'd thought he truly loved Christina. Thought he would settle down, take his vows seriously.

She was the oldest of five girls, her dad's very own United Colors of Benetton collection. Blair and Samantha were biracial, a mixture of African-American and white; their mother, Margarite, had been her dad's first wife. He hadn't married Piper's mother, who was of Creole descent. He'd managed to ruin marriage number one. Outside forces got in the way, those pretty young things. His second marriage lasted a year and hadn't produced any children, thank the Lord. Kennedy and Taylor were also biracial, produced from wife number three; Christina, their mother, was of Vietnamese descent. Somehow he'd manage to keep Christina, until now that is. Twelve years down the drain. She hoped not. So if her life was upside down for a few days, maybe a few weeks, she could handle it. Her sisters deserved no less from her.

—⚓—

Third week in June

Joe entered Lights Out the next day and found Piper behind the counter, handing money to a customer. He walked over and stood, now next in line. She looked up and smiled.

"Joe," she said.

"Piper," he said, his eyes never leaving hers.

"You having your usual?" she asked.

What, no sexy banter this morning? he thought, surprised. He wanted to nail down a time and place. He moved in closer to her ear, eyes locked on hers as he did so. He could hear her breathing change and inwardly smiled.

"So," he said softly in that low voice of his, pulling back to look into her eyes.

She tilted her head to the side, her eyes pointed left. Joe followed her eyes to land on one of the girls from yesterday. He hadn't noticed her standing there. He was rather focused on Piper and what hadn't gotten resolved between them yesterday.

"This is my youngest sister, Kennedy," she said, looking at Joe. He smiled at her sister.

"This is Joe," she said, continuing with the introductions. "He comes in most mornings and usually wants a large coffee, black," she said.

Kennedy stood staring at Middleweight, appreciation in her eyes. All ages were vulnerable to the pretty ones, Piper thought.

"Sometimes he'll add a bagel," Piper added. "So what do we need to do after we've taken his order?"

Piper asked of her sister, continuing with her instruction.

"I need to get his coffee," Kennedy replied, seeking confirmation from her sister's eyes.

Piper nodded. She and Joe watched her take a cup, set it underneath the dispenser, hit a button, and watch the cup fill. She was dressed in a too-big Lights Out employee shirt that fell over her arms and a too-big apple green apron tied around her waist.

"My sisters are living with me for a while," Piper said, her eyes on her sister while she talked to Joe. "They're getting settled in at my home and will be working here with me. Can I bring your bagel out to you this morning?" she asked him, hoping he'd realize that she didn't want to talk right now.

"Sure," he said, understanding her message. She wanted to talk away from her sisters. He handed over a five to Piper, who passed it to Ken, who punched in the order into the cash register. Piper moved over to stand behind her to supervise the transaction.

"Great job," she said, continuing to watch her sister as she made change and handed it to Joe.

"Thank you," he said, giving Kennedy a soft smile.

Ken smiled back, shy now. "Thank you for coming to Lights Out," she said. Piper lifted an eyebrow. She gave a bemused grin to Joe.

"Your charm is limitless, it seems," she said, chuckling.

"And don't you forget it," he said to her and winked at Kennedy, whose smile widened. "See you in a few," he said, walking away.

Her sisters, he thought, walking over to find a seat, running the implications of that through his mind. It was an interesting development, and one he hoped didn't change anything for him.

A few minutes later Piper placed the bagel on his table, interrupting his perusal of e-mail.

"So," he said, giving her a smile.

"My sisters are going to be with me for a bit."

"So you've said. The two girls from yesterday, the ones that came in with your father?"

"You know he's my dad?"

"I do now," he said, smiling at her. "You didn't tell me. Why?"

She shrugged.

"Ken's ten and her older sister, Taylor, is twelve. They're spending some time with me until their mother returns."

"Returns from where?" he asked.

Piper looked back over at the counter. Estelle was working with Ken now, the line not long.

"Vietnam. It's a very long story. Not sure I have all the pieces to it yet," she said, looking back at her sister. "My dad asked me to take care of them for a while."

"How long is a while?" he asked, holding her hand.

"Don't know."

"We could still hook up. Babysitters work well,"

"I'm sure, and maybe I'll take advantage of one, but not now. They just got here. I want them to get settled in first."

"So that's a 'no.' "

"Yes," she said, looking into his eyes, disappointment reflected back at her. "Sorry."

He was quiet. "Let's just wait and see how it goes. They and you may adjust sooner than you think, or they may leave sooner than you think."

"Maybe so," she said.

Chapter 4

Fourth week in June

Piper walked into the bedroom located immediately next to hers on the second floor, where all of the bedrooms were situated. This was Ken's room now, and signs of her sister settling in were evident as she looked around the room—nail polish, clothes, and girl-power-themed DVDs littered the floor.

Her dad had been correct in his assessment of her home. It was large enough for the children and their stuff. But who knew they could use so much stuff?

She felt the buzz of her cell against her butt. It was tucked into her back pant pocket.

"Hello," she said, cautious, not recognizing the number.

"Hello, Renee. It's me, Christina."

"Christina. It is so good to hear from you. How are you? Where are you?" she asked, walking out of Ken's room and entering the hall leading to her bedroom.

"I'm fine. How are Ken and Taylor?" she asked.

"They are okay, but they miss you." It was quiet on the phone for a second, and Piper could hear Christina crying.

"I'm sorry that you have to take care of them. That was not my intent. I wanted your father to take care of his kids. They are his kids," she said, her voice changing from tearful to angry. It was quiet for a few more seconds. Piper could hear her revert back to the crying again.

"I'm sorry. My mother's been ill, is ill, and I hadn't known. Plus your dad…" she said, stopping, not finishing her thought. "Between leaving and my mother's illness, I can't seem to get it together," she said.

There was a pause. "Did you get the list of things to do for the girls? I left one at the house for your father," Christina said, angry again.

"Yes, I have it."

"How is your mother?" Piper asked, hoping that was a safer topic than her father.

"Oh, Renee, I don't know if she's going to make it. She has cancer. Do you know I haven't seen her in thirteen years? I left her because of your dad. I chose him over my family. She didn't want me to marry him, said he was too old."

Renee didn't know which way to go now, what to say.

"What do you want me to do?" she asked.

"Would you take care of the girls, please? I feel comforted that they are with you. You know what your dad is like."

"When do you think you might be back?" she asked.

"I don't know. I don't know what I'm going to do. I thought about coming back for the girls, but with school starting soon and taking care of my mother. He couldn't do this one thing I asked. I've given up so much up for him, and this one thing, to take care of his children, he couldn't do. Is that too much to ask?"

Renee didn't know how to respond to that one, either.

"The girls seem to be adjusting, and I'm getting to know them, which is an upside," she said, hoping her humor would help.

"Are there any good schools near you?" Christina asked.

"I don't know."

"Would you check into that for me? I don't know how long I'll be here," she said. "There will be things they will need in order to be enrolled. Your father can help. You'll need to make a trip to San Antonio to get those for me. Thank you so much. I'm glad the girls can depend on you. Mac is such a…" She thought better of it, and stopped talking again. It was quiet on the phone.

"I miss them so much," she said and started to cry again.

"Maybe if you come back, Mac might be ready to discuss it with you. Maybe he would listen to you now."

"I don't know," she said, sounding lost. "I've got to go. I'll call soon to check on the girls. Thanks, Renee. You don't know what this means to me, knowing that you are watching over them. Can I talk to Taylor?" she asked.

"Sure, let me go get her," Renee said, walking out of her room and down the hall to Taylor's new digs.

She knocked, noting the Do Not Disturb sign hanging from the door.

"What?" she heard through the door.

"It's your mom calling," she said, listening as the door opened and an arm reached out. Piper placed her phone in Taylor's hand and the door closed.

Okay, she thought, and walked over to the top step leading downstairs. She sat, waiting.

What a mess. Christina was a nice woman, a few years older than her twenty-seven. She met and married her dad at age twenty and had Taylor a year later. At twenty Piper had been intent on partying, away from home, away from the watchful eye of her Pops and couldn't imagine being married to her dad at such a young age. Not her life. She sat for about five minutes before the door opened and Taylor walked down the hall, looking for Ken.

"She wants to talk to you, Ken," she said, handing the phone to her sister, who walked over to the entrance of her bedroom. Taylor walked over to sit on the top step with Piper.

Ken talked for about fifteen minutes and brought the phone back to Piper, moving beyond her and taking a seat on the step below.

"Christina?" she said into the phone.

"Renee, thank you again for taking care of my girls. I'll call you later on in the week to check on them. This is the number to my mother's home. My cell doesn't work here, but I'm going to get a new one today. Call me here if you have any questions about the girls," she said, and was then quiet for a few minutes. "I just need time to figure this out," she added, before hanging up.

"So, looks like you're going to be stuck with us for a while," Taylor said.

"It's not so bad having you guys here. It could be fun. You'll get to know me and I'll get to know you."

Taylor sighed.

"Hey, I'm not that bad," Piper said, a smile in her voice, hitting her shoulder into Taylor's. "We could work," Piper added, smiling at Ken, who smiled back.

"I guess," was the response from Taylor. Not the excitement she'd hoped for, but she hadn't had to leave her home, move in with someone she saw three or four times a year, start a new school, in a new city, while her parents were doing who knows what. Renee hit Taylor's shoulder again and smiled. Taylor gave her a weak one back this time.

—⁊⁊—

First week in July

Piper looked in the window, groaning at the long line that was visible. They had been late again; when did getting out the house becomes so difficult?

She hopped out, grabbed her bags, and waited for Ken and Taylor to disembark. They joined her on the sidewalk.

"Got everything? Everyone?" she said, locking her car and walking to the front door, the girls trailing along behind. She opened the door and watched as her troop marched inside, a single line, Taylor with her load, followed by Ken with hers. They marched through the shop, heading to the back toward Piper's office to drop off their stuff.

"Hey, Estelle," she called out, "I'll be there in a second." She smiled at the customers as she passed. Of course he was here, at the back of the line, watching her as she moved toward her office. She hadn't seen much of him because of her recent tardiness. The few times she had, he'd continued where he'd left off, still flirting, still smiling, teasing, not giving up apparently, which surprised her. If she'd had his looks, she would have moved on by now. Knowing his type, she was surprised that he hadn't.

Not much for teasing this morning, she just gave him a smile, lifted her eyebrows, and kept on walking into her office, dropping her junk on her desk and starting up her computer for Taylor.

"Taylor, you and Ken get situated. I need to help Estelle out front."

"Sure, but I call the computer." Ken said.

"Don't think so," Taylor responded, sitting in the chair behind the desk. Ken looked at Piper for help.

"Taylor, let's allow Ken to go first this morning."

"Don't think so," she responded back, as if that was enough, end of discussion.

Piper wasn't doing this this morning. "Ken, help me at the register. I can see if all my training is paying off. I'll let you try it without me, I'll just look over your shoulder," she said, standing in the office door looking back at Taylor, hoping that was enticement enough. "Then in one hour it will be Kennedy's turn."

"She always gets her way," Ken said, following Piper up to the front.

"Not always," Piper said.

"You'll see. You have to get tougher, Piper, or she'll run all over you."

"Thanks. I'll keep that in mind," she said, walking into the kitchen, pulling an apron from her stack, and handing one to Ken. She tied it over her black capris and black Lights Out polo with the green boxing gloves embroidered on the pocket. Ken did the same.

"Sorry I'm late, Estelle," she said, trying to muster up some energy this morning. How did mothers do this on a daily basis?" she wondered. Ken trailed along and stood beside her at the counter.

"Hi, Kennedy," Estelle said.

"Hi," Ken replied, ready to go. Piper was learning that this little sister liked being in charge.

"Motherhood is something else," Estelle said, a smile on her face, moving over to take on the drinks now that Piper would take over the mic.

"Joe," she said, smiling but not feeling it today.

He smiled at Piper's youngest sister.

"Large coffee, black," Ken said, standing up straighter, her smile in place.

"With a bagel, and you can bring it out to me. No hurry," he said, looking at Piper as she placed his coffee on the counter. He handed her a ten.

"Keep the change," he said, winking before turning and walking away.

"Thank you, Joe," Kennedy said. Piper lifted her eyebrow. So he was Joe now.

Piper watched him walk away. He was dressed more formally than usual; there must be something going on today. Ken hit her with her shoulder, pointing to the next customer in line, who was amused by Piper's interest in Joe.

Joe found a seat near the front window. It was sunny outside, on its way to another scorching and typical summer day in Austin. He would only be here an hour and then it was off to San Antonio. He hadn't quite given in to her no, not after what he'd experienced. He was so psyched for more.

"Piper."

He heard her name and looked up, and watched as her other sister marched over to the counter.

"I guess I can help," she offered, more put upon than excited.

"We don't need help, do we, Pipe?" Ken said.

"We could always use help," Piper said, looking at Taylor. "How about you pick up some of the empty plates on the table?"

"Not what I had in mind," she said. "I want to learn how to work the counter, like you've been teaching Ken."

Piper took in a huge breath of air. "Let's start with the little things," she said, walking around the girls into the kitchen, where she pulled out a towel, handing one to Taylor and one to Ken.

"I can manage the line for now. This would be a big help to me," she said, turning them around to face the room and giving them a push in the direction of the tables. "After you're done, I'll start to teach you how to work the counter," she said to Taylor.

A few minutes later, Piper grabbed Joe's bagel and walked over to his table, placing it in front of him.

"Thanks," he said.

"You're welcome," she said, taking a moment to take in Taylor's not-so-fast progress. Ken had cleared two tables to Taylor's one.

She sighed again. He reached for her hand, preventing her from leaving.

"How's it going?" he asked, eyes moving to watch her sisters.

"Okay. Takes some getting used to."

"You'll adjust."

"Hope so."

"Free time?" he asked, eyes hopeful.

"Not much," she replied and watched the disappointment register in his. What was up with this?

"Still no, then?" he asked.

"Sorry, still no," she said, glancing at the counter and the line beginning to form again. She looked back at him, her hand still in his. "Don't take this the wrong way," she said, looking at her hand held between his. "But I'm surprised that you're still here, pursuing this. You could have anybody, and although the sex between us would be good, it's probably okay with any other woman you'd pick. I'd thought you'd have moved on by now." She watched irritation swim across his face before it disappeared, quickly.

"Why is that?" he said, voice neutral in tone, his hand quietly holding hers.

"I don't know. You're really handsome, you know that, and it's just been my experience that your type moves on when it's not so easy."

He didn't say anything. Irritation passed over his face again, and just as quickly was gone.

"Don't get angry. I'm just being honest. I like you, like the way you banter with me, but I didn't think it was more. You asked for the hook-up, remember? And I was really with you at first until my sisters arrived and I don't know when or if I'll be there again. That's all I'm trying to say. Sorry if that didn't come out right or if I hurt your feelings."

"No, you're good. It *was* a hookup request, my idea, and a good one, probably," he said, smiling, squeezing her hand before he let it go.

"Good seeing you again, but I'd better get back. See you later," she said, walking back to the counter.

"Yep," he said to her departing back. "See you later."

Second week in July

They entered the shop this morning on time, fourth time in a row. Yes! You go, girls, she thought. The girls no longer went to the office first, but handed their bags off to Piper at the door instead, waving to the customers they'd gotten to know. They were a family now.

Ken and Taylor went to the kitchen, washed their hands, and tied aprons around their waists. Today Taylor was helping at the counter; Ken would clean up and refill coffee for those customers sitting at the tables. They'd agreed to take turns with these two assignments.

Piper went to the office, put their bags away, booted up her computer, and walked back out and to the kitchen to wash up, watching her sisters confidently assisting her customers. They'd gone shopping last weekend in search of black clothes to wear to match the employee polos. They wanted to be official employees. She grabbed a purple apron from her stack, tied it around her waist, and walked to supervise.

"Good morning, Mr. Hugo," Taylor said, perky and serious.

"Good morning, Taylor. I'll be having my usual."

"You're off early this morning. Do you have to work a double?" she asked.

"Nope, the owners finally decided to hire some extra help," he said.

"I see. So that will be just black coffee for you this morning?" she asked formally, like the butlers of old.

"Yes," he said, trying to match her in gravity.

"Would you like any pastries to go with your coffee?"

"No thanks," he said, watching her take his money and give him change. He placed a dollar in the tip jar. He'd handed his cup over to Piper, so it was filled and ready to go, her speed not hampered at all by her sister's presence.

"Hello, Ms. Ellie. Non-fat latte for you this morning?"

"Yes, and you are doing such a great job, Taylor," Ellie said, handing over her card which Taylor used slowly, while Piper looked on.

"Thank you," Taylor said, and Piper smiled at Ellie, thanking her with her eyes for the patience she had showed her sisters over the past few weeks.

Piper looked up into the eyes of Joe and smiled. She hadn't seen him in a while. She'd been busy with the girls, and his attendance had dropped off. He'd seemed different since they'd talked. He still teased her, but nowhere near as intensely as he used to. Guess he was moving on.

"What's up? I haven't seen you in a while," she said.

"My work and your sisters," he said with a smile.

She nodded in agreement. "Your usual?"

"Just coffee today," he said.

Taylor had placed a cup under the dispenser and stood waiting for it to fill. He handed his card to Piper, who swiped it and handed it back, along with a copy of the receipt. Taylor handed him his order.

"Thanks," he said, giving her his smile and turning away. He found a table toward the back and pulled out his laptop. He had a quick thirty minutes before heading on to Belton. He looked around and found Piper was back to teaching her sisters at the counter.

He'd been impressed with the care she'd shown them. There was more to her than met the eye. He knew her sacrifice first-hand.

He'd liked her from the beginning, with her smart mouth, sharp comebacks, and lovely body. He just didn't do more than the lovely body parts these days, not any day, really. She'd been correct in her assessment of him. Women and commitment were roads he didn't travel much—more like at all—especially now that Shane was a permanent fixture in his life.

Women. He liked them in bed—loved them in bed—but hadn't found any he'd wanted to risk more with, so he kept them at a distance. When and if he settled, and he had a huge doubt about the if, it would be with an old-school woman, a partner, willing to put family first. He wanted one who would dig in with him for the long haul, make a life with him, one who had his back and he hers, and honestly he'd given up searching a long time ago. Hadn't thought they made that brand anymore. Until now. But she didn't think much of him, thinking back to her words that day. He chuckled. It was an image he'd worked hard to portray, and there was no use allowing his feeling to be hurt now because she'd believed him.

Chapter 5

First weekend in August

Sunday night, two weeks later, Joe sat in a car parked out in front of Lights Out Coffee, for what he knew to be poetry night. He hadn't been here in a while—two weeks, to be exact—not that he'd kept track. Work had kept him busy, and he'd decided to let Piper go. Danger lay there. She was more serious than he wanted, so he'd gone back to some of his other coffee haunts. He also acknowledged that her remarks had bothered him, and more than he thought possible. Another surprise.

She'd been on his mind, even without seeing her daily. Another bad sign. She'd show up at night, mostly before he dozed off, nude, legs wrapped around him. If he felt kinky, she'd show up with her hair in those two puffs and those Ropers on her feet, golden brown skin in between. She was always plaint, pliable, and completely at his mercy. Her eyes were usually closed, mouth parted, pleasure profound on her face as he…

"Joe."

He heard his name and turned to its source: Rachel.

He was here at the request of Rachel, a woman he'd met from work, his date for the evening. Their third date. He'd found a sitter for Shane, his nephew, and he'd agreed to dinner, but she had a surprise for him she thought he might like. She'd done the driving tonight. Shane's sitter was late again, so it was faster for her to swing by and pick him up; her suggestion.

Surprise for him, all right; they were here for poetry night, of all things. He didn't do poetry. He was nervous, here with a date, worried that Piper might get the wrong impression of him, her words under his skin.

"I'm sorry I didn't tell you, but it was a surprise," Rachel said, looking over at him, reaching for his hand, bringing him back to the here and now.

"You may like it. And anyway, we can't sit here all night," she said.

Fine, he thought, getting out of the car, walking to the door, waiting for her to lock up her car.

He and Rachel entered the shop. He was again surprised by the size of the crowd, surprised at the popularity of this place, for any event, it seemed.

"Isn't this great?" Rachel asked him, reaching for his hand and leading him toward a booth located near the front of the room. The tables closest to the stage had been taken.

"Yep," he said, sliding into one side of the bench, she taking the seat across the table from him.

"I love this place. I love the new location. The other place is so small. Ever been there?"

"Nope," he said.

"Interested in poetry?" she asked.

"Nope."

"Too bad. I brought some with me that I'd like to share with you," she said.

He gave her a nod. It was better than anything else he could think to say.

"You want something to drink?" She opened her purse and pulled out her wallet. "My treat, for you being such a sport and coming with me," she said, leaning over the table, placing a quick kiss on his lips.

He hadn't been given a choice, since she'd been the one driving. He didn't voice that, though.

"Coffee, black," he said, his eyes darting around looking for Piper. Quickly catching himself mid-search, he turned his attention back to the one he'd come here with, Rachel, as she left the table. He followed her with his eyes as she made her way to the counter to place their coffee orders.

Piper stood behind it; her eyes caught his and moved away. She stood next to her sister, Taylor, the one Shane's age.

He glanced over the room, taking in the many different kinds of people here. Who knew there were so many people interested in poetry?

He found Rachel again. She'd gotten her drinks and had moved on, and was now standing at a table near the stage, bent over it with pen in hand, writing. His eyes roamed over the crowd again, looking up as she returned to their table.

"I signed up to read tonight. The line is starting to form," she added, again pointing to a line with three people standing in it; Piper's younger sister was second, a sheet of paper in her hand.

He inwardly groaned, dropping his head to his chest. His hand went to rub his forehead. Poetry from all ages. He looked at his watch, wondering what excuse he could use to get out of here.

"I'm fourth," she said, bringing his attention back to her. "And I've got to tell you, I wrote this poem with you in mind. I'm going to read it tonight."

Fuck me, he thought, but gave her a smile. "Should be interesting."

"It's good," she said, turning her attention to the stage as Piper walked up to the mic.

"Thank you ladies and germs," she said, the mic in one hand. He let out the breath he'd held, unaware that he'd been holding it, his attention so drawn to her.

"Thanks for coming out tonight," she said, looking around the room. "I'm turning you over quickly to Thomas, the guru of all things poetry, the planner and host of tonight's event. I'll be at the counter if you need anything coffee-related," she said, stepping off the stage.

A tall, young African-American man strode up to the stage—hopped on, actually, all youthful vigor. He looked to be in his early twenties, still in college probably, funky Frank Sinatra hat on his head, smooth face except for that patch of hair on the bottom of his chin.

"Thank you," he said, big smile, white teeth, contrasting his smooth brown skin. It was the kind of smile that said I know I look good. Joe knew that smile. He owned one.

"Let's give a hand to Piper, the owner of this place and our personal barista for the night," he said in a low voice. Joe thought he was probably trying to be sexy as he looked at Piper like she was the only one there.

Needs work, Joe thought, but watched as Piper smiled back and blew him a kiss.

"You all know the drill," he said, giving off that sexy intellectual vibe. "Sign in and spread some love, some rhythm, some rhyme. We welcome you to Sunday night poetry and coffee at Lights Out. Now without further delay, let's welcome up Jasmine, that sweet smelling flower that tantalizes the senses and delights the soul," he said. The crowd laughed, hollered, and clapped. She must be a regular, Joe mused, controlling his impulse to gag at the flowery introduction.

A tall, thin woman, her bald head a nice pink color under the lights, walked onto the stage, regal in her bearing. She raised her arms above her head, fist clenched tightly, and shouted at the top of her lungs, "Shoot 'em up! Shoot 'em up! Shoot 'em up! Take it to them! Take it to them! Take it to them!" The crowd was startled by her volume and the content of her message.

She then lowered her arms, bringing them together in front of her chest in a prayer-like pose.

Applause sounded. Well, apparently she was done, Joe thought, looking around the room, taking in the pleased expressions on the faces of those present. He totally missed that one.

"Wasn't that great?" Rachel asked.

"Yep."

"I'd better get in line," she said, getting up and walking to stand behind a man with pink-colored dreads.

This is going to be a long night, he thought, rubbing his forehead again, watching as the emcee came back up and introduced Piper's little sister, Kennedy. She was shy, walking onto the stage, child-sized employee uniform on, her paper clutched in her hand.

"The name of my poem is My Dogs," she said, eyes darting between her paper and the crowd, paper and the crowd, then back to the paper. "My dogs. McKenzie and Pepper," she began, a quick peek at the audience and back to the paper. "Good dogs, loyal dogs, smart dogs. They are man's best friend, my best friends. I love them." She looked up at the crowd expectantly. She was done, he guessed. Applause sounded, mixed in with a few whistles, and her smile appeared and then widened on her face at the onslaught of approval from her fellow poets.

He listened to the next two before turning his attention to Rachel as she was introduced and took to the stage. She looked like a gypsy—she was small in stature, with short, dark curly hair that fell to her shoulders.

"I'd like to dedicate this to a wonderful man. I've known him for two weeks, and tonight is our third date," she said, to cat calls and whistles of innuendo. "Don't laugh," she said, her eyes teasing and playful. "You know when it's your soul mate," she said, and began to read something about him and the night sky.

Piper smiled, caught Joe's eye, and laughed. He looked embarrassed. As well he should be, she thought. She wasn't bothered that he'd brought along a date, and not really surprised. Joe was Joe. Okay, so she was bothered, but she'd told him no, she reminded herself.

She looked at him, his attention now focused on his date, face unreadable. What could he be thinking, having some woman wax lovingly about you naked under the night sky?

She laughed out loud at the part of the poem, a verse about the poke from your spoke giving her hope. Yikes, she thought, covering her laughter with a cough. Girlfriend, Piper wanted to tell her, that poem was not a good idea, and probably wasted on Joe.

He turned and caught her eye and smiled. She smiled back, trying not to laugh, moving her eyes and eyebrows up in question. Did he sink lower in his chair before he shrugged at her silent question?

It went on like that for the next hour, poets reciting, some loud, some soft, some with guitar accompaniments, some with portable keyboards, a few drums, some really long ones about the war, living free, and his personal favorite of the night, to tea or not to tea— an ode to the tea bagging community of America.

Joe drank his coffee, waiting for a chance to leave, and finally it presented itself. The poets were taking a break. The god of the non-poetic had finally answered his prayers and he'd talked Rachel into leaving. He was sitting there waiting for her to return from the ladies' room, pleased that he was finally getting out of there.

Piper had been walking throughout the shop. He'd kept an eye on her, coffee carafe in her hand, refilling coffee cups, now standing next to his table.

"Under the night sky? Really, Joe? Had I known you were all that, I'd have made time. We could have used my office; forget about going somewhere else,

Mr. 'I've got women writing poems in my honor,' " she said, one eyebrow lifted before she started to laugh.

"Hey, you had your chance," he said, falling into her smile.

Both of them looked up as Rachel joined him, sliding into the seat with him, entwining her arm into his, pushing herself closer to him.

"Nice poem," Piper said to her.

"Thank you," she said, smile wide, pushing herself even more into Joe.

"Well, have a good night, you two," Piper said, winking at Joe. "Might want to take it indoors this time," she said, and chuckled.

He laughed, but caught himself before Rachel noticed. Piper watched him pass her on his way out, taking note of his hand entwined with the woman's.

—⁂—

Joe rolled over and looked to the space next to him, now empty, and inwardly groaned, hoping that Shane wasn't awake. He'd overslept, meant to get up and get her out long before light and before Shane woke up.

He sat up, throwing his legs over the side of the bed, running his hand through his hair. Usually he limited women and their overnight stays, but it had been a while for him and the sitter said Shane was asleep when he arrived home after leaving Lights Out, so he thought he'd quietly tiptoe her in and quietly tiptoe her out in the morning. Things hadn't worked out quite the way he planned. Hell, the whole night hadn't gone according to plan. He was still smarting from running into Piper, her laughter, her grin, her assumptions that she knew him.

He stood up, grabbed his pants, slid his legs into them, found a t-shirt and pulled it over his head and went in search of Rachel of the Night Sky. He still couldn't comprehend how she'd come up with that.

Where had she gotten off to, he wondered, walking over to check the adjoining bathroom. No sign there. Maybe she left early, on her own, but he doubted that. She had been pushing for more lately, wanted to meet his nephew—proof she could do family. She couldn't do his family. Shane was enough for him. He didn't mind, in fact he loved his nephew, hadn't thought twice about where he would live after his mother left. Of course it would be with him. But it still put him with children sooner that he'd expected, if at all.

He played dad growing up, starting at the ripe old age of ten. His father and mother had not been anywhere near responsible for him and his sister.

He headed down the hall, looking under Shane's door. It was dark. Hopefully he was still asleep. He entered the kitchen and yes, there she was, standing next to the coffee maker, bra and panties on. Not the best way to start the morning with kids around, but she didn't know that. She turned, smiling as he walked over to her. He pulled his t-shirt over his head and handed it to her. She looked at him, surprised.

"In case you run into my nephew," he said, reaching around her for a coffee cup.

"Thanks for making me coffee, Rachel," she said, to him, a little irritation creeping into her voice. "And I didn't know he was here," she added.

"Thank you," he said, pouring a cup and leaning against the counter. She slipped over closer to him, squeezing in, lifting her face and placing a soft kiss on his lips.

"I had a good time last night. Thanks," she said.

"You're welcome."

"What are you doing today?" she asked.

"Not sure."

"Want me to stay a little longer?" she said, moving her hand to the button of his jeans.

"Not today. I usually spend time with my nephew on the weekends, plus I've got to catch up a little on work," he said, looking at her. Her hand stopped mid-button at the look he gave her.

"I could hang out with you, too. Or maybe we could get together tonight? Want me to call you?" she said, not quite ready to give up the ghost.

He shook his head. "Let me call you," he said, taking the coffee cup from her hand. "My nephew will be up in a little bit. I try not to mix my personal life with his." He took her hand and lead her back down the hall to his room. He closed the door and started looking around for her clothes. He handed them to her. She snatched them from his hand and turned her back to him.

"I'll wait by the front door," he said, closing his bedroom door behind him as he left the room. Joe, you could have handled that better, he thought, ad-

79

monishing himself. Yeah, but it wouldn't have been nearly as effective. Rachel and her night sky would not be calling him again, he thought.

—⁓—

"So are you ready for school?" Joe asked Shane as he stood inside the door of his room.

"Been ready, stay ready, born ready," Shane said, looking at his uncle and laughing. That was the line they shared with each other, a habit they started right after Shane had come to live with him. He loved this kid, couldn't imagine loving his own flesh and blood more.

Shane had been so shy, so unsure of himself when he came to live with Joe, and now he was not the same kid anymore. A stable home seemed to worked for him.

At first Joe wasn't sure what parenting an elementary-aged child required, but he'd known what unstable looked like, so he started out by doing exactly the opposite of the way he'd been raised. So far, so good. Between he and Reye, and the teachers and principal at school, they'd gotten him on track. Success at school had helped to build his confidence.

Had he known Reye would have been what he was looking for, he'd have treated her differently in the beginning of their relationship. Not that she would have been interested. She loved Stephen.

School started tomorrow. His mind moved away from its musing and moved on to his internal list of what Shane would need for the day.

Chapter 6

It isn't so bad here, Taylor thought, looking around the room at the kids sitting at the tables surrounding her in her homeroom at her new school. A Mr. Marshall would be her homeroom teacher. Homeroom was their first stop here at the beginning of each day. She also had Mr. Marshall for math.

Piper had insisted on walking her to her class. Thankfully, her sister hadn't been the lone parent. There were parents everywhere at this school. Most trailed behind their kids, but others stood talking to other parents in clumps in the hall before class and talking to teachers like they were old friends.

In her old school parents hadn't been allowed in. Kids were dropped off at the door. But this was a different kind of school, she could tell that already. There were different kinds of kids here, too. Maybe she would fit in.

The kid next to her rocked back and forth a little, autistic, she believed someone had said. They didn't tease him, a new concept for her, and the other children seemed to be used to him. That in itself was interesting. His name was Sebastian, and he spent a lot of time on the computer.

The girls had also been a surprise. They were actually friendly to her. A few had come over and introduced themselves. Judith, Heather, and Sarah, she believed those were their names.

No needless teasing about her baseball cap, her jeans, questions about her wanting to be a boy. No, she wasn't a boy and didn't want to be one. She just liked what the boys did, and she wasn't interested in clothes—jeans, a shirt, and sneakers were all she needed.

"Hey. You're new here?"

Taylor looked up into the face of a boy, blond hair falling to his shoulders, sporting a Brazilian soccer shirt.

"Yes, I am."

"You'll like this school," he said, walking around the table and pulling out the chair next to her. "I've only been here two years," he said, sitting down. "Most of the kids have been here since pre-school. I saw you talking to Heather, Judith, and Sarah. They're nice, too. Most of the people here are nice."

He talks a lot, Taylor thought.

"My name is Shane. Shane Sandborne. What's yours?" he asked.

"Taylor Knight."

"Where you from?" he asked.

"San Antonio."

"I used to go to a different school before coming here, when I lived with my mom. Kids there were mean, plus I had a hard time learning things."

"Is it different here?" she asked.

"Yeah," he said, looking over at her. "I like the hat," he added, pausing for a second. "I'm going to sit next to you, look out for you, since you're the new kid. Have any questions, just ask me."

Taylor returned his gaze and nodded her head. "Okay. Nice to meet you, Shane," she said.

Their teacher Mr. Marshall had moved to the front of the room.

"It is time to begin the day. We have a new member joining our classroom this year," he said, and Taylor inwardly groaned. She hated the introduction of the new student more than she hated being the new student.

"We have a special way of introducing our new kids in this school, so stand up, guys," he said. "You know the drill."

Taylor watched as the kids formed a circle, like a football team would do before the start of a game to pump themselves up. The circle started moving, rocking from side to side, children's arms wrapped around the shoulders of the students next to them. Mr. Marshall started talking, his voice a hair above a whisper.

"This year, we are excited to have a new student in our class. Her name is Taylor Knight," he said, moving side-to-side along with the children. "Taylor hails from the city of San Antonio, has a little sister also attending our school, and loves basketball. Let's give it up everyone, for Taylor," he said. The circle started to clap in unison.

"Follow me, Taylor," Mr. Marshall said to her, and she did, walking around the circle and high fiving the kids like she was the starter of the game. She laughed. They were all laughing and smiling by the time she completed the circle.

"Thank you, students," Mr. Marshall said, scanning his students. "We are happy to have you here in our classroom. Take your seats, kids, and let's get this party started."

Taylor took her seat next to Shane, who looked over and smiled. He leaned over and whispered in her ear, "Told you that you'd like it here."

She sat back and reached for the schedule Mr. Marshall was currently passing out to the class. Maybe she would.

———

Piper pulled in to the school parking lot, at the end of the first day. Her eyes searched for an empty spot. This was a small school; about 300 kids from grades pre-K to eight were housed in a three-story brick building situated on two acres of land, surrounded by an older, established neighborhood.

Lots of land, but not so much parking, Piper thought as she made her second pass through the parking lot, finally finding someone leaving.

She walked into Ken's class, noting the many parents here—old hands, apparently. She smiled at the teacher, Mrs. Samson, who stood talking to an older woman, maybe someone's grandmother. She had Mrs. Samson, an older woman in her sixties, earlier that day.

Piper stood for a second, observing Ken in the midst of play. She had missed having the girls with her today.

Ken spotted her and walked over to meet her, a smile in place, taking Piper's hand in hers and moving them toward her teacher. Mrs. Samson stood in the middle of two sets of parents, and Piper and Ken walked over and stood quietly waiting their turn. About three minutes later, Mrs. Samson turned to them.

"Hello, Piper, nice to see you again," she said, pulling Kennedy's body into her side. "I enjoyed having your sister in my class today. She is going to be fine," she said, taking Piper's hand in her free one with a grip that would have made a wrestler proud. She was strong for her old self, Piper thought, trying not to grimace.

"I'm glad. I was a little worried."

"Don't be. She'll be fine," Mrs. Samson said, letting go of Piper's hand. "I'm going to have a really special class this year, I can tell," she said, squeezing Kennedy, who seemed pleased by the attention and the hug.

"And while you're here, there are some volunteer sign-up sheets for upcoming activities that will require our parents' assistance. Feel free to make use of them. We need drivers for field trips, hosts for parties, so find something you like. And always feel free to call if you ever have any concerns or questions about Kennedy," she said, dismissing Piper nicely and politely, as there were parents waiting in the queue to talk to her now. She gave a final squeeze to Kennedy. "I'll see you tomorrow," she said, looking down into Ken's face.

"Let's go see what we can sign up for," Piper said, looking over at Kennedy after they'd moved away from the teacher. They walked over to look at the sign-up sheets.

Who knew there was so much to do? Piper put her name down for two field trips and signed up to help with the Halloween carnival. That sounded like fun, and it was a ways off. They collected Ken's backpack and headed out the door to check out Taylor's room.

Piper felt like a salmon heading upstream as she and Ken made their way toward Taylor's room, which was located at the opposite end of the building. When they reached the door, Ken let go of Piper's hand and ran into Taylor's classroom, searching for her sister like some seek-and-destroy missile. Taylor stood talking to a blond haired kid about her age.

Piper watched them from the doorway, admiring the way Taylor introduced Ken to the boy. She was glad that they were more friends than enemies, as she knew some sisters could be.

Taylor seemed happy, her smile large as she talked to the little boy before moving off with her sister's hand in hers to talk to three other children standing nearby.

Piper looked around the room. There was a sign-up table here, too. Piper walked over to it, looking at her choices.

There was a sheet for help with the science fair. She used to be okay in science; maybe she could help with that and Halloween. She was thinking it over when Taylor appeared at her side, with her boy buddy in tow.

"Piper, this is my new friend," she said.

"Hi, new friend," Piper quipped. Taylor rolled her eyes and the boy smiled.

"His name is Shane," Taylor said.

"Hi, Shane. Nice to meet you. Are you new to the school, too?"

"No, I started last year. This is my second year," he said.

"Are your parents here tonight?" she asked, looking around the room.

"No. I live with my uncle. He's my legal guardian, and I've been with him for the last two years, since my mother got sick," he replied, earnest and sincere.

"I'm sorry. I hope your mother is better now?" she said. Shane's face shifted and turned cloudy.

"I think so," he said.

"You're lucky to have someone care for you. He must be a nice man," she said.

"He is the best. He should be here soon," Shane said.

"Can we stay and meet him?" Taylor asked, eyes pleading.

"Sure," Piper said, still caught in the euphoria of the girls making friends.

"I'll bring him over when he gets here," Shane said.

"We'll be over there," Taylor said, grabbing Shane's hand and pulling him along behind her and back toward the corner filled with other children. They were having a good time, occupying themselves while their parents visited with the teacher or looked around the classroom. Ken tagged along, watching her older sister and this new boy with a this is an interesting development look in her eyes.

Piper went back to considering the Halloween carnival. She could volunteer for both of the girls' classes in one night. She decided to also sign up for the spring trip to the water park and a trip to the humane society.

Having completed that task she looked up, scoping out the other parents. And then she watched Joe walk into the room, looking good enough to eat. She hadn't seen him in what, a month at least, not since the poetry night. He'd stopped coming by the shop.

He'd come from work, and was dressed professionally in a light blue dress shirt, open at the throat, tucked into nice dress slacks. The whole ensemble appeared expensive.

Did he ever have a bad hair day, a bad anything day? she wondered, continuing to watch him. He was fine. She couldn't deny that, didn't even try.

Don't tell me he has a kid, she thought, looking around for offspring that matched him. Was he married? What a disappointment that would be. She watched him as his eyes scanned the room, meeting up with hers. He was surprised. She could read it in his eyes. He smiled at her and she returned his with one of her own.

"Uncle Joe!" She watched as Shane dashed over to his side. Taylor followed behind, cautious in her approach, recognition in her eyes, too. Piper watched as Joe smiled at Shane, and noted the love reflected in his eyes.

"Uncle Joe, this is my new friend, Taylor," Shane said, reaching for Taylor's hand, pulling her to stand next to him. Joe looked over at Taylor, who smiled shyly back at his uncle.

"You've been to my sister's shop," said Taylor.

"Yes. Lights Out Coffee," Joe replied.

"So you know her sister Piper, too?" Shane asked.

"I do, actually," he said, looking at Shane.

Piper walked over to stand behind Taylor and Ken.

"Piper," Shane said, looking up at her with pride for his uncle displayed in his eyes. "This is my Uncle Joe. Joe Sandborne," he said.

"Your uncle, imagine that. Hello, Joe. I can see the resemblance." she said, looking between the two of them, noting the blond hair reaching both their shoulders. Different eye colors, though.

"So Shane's your nephew?"

"Yes."

"Joe, can I show Piper and Kennedy my locker? We'll be right back," Shane said, looking between the two of them.

"We'll need to get going soon, so don't be long," Joe said.

"I won't." Shane turned and pulled her sisters along behind him. Joe and Piper watched the kids move away. She turned to look at him, feeling suddenly nervous.

"So," she said.

"So," he replied and smiled.

"How long has he been with you?"

"Two years."

"What happened to his mother?"

"Long story," he said. That was clearly the end of that.

Okay, she could take hints.

"How do you like the school?" she asked.

"I love it. It's been great for Shane. We've been very happy here."

"Good to know."

It was quiet for a moment.

"How long are you going to have your sisters?"

"It looks like it may be the entire year, or the first half at least."

"You okay with that?"

"Getting used to it," she said.

"It gets easier," he said.

The kids came back over.

"Well, we'd better get going," he said. "Say good-bye to Taylor. I need to talk to your teacher for a second, and then we'll leave," Joe said to Shane.

"Sure, Uncle Joe. See you tomorrow, Taylor, Kennedy. Nice meeting you, Piper," he said, walking to stand at his uncle's side.

"See you around. Nice to meet you, too, Shane," she said to Joe, smiling at Shane before following Taylor and Kennedy out the door.

—⁂—

"So the two of you like school?" Piper asked, pulling out of the school's parking lot a few moments later. She listened as Kennedy talked about her first day.

"You like Shane?" Piper asked Taylor after Kennedy quieted.

Taylor looked over at Piper, assessing.

"I like him as a friend," she said. "Not interested in boys yet. It's too early for me."

"Good to know. I'm going to stop by Target and pick up the rest of your school list, and then we'll head to the coffee shop," she said. "You guys hungry?"

"Nope."

Kennedy started telling her about each of the kids in her class, full descriptions, and Piper let her mind drift, happy that the girls were happy, reflecting on her surprise at seeing Joe. He had a kid, his nephew, and like her, he was taking care of his own, choosing family over himself.

She thought back to the last time she'd seen him. She remembered the woman, her expression as she read the poem about him. Piper had seen naked and unguarded want, maybe even love in those eyes. That was a frightening proposition, because she didn't think he did love; sex, yes—mind blowing, leave your heart in tatters sex—but sex only, not love.

She missed seeing him, missed sparring with him. She liked that he'd pushed back and wasn't intimidated by her assertiveness. And now, a family-first man. What a surprise.

—⟋⟍—

"So how long have you known Piper?" Shane asked while Joe drove them home.

"About two or three months," he said.

"You've been to their coffee shop?"

"Yep."

"You have to take me there sometime," he said.

Joe nodded, but knew he wouldn't if he could avoid it. What a surprise to see Piper again, although it shouldn't have been. It made sense. The school was in close proximity to her shops, and her dad could probably afford it, but he hadn't thought the girls would be with her on a permanent basis.

And he was back to being impressed with her and aroused, as sick as that sounded, all over again. He'd actually missed seeing her in the mornings, a little foreplay with his coffee. He thought she was easy to be around, funny and welcoming to her customers, to people in general. She seemed to take life as it came, just went with the flow, made the best of it, and there was something very sexy in that, especially for him.

Her physical presence was another pull, and probably always would be. She'd looked good today outfitted in a dress that clung to her figure. It had been an enticement from the beginning. He didn't think her beautiful, and still didn't. But she'd gotten his attention tonight, attractive in her own way, her hair curly around her head, freckles dusting the top of her cheeks, lips full and shiny. When she smiled she was pretty, or maybe he thought so because he admired the person underneath the skin.

"So, are there any new kids besides Taylor?" he asked, letting Shane take him into the world of the fifth-grader, content to think of something other than Piper.

Chapter 7

Piper sat in the living room of her home. It was Sunday evening, and she'd sat through two half-hour programs with Kennedy on a few of the children's channels. Kennedy had taken off, needing to prepare for school.

She'd remained behind, flipping through channels, feet up, thinking of Joe. He was officially taking up space in her mind now. He'd chosen to raise his nephew, and that made quite the impression on her. In fact, it was responsible for moving him to her eligible-for-more-than-just-sex category.

Her phone rang, interrupting her thoughts. It was Margarite, her dad's first wife.

"Hello, stepmother number one," Piper said playfully. She loved her dad's first wife. Their relationship hadn't started out great but, over time, Margarite had hung in there with her and helped her navigate through her teen years. Piper now appreciated the patience that Margarite had shown her.

She and Margarite made it a point to talk at least once a week. She communicated with her first set of sisters on Facebook weekly.

"So, how are you and the girls?" Margarite asked.

"Fine. School's rocking along. No scarring of children on my watch," she answered.

"I'm sure you're doing fine with your sisters."

"Let's just say that I'm not doing too bad. Plus, they're easy, not like me growing up, fighting with you all the time."

"You were fine, once we got to know each other."

"You don't have to pretend with me, I was there," Piper said, laughing.

"So how are the shops? Keeping you busy, along with the girls?"

"Not too much. I've done some extra hiring to cover for me. I wanted to have two people on the clock, and one of those used to be me, but Daddy Warbucks of the deep pockets is helping out financially, so I'm free to some extent. I'm at the shop while the girls are at school and some evenings and weekends, but not too much."

"And how are the parents?" she asked.

"Christina and Mac?" Piper responded. "Who knows. She's at least talking to him on the phone now, but he's not in the sharing mood with me. Really tight-lipped about what's going on between them. I do know that her mother is not getting any better. They don't expect her to live past six months, but you never know. I think Christina wanted to bring her back to the states, but her mother's refused."

"I'm sorry," Margarite said.

"Yeah. Me, too." It was silent for a second. "So what are you up to? How's Freddy?" Piper asked. Freddy was Margarite's second husband, and a keeper.

"Fine. Busy at work. If he's not there, he's holed up in his garage tinkering with his old cars. Told him

I needed to change my body type to a '67 Chevy and maybe he'd notice me more," she said, laughing.

"How about you? Are there any new men in your life?"

"Are you kidding me?"

"Well, you're still young. There is still hope. I may see some grandchildren out of you yet."

"Don't hold your breath," Piper said, laughing again. "I'm changing the subject now. I realize it's way early, but what are you and the girls' plans for Thanksgiving?" Piper asked.

"I don't know. I'll check. Why?"

"If Taylor and Kennedy are still with me, and I think they will be, I'll probably be going to visit Nanny and Pa. And since I'm making a trek your way, I thought Blair and Samantha could meet me in Raywood for a day. Nanny would like to see them, see how much they've grown, and they could hang out with Kennedy and Taylor, spend some time getting to know them," she said.

"I'll talk to them about it," Margarite said. "Listen, Freddy just walked in. He had to work late today. I'll chat with them and call you next week. You take care," she said, hanging up.

Piper hoped Blair and Samantha could make it; she wanted them to meet Ken and Taylor. She hoped that all five of them could hang out. She felt proprietary toward her four sisters. Being the oldest, she had been around when Blair and Samantha were born and grew up with them. She wanted that for Ken and Taylor.

She may have teased Margarite about being her stepmother, but she had been more like a mother to her than the one who'd given birth to her had ever been. Her Nanny had been there for her in the beginning, and Margarite had taken over after age twelve.

She'd raised Piper, suffered through her teenage antics and angst, and saw her off to college. What could have been a difficult time for her, with her dad remarrying and producing two new siblings, Margarite had transformed into a family where Piper had felt vitally needed and loved.

─ᴍ─

Second week in September

Piper stood along the wall outside of Ken's classroom waiting for her to be dismissed for the day.

"Hey, Ken. How was school?" she said, reaching for her sister's lunchbox.

"Good. We are going to the zoo tomorrow. We are supposed to remind our parents," she said. "Are you coming, Piper?"

"No, didn't sign up to drive for that one," she answered. "Ready?"

"Yes."

"Let's go wait for your sister."

Taylor preferred to come to them, instead of them coming for her. She was in fifth grade, soon to be middle school, and didn't need her sisters meeting her at the door. So Piper and Ken found two chairs near the office to sit and wait. They didn't have to wait long. Five minutes later, Taylor approached them with Shane two steps behind.

"Can Shane come to the coffee shop with us today?" Taylor asked. No hellos, just getting right to the point.

"Uh, doesn't your uncle normally pick you up?" Piper turned to look at Shane, feeling a little put on the spot. "I bet he has plans for you," she added, hoping so.

"Nope, he doesn't, and he wouldn't mind. Plus he's been late the last few times. I can call and ask him now. I'll tell him I'm going home with you. He wouldn't mind, I've done it before. It's okay as long as he knows the person and their parents."

"Wow," Piper said, impressed by the sheer number of words he'd gotten out without taking a breath.

"Come on, Piper. He's my friend. You know his uncle and he knows you," Taylor said, pleading her case.

Piper sighed and looked over at Ken, who sat smiling at Shane, her new crush in place.

"I'll call my uncle right now," Shane said, somehow reading her. He knew adult indecision when he saw it.

"I bet he's busy."

"No, he told me I could call him anytime," Shane said, dialing the number as he talked.

They all watched Shane, waiting.

"Uncle Joe. Taylor has invited me to go home with her. Her sister, Piper, says it's okay. We're going over to their coffee shop. I've never been there. Remember you promised to take me. You can pick me up from there."

He had that talking without breathing thing down pat, Piper thought.

"No, she's sitting right here," Shane said, looking at Piper and smiling before handing her his phone. "He wants to talk to you," he said.

"Okay," Piper said, taking the phone from his hand. She stood up and walked away from the bum-rush trio.

"Hello," she said, shy now, tentative even.

"Hey," he said, smooth as warm caramel candy.

"The kids just sprang this on me," she blurted out, wanting him to know it wasn't her idea, like she was using the kids' friendship with his nephew for more.

"No problem," he said agreeably.

"I mean, it's not that I mind. I don't, but I can understand if you have a problem with the short notice and all. We usually go back to either one of the two shops, do homework, snack, and I work a little. Then we head for home. Shane is welcome to come with us if you want, but I understand if you don't. It's such short notice, we can do it some other time," she said, looking back at the kids, who were seated, waiting and watching her.

"It's not a problem, Piper, really. I can pick him up from your shop. Just tell me which one."

"The new one; the one you usually come to. We'll be there until about six or six-thirty. Will that work for you?"

"Yes. Let me call the school, give them permission."

"Okay. The kids will be pleased."

"I'm sure they will," he said. "Let me talk to Shane for a second, and then give me five to call the school."

"Sure," she said, walking back and handing the phone to Shane. She watched as he nodded his head and said yes a few times before hanging up.

"He's going to call the school now, and then we can go," he said to Taylor.

Another ten minutes and they all loaded up in Piper's car and she drove the five minutes it took to get to the shop. She parked and they headed in, Taylor securing a booth near the TV. No surprise there.

Piper noted the comfort and ease with which her sisters moved around the shop, delighted in the knowledge that they felt like they belonged here. After securing three strawberry banana smoothies, they started in on their homework, with Ken sitting next to them, working on writing or something. Mostly, though, she gazed at Shane.

Homework took about an hour to complete, so then it was time for play on the Wii, the reason behind the focus and dedication to homework. Whatever worked, Piper thought, watching them.

She worked the counter and cleaned. Cleaning was a job that never ended, either at home or here. Piper turned at the bell that rang when the door opened. It was Joe, dressed for work.

He scanned the room for his nephew and smiled when he spotted him toward the back of the shop, dancing, playing on the Wii. He needed to get going; still had dinner in front of him.

He turned and found Piper's eyes on him. She was back at the counter, leaning against it, her arms crossed, watching him. Her hair was in those puffs, his favorite of her hairstyles, a smirk at her mouth. He took a few steps, closing the distance between them.

"Thanks for letting Shane come with you," he said.

"It worked out well, actually. He kept Taylor entertained, gave her motivation to complete her homework quickly, not drag it out like she usually does."

They were quiet, watching the kids play.

"So how was your day?" he asked.

"Fine. Yours?"

"Fine," he replied. They went back to silence again, watching the kids finish the dance. She was nervous again. Joe looked down at this watch.

"Getting settled in to school?" he asked.

"Yes, figured out how to check grades online," she said.

"Good thing to know. You're welcome to call if you have a school-related question. I might know the answer."

"Thanks," she said, watching her sister and Shane, laughing as Taylor missed a step. "You know if you need any help with Shane, feel free to call. My sisters like him and it would be easy to pick him up when I grab the girls."

"Thanks," he said, looking at her, pleased by her offer. "Well, I'd better get going," he said, heading toward the corner to the kids. She pushed away from the counter and followed him over.

"Shane, dude."

"Hey, Uncle Joe. I'm almost done here. I'm winning."

"That's good, but we need to get moving. Tell everyone thanks," he said, reaching for Shane's backpack from the floor.

"Thanks for letting me come home with you today," Shane said, stepping off the mat.

"We enjoyed it. You have to come back another time, maybe on the weekend, and you can stay longer with us."

"Can I come this weekend?" Shane asked his uncle.

"We'll see," Joe said. "Thanks again," he said to Piper before he and Shane walked toward the front door.

She watched them leave. She glanced at her watch—6:30. It was pushing past time for her crew to head home.

"Let's go, girls," she said, turning and heading toward her office.

Chapter 8

Joe was tired. He had gotten home later than he liked two days in a row; at eight yesterday, and now he was walking up to his door at eight-thirty. Thank God it was Friday. Fortunately he'd found a sitter for Shane who seemed to be working out okay so far. She'd picked him up from school both days he ran late. She was a college student, a little flighty, but sweet.

Joe unlocked the front door, and was surprised to walk in and find several people in his home. There seemed to be a party going on, and he hadn't gotten his invitation. There were kids present—well they weren't kids really—maybe nine years younger or so than him. He wondered when he'd gotten old. They smiled, said hi, and he smiled back. He walked toward the kitchen, where he found yet more party guests.

"Hey, Joe, you're home early," the sitter, April, said, all chipper. She opened the door to the refrigerator, pulled out his gallon of milk, and walked to the counter, where she poured some into a bowl. Empty egg shells sat in an egg carton next to the bowl.

"I'm making an omelet," she said, putting the top back on the milk, picking up the fork and beginning to stir. "Some of my friends were hungry, so I decided to make enough for us all. I told them you wouldn't mind, that you'd be cool with it."

"Where's Shane?" he asked.

"In his room, I think."

Joe turned and walked out the door toward Shane's room. Yep, there was Shane, sitting on his bed, watching as two other college-age boys sat on the floor, controllers in their hands, playing a video game.

"Hey, Uncle Joe," Shane said from the bed, smiling before pointing to the two young men seated at the foot of his bed, feet stretched out before them, crossed at the ankles, bodies twisting as they gave chase to some alien on the screen.

"Hey, dude," they said in unison, eyes darting in between Joe and their game.

Joe turned and walked back to the kitchen.

"April, I'll take over from here," he said, holding his hand out for the fork, turning off the heat on the stove. "It's been a long day. You and your crew should leave."

She seemed startled.

"Is there a problem?" she asked.

"Nope, just wanted you and only you in the house with Shane," he said.

"What's the big deal? I know these guys. They're harmless," she replied.

"I'm sure, but it's not what I hired you for. So, again, thanks for taking care of Shane." He reached for his wallet, took out enough to cover what he owed her, and handed it to her.

"I don't know what to say."

"Nothing is required. Come on, I'll see you out," he said, waiting as she walked out of the kitchen and called out to her friends. They came, the two from Shane's room, the four from the front, bewildered at first, and then angry, but leaving, which was all he cared about.

"So I'm not working here anymore?" she asked.

"No, you are not. Oh, let me have the key to the front door," he said. The confused expression on her face was priceless. She reached into her purse and pulled his key from her ring, gave it to him and followed her friends out of his home.

Okay, back to square one, Joe thought, heading back to the kitchen as Shane walked into the living room.

"Where did everyone go?" Shane asked.

"Home. You hungry?" Joe asked.

"Nope, I treated April to Jack in the Box on our way home from school. Used my allowance," he said proudly.

Joe inwardly groaned and rubbed his forehead. "I'm going to clean up the kitchen then. I could use some help and conversation," he said. He could use some sleep, but he liked to talk to Shane find out what was going on in school and his life.

"Sure," Shane said.

"So how is school?" Joe asked, walking in the direction of the kitchen.

"Fine. Taylor and I have been assigned a project together," Shane said, following him.

"Really," he said, walking to the sink, putting the stopper in while reaching below for some soap.

"I like her a lot. She plays soccer and basketball," he said.

"That's good," Joe said, running his hands through the water and moving to stack plates. He ran them through the suds before putting them in the dishwasher—a habit he'd picked up from his foster mom, one of the many household tips she'd taught him. He spent many a night in her kitchen, helping her clean up. She listened to his seventeen-year-old self, his anger and hurt. That was all so long ago.

"Basketball, huh?" he said to Shane.

"Yep. And she's smart, and pretty, and fun," he said.

Joe listened as Shane moved on to the other parts of his day and his life. He allowed his nephew's voice to quiet some of the stress he'd felt from work, reminding him of work's place, behind his family. Shane was his family. He'd worry about finding a new sitter tomorrow. Tonight he'd just enjoy his nephew, maybe watch a movie or a game or something and fall asleep on the couch. Sounded like a perfect ending to this week.

—⁓—

The following week Piper walked down the hallway searching for Taylor's locker and a forgotten assignment. She found the locker and placed Taylor's assignment in the blue folder as per her sister's instructions. Might as well snoop a little, now that she was here. She was surprised at how neat and tidy it was. It was color-themed with coordinated shelving, a mirror, and pencil holders magnetically clinging to the inside of her locker. This generation had all the cool stuff.

She closed the door. It was quiet in the hall. She made her way down the hall, headed toward the exit, until she heard that voice—Joe's voice. What is he doing here? she wondered, moving toward the sound, which was coming from a classroom.

The door was open, providing a clear view to the inside. She would be able to peer in if she stood a ways back. She didn't want to be seen, just to see, and this spot afforded her the best opportunity to do both.

It was the computer lab. Kids were sitting around computers while Joe, of all people, talked. Was he teaching? She listened for a second and yep, he was indeed lecturing, making jokes, and explaining something computer-related to the kids. She watched him smile—a full one, with nice teeth between soft and supple lips.

"Ms. Knight," someone said from behind her, causing Piper to nearly jump out of her skin. She turned to find Mr. Marshall, Taylor's homeroom teacher, standing next to her, his smile open, eyes interested.

Not now, she wanted to tell him, and wanted to hold her finger to her lips to tell him to lower his voice.

"Hi, Mr. Marshall," she said, keeping her voice low, hoping he would follow suit and not alert Joe to her presence. He smiled back, his eyes roaming over her.

"Good to see you, Ms. Knight," he said, giving her a once-over. Talk about a lack of subtlety.

"If you're looking for Taylor, she's not here. This is the computer lab."

"Yes, I know. It's okay. I was just leaving. Taylor forgot something at home and I just dropped it off, put it in her locker," she said softly, hoping to slink away.

Not today. Mr. Marshall's voice didn't do soft.

Joe's head popped out of the door of the class-room. "Piper, Mr. Marshall," he said in greeting, giving them a smile.

"Oh, hello, Joe. We apologize for disturbing your class. I was on my way to my room when I found Piper standing out here in the hall," he said.

Joe smiled, gave her an I'm busy working, you're interrupting look, and closed the door.

"Well," she said.

"He volunteers to teach sometimes. Computers are his area of expertise," he said, looking at her, offering an explanation in case she was offended. "Parent volunteers are the lifeblood of the school," he added.

"Oh, that's nice. Well, I guess I'd better get going."

"Sure. Take care," he said, turning to leave. Piper waited a second, allowing him to leave, listening as he walked away. She wanted one more glance, she told herself, standing on her tiptoes to look into the small square of glass at the top of the door of the computer lab. She found Joe again, bending over the shoulder of a boy, and watched him point to something on the screen as the child's face lifted into a smile. He moved away. She watched his back, and then lower—it was nicely dressed in slacks, belt, shirt tucked in. She sighed.

She'd lost him. He'd moved out of her range of vision. She continued to peer in. Where was he? Her question was answered a few seconds later when his head popped in front of the window. She jumped back, startled and shaken, and caught his gaze. He made a face and she laughed.

—⁓—

Her father had taken the girls for the weekend and, lucky her, McKenzie and Pepper went along, too. She'd taken the day off from the shops as soon as she finished grocery shopping for the week. She grabbed her green bags from the back of her car—pulled out her BlackBerry, the source of her grocery list—and headed into the store.

Piper reached for a cart and stopped first in produce. She looked down at her list.

"Joe."

She heard a little boy's voice call out from behind her. She knew that voice. It belonged to Shane. She kept her head down and scooted closer to the cucumbers. She wore one of Taylor's hats on her head this morning. She pulled the bill lower and listened for the sounds as they passed her by, turning over the cucumbers and looking at them but not really seeing them.

They were passing her. She turned to look, slowly moving her head to her left. Yep, it was them. Shane was walking beside a lady who was seated in one of those riding carts with the big wire basket in front. She looked to be in her 70s, maybe even older. Joe was pushing his basket bringing up the rear, a smile on his face, baseball cap on his head, hair behind his ears brushing his shoulders.

God, it wasn't fair that he should always look good.

"Mrs. Lewis, would you like me to get you some grapes?" she heard Shane's voice say.

"Yes, thank you, young man," the older woman said.

Piper watched as Shane lifted a bunch of grapes, placed them in one of those clear plastic bags, and placed it in the older woman's cart before going back and doing the same for Joe. Joe was adding bananas to both of the carts, smiling and talking to the older lady. Whatever he said caused the woman to smile.

What the hell was going on here? She hung back, watching them as they continued their shopping for the older woman and themselves.

Please don't let him be helping that older woman. Please don't let him be a really nice guy, she thought as she continued to hang back, watching as they finished with the produce section and moved on.

Shoot, she said to herself. She was here to shop, too, not to just watch them. She hurriedly gathered the produce she needed.

Where did they go? She quickly glanced down the aisle closest to the produce section, not wanting to get caught snooping but not wanting to lose them, either.

She pushed her cart, feeling like an inept spy, eyes down, glancing out of the corner of her eyes as she passed each aisle. Okay, they were not in the condiment section. Nope, not in the baking aisle, either. Oh, there they were, near the meat. Piper ducked in to an aisle, staying near the edge, peeking out. They were at it again. Joe had a package of pre-cut chicken in his hand, smiling. Who knew he could smile so much. He was talking to the older lady and she laughed and returned Joe's smile.

He was something else when he laughed, in a whole other category. Shane was standing beside him talking, too, looking between the older woman and Joe, a picture of youthful happiness. What a nice picture they made, Piper thought. Wonder who that was? His grandmother? She didn't think he had family around here.

The trio turned the corner, and Piper checked her list, gathering the items she needed quickly before checking and making sure the coast was clear.

She pulled out into the main aisle, headed toward the meat section herself, on the lookout for them. They were in the milk section. She would have to pass them, but maybe if she walked quickly and kept her head down, they wouldn't see her.

"Piper!" she heard just as she cleared the aisle.

It was Shane's voice. She increased her pace, hoping to turn into the next aisle. Maybe he'd only think he'd seen her, but then she heard footsteps running toward her. Crap.

"Piper," Shane said, catching up to her. "It's me, Shane," he said, all smiles.

"Hey, Shane," she said, returning his smile.

"I told Joe it was you," he said.

"Oh, he's here with you?" she asked.

"Yes, we are here with my neighbor. You have to meet her."

"No, I wouldn't want to interrupt. I bet you guys just want to shop."

"No, she's a really nice lady, like you. We shop here all the time. She used to watch me for my uncle sometimes. Come on, please," he said.

"Sure."

Always a sucker to please, she followed Shane back to his uncle and the little older woman. Joe was putting coffee creamer into her basket.

He looked up and caught her eyes. She wanted to laugh. He seemed so uncomfortable, like he'd been caught with his pants down. No, scratch that— that probably wasn't something he'd be embarrassed about.

"Hi, Piper," he said, back to cool-as-ever. The uncomfortable face had been put away.

"Hi, Joe," she replied.

"This is my neighbor, Mrs. Lewis," Shane said. "Mrs. Lewis, this is the lady with the coffee shop, the one with the two sisters," he added.

"Hello, dear," Mrs. Lewis said, smiling, her eyes twinkling.

"Hello," Piper said, smiling back. "Don't let me interrupt your shopping."

"No, you're not interrupting at all. I like company, the more the merrier. Joe and Shane are kind enough to take an interest in an old woman. They shop with me once a month. My grandchildren live in Dallas and I don't get around like I used to," she said.

"That's nice of them," Piper said, eyes flickering to Joe, who was studying a milk carton like he personally knew the missing person listed on its container.

"It was nice meeting you."

"Taylor's coming home tomorrow?" Shane asked her.

"That's right."

"Well, goodbye," she said, smiling at Shane and Mrs. Lewis before braving another glance at Joe. He looked back at her, his face back to that unreadable mask again.

"Bye, Joe," she said.

He gave her a nod, and watched as she turned and walked away.

—∿—

Third week in September

Joe entered his home. It was seven-thirty, and he was home early. He was very proud of himself. He pulled up short at the sight of his newest sitter with a girl on his lap, lips locked. They broke apart when they heard his foot hit the floor. He had done that intentionally.

"Sorry, Joe," Jim, the new sitter, said. "My girl-friend stopped by," he added for clarification.

Joe nodded. He could see that.

"Where's Shane?" Joe asked.

"He's in his room."

Joe watched as the two stood up from the sofa, the girl putting her clothes to rights while Jim adjusted himself.

"Will you need me next week?" he asked.

"No, I don't think so. You might as well leave me the key," Joe said, his hand out to Jim. The younger man dug into his pocket, pulled out a set of keys, and removed Joe's from his ring. Joe watched as they gathered their bags and left. He sighed.

He walked down the hall to Shane's room. The door was open and Shane lay on the bed, reading. He looked up and smiled.

"Hey, Joe."

"Hey, buddy. How was school?"

"Fine," he said, watching his uncle walk into his room and take a seat next to him.

"Tired?" Shane asked.

"Yep," he said, looking around the room. "You cleaned your room?"

"Yeah, well, I got done with my homework, and since Jim's girlfriend was here, I stayed in my room. Got tired of playing video games."

"How long was she here?" Joe asked.

"Since after school."

Joe nodded.

"Hungry?" he asked.

"Yep."

"Well, let's see what we can scrounge up to eat," he said, standing up from the bed, stretching his arms above his head. He let out another yawn. "Did you tell me your homework was done?"

"Yep."

"Good. Give me ten for dinner," he said, walking out of Shane's door.

"Sure," Shane said, watching his Uncle Joe leave. A few minutes later he heard Joe moving around in the kitchen. It was probably going to be an omelet night, his uncle's standby when he had to come up with something quick. Good thing he liked omelets. They had a lot of them lately. He was lucky to have his uncle, and he knew that. Life with his mother had taught him that. He still missed her, though. But he didn't tell Joe that.

He missed her holding him, the way she smelled, the way she smiled and sang to him before things got bad. It hadn't always been bad. He didn't talk about that with his uncle, either; it was a kind of sore subject. He sat up and put his book away, deciding to go help his uncle in the kitchen.

—⁂—

Shit. Joe looked at his watch. He was going to be late picking up Shane. He had gotten tied up in a meeting, one that he couldn't leave. He checked his time again. It was four o'clock and he was in San Antonio, at least an hour and a half drive on a good day, not rush hour traffic. He would never make the six o'clock deadline at the school.

Fuck, he thought, trying to figure a way out. He could call Reye, but he hated to do that. She was absolutely on his last-ditch list. Who could he call?

Piper popped into his mind. He could call her. She'd offered, but he wanted to stay clear of her if he could. She was too much of a pull for him, especially after their run-ins at school and the grocery store. He'd caught that *you're much more than I thought* look in her eye.

He looked at his watch again, gritting his teeth, and made the decision to call her. He stood and quietly left the room. Maybe he could reach her at the shop before she left to get her sisters. He found the number to her coffee shop on his BlackBerry, hoping she was at this one and not the other location. He was a lucky dog; he heard her voice after the first ring.

"Lights Out Coffee." She sounded all perky and bright.

"Piper. This is Joe, Shane's uncle."

"Hi, Joe," she said. He could tell she was surprised.

"I've got a huge favor to ask of you. I'm tied up here in San Antonio and there's no way I can get back there before six to grab Shane, not with traffic getting out of here. Not sure when I'll be leaving, actually. Could you grab him, and I'll pick him up from your shop?"

"Sure," she said.

"Okay." That was easy. "Thank you. The single most challenging thing about Shane is the child care issue, at least until he's old enough for me to leave him alone," Joe said.

"I understand. It's no problem. You'll probably need to call the school so that they can let him leave with me."

"Sure, sure. I'll call now. Thanks."

"Hey, before you go, let me give you my cell number," she said.

"Right," he said, surprised he'd forgotten to ask. He waited as she gave him her number.

"See you later," she said.

"Yeah, and thanks," he said, disconnecting, relieved at finding an answer to his dilemma but bothered by the realization that he was pleased with the possibility of seeing her, too.

—⚊—

"In 1.7 miles, turn left onto Saddleback Street," said the lovely British-accented voice on Joe's navigation system. He'd plugged in Piper's address before leaving San Antonio; he was running later than even he'd expected. She'd called to let him know that she was taking the kids to her home and that he could pick Shane up from there.

Saddleback Street was only about five minutes away from his house. He turned onto her street, which ended in a cul-de-sac with Piper's home smack dab in the middle of it. It was lit up like a Christmas tree. Every window was lit. It was a large home, larger than what he'd thought one person would need. This could hold a family of four or five easily. Maybe she was planning on a large family someday. Her drive was empty. He pulled in and parked.

He got out and walked to her front door. He could hear music coming from inside, the faint strains of zydeco. Not surprised by that. He rang the doorbell and waited. No answer. He waited a second and rang it again, pressing the bell longer this time.

Piper was upstairs and someone was at the door. She hadn't heard the doorbell, but she didn't need to. McKenzie and Pepper were doorbell hounds. One ring sent them into a frenzy of barking, and then headed toward the front door in search of prey. It was enough to send any burglar scurrying away, and fast. Must be Joe. She'd waited at the shop for him an extra thirty minutes before calling to let him know she was going home.

She walked down the stairs and over to the door. "You two have to move for me to see who this is," she said to her two guard dogs, who were barking away.

They kept right on barking. She took her foot, gingerly pushed them to the side, and opened the door.

"I see you found us," she said, stepping back to let Joe enter.

"Yes. Sorry I ran late. I'm not usually this late," he said, stepping into her home. The two dogs, barking furiously as he entered, stopped for a second and stepped over to give him a sniff. He watched them. One sniffed and moved on, the other stood there and looked up at him as if to say, You better watch yourself around here, dude. After getting its point across, it turned and followed its friend upstairs.

"Pepper and McKenzie, brother and sister," she said, watching them head back upstairs where their favorites resided. "Let me put this up and I'll be right back," she said, walking away from him. He watched her shorts-clad hips move, her ponytail resting at the very top of her head, puffy, bouncing along to the same tune as her butt. He looked around, taking in her home, which was cozy but cluttered.

He stood at the base of the stairs, his back to her front door, and looked straight ahead to what must be the kitchen, where Piper had disappeared. He could see parts of the counter and table; a small vase of flowers stood in the middle of the table. Her dad's money, he thought. This was a very large space for one woman.

To his left was a large, open living room. He walked over to it, taking in a large sectional couch, carpet on the floor. Someone was into pictures. They were everywhere. Tennis shoes of all sizes lay near the coffee table, Shane's included.

"Sorry about the mess. It's a permanent fixture for me, it seems. I can keep the shop spotless, but not home. But hey, home is where you should be comfortable, don't you think?"

"Yep," he said, turning to her, eyes roaming over her head to toe as she came to stand in front of him, toenails painted pink with yellow flowers on them. She followed his eyes.

"Ken's idea," she said. "She is going to make a beauty out of me yet." He smiled.

"I bet you're ready for Shane," she said, noting his silence at her comment. "He's a great kid, by the way, and that's a compliment to you since you've had a hand in raising him."

"Thanks."

"Let me go get him. You can come up if you want," she said, turning and taking the stairs, two at a time. He followed, working hard not to notice the size of her cheeks now that he was up close and personal with them. Yep, they were a nice size, small enough for one to fit nicely in each hand.

He turned away, glancing at the pictures on the wall leading up to the second floor. There were pictures of family, and of her father in his boxing gear, and with his arms around women Joe didn't recognize.

"Shane, your Uncle Joe is here," Piper said as she entered the room located just off the top of the stairs.

The kids were sitting on a small sofa, locked in mortal combat.

"Shane, take him out!" Taylor shouted, moving her body as if she had a gun in her hands instead of a controller.

"I did. Yeah, you're dead. We're almost to level five. Can I have a minute more?" Shane asked, looking quickly over his shoulder at his uncle.

"Nope, save it for later. Thank Taylor, Kennedy, and Piper for taking care of you, and let's go," Joe said as he entered the door of some type of game room, maybe more like library. He looked around, taking in the bookshelves on all but one wall, which held a flat screen and a small fireplace. Video games were shelved with DVDs and a huge CD collection. They vied for room on the shelves with some books.

"You've got school tomorrow, and so do they," he said, looking around at the room, searching for Shane's gear.

"Thanks, Piper, I had fun. Can I come back tomorrow?" Shane said, setting his controller down before standing up.

"Let's give Piper time to rest between visits," Joe said before she could answer. He picked up Shane's backpack from the small sofa.

A few moments later, he and Shane led the way back down the stairs, Taylor and Piper bringing up the rear, the dogs running from behind the crowd to the front of the line, reaching the door before all of them, managing not to trip anybody. The dogs were giving a final sniff to Joe's shoes while Shane grabbed his from the shoe pile.

"Thanks again for bringing him home with you, especially given the short notice," he said.

"Don't worry, we enjoyed having him," Piper said, opening the door, watching as Joe and Shane walked through. She and Taylor stood there and watched them get into their car and drive away, giving them a final wave.

"Shane's my best friend," Taylor said.

"You don't want a girl for a best friend?"

"Nope. Girls are work," she said. "Like you one minute and the next minute they don't. Too much trouble. Shane always likes me."

Piper locked the door, set the alarm, and couldn't argue with her sister's logic.

"Well I'm glad you have a friend. Shane is a nice kid. It's always nice to have a good friend."

"Did you have friends growing up?"

"Yeah, like you, they were more male than female. Plus I had your older sisters, Blair and Samantha, for company when they weren't getting on my nerves," she said, walking to turn off the lights in the living room, Taylor trailing along behind her.

"I don't know them that well," she said.

"We'll have to fix that," Piper responded, reminding herself to check with Margarite again. "They are nice, and fun. You would like them." Piper headed toward the kitchen to lock up in there.

"Where are they now?"

"Samantha, the oldest, is in her first year of college at Rice University. Blair is a junior in high school."

"I wish I were around them more. I like being here with you. Sometimes I feel different, not like I belong. You know, being from two different parents. It would be nice to know my sisters, though, since they are kind of like me."

Piper was surprised, but maybe she shouldn't have been. It was hard trying to find where you fit in, even when it was clear who you were. She couldn't imagine having to make a choice.

"I know. I'll see if I can get us together, soon, I promise," she said, pulling Taylor to her side, walking out the now dark kitchen headed back to the stairs.

"We'd better get ready for school tomorrow."

Chapter 9

A week later, Joe walked into Home Away From Home on his lunch hour. He hadn't been by since school started. But today he wanted to ask Reye's opinion about something as well as bring her up to date on Shane. He could have called, but he liked seeing her in person. He considered her a good friend, one of the few people who he felt truly cared about him and Shane. He didn't talk about himself much, and she knew more than most, which wasn't a lot. She wasn't pushy. That was one of his favorite traits in anyone.

He'd been feeling out of sorts lately, the upheaval in finding a permanent sitter for Shane, he guessed, and maybe this uncompromising desire to have Piper in a purely sexual way pitted against this fierce need to protect his heart, although it usually hadn't been this much of a struggle.

He rapped his knuckles on the side of the door in warning before he opened the screen door and strolled in. She was heading to him, a smile on her face. She was almost as tall as him, spiky locks on the top of a heart-shaped, beautiful face. Her smile widened.

"Hey, stranger," she said, walking over to give him a hug.

"Hey," he answered, returning her hug, letting himself be comforted, surprised that he'd needed it. He pulled out of her embrace.

"So what brings you by?" she said.

"Nothing. Just wanted to let you know Shane was doing well. No problems with school, fitting right in so far."

"That's great. He's a great kid. You've done a lot for him," she said.

He brushed it aside, his habit to always underplay his commitment to his nephew.

"So how are the sitters?" she asked, walking to the couch placed in the room that held her computers.

She sat, and so did he.

"Not much luck," he said. "I came to the end of your list three weeks ago. I've been using the lady next door, Mrs. Lewis. She has grandkids of her own and felt sorry for me, but it's getting old. She's getting old."

"Sorry."

"It's okay. Who knew it would be so hard to find competent help," he said, looking out the front door. "How is Stephen?"

"Fine. Busy at work," she said.

"So he was a good decision for you, a good mate for you?" he asked, looking ahead.

"That came from nowhere, but yes, he is," she said. "Why?"

"No reason, just making sure," he said, his eyes moving around the room. "There is a woman I know. She's taking care of her two younger sisters while their parents work out their lives. Not formal custody like me, but acting as their parent now. They attend Shane's school.

"She watched Shane for me once. I couldn't get away from work in time to pick him up from the school's aftercare program. He loves being with her and her sisters, and is always asking to go home with them. One of the girls is in Shane's class, the older one, who is actually turning into a good friend to him," he added, looking at Reye now. "I've been thinking about hiring her to pick him up for me, you know, on the days I'm working late or get tied up."

"Sounds like a reasonable plan to me. She must be nice if you are considering her." Reye's tone was tentative, almost inquiring.

"She is, actually, owns the two Lights Out Coffee shops. You're familiar with them?"

"I've not been there. But I've heard of them, good things, too," she said, masking her curiosity.

"What do you think?" he asked.

"You should ask her. Sounds like the perfect plan for you and Shane."

"I wouldn't need her every day, just a couple of times a week," he said, pausing. "And maybe someone to call in case of emergencies. You know, if I get hit by a truck, someone he could stay with."

"If you get hit by a truck, I would take him," Reye said.

"I know, but I wouldn't impose, and you have a husband now."

"Stephen doesn't mind. He likes Shane as much as I do," she said.

"It would be perfect, her taking care of him," he said. "Her shops are located close to school and close to her home. Shane is in her sister's class. They are good buddies, so why not encourage it? You know, it can't hurt for Shane to have one good friend. Everyone needs that, right?" He was rushing through his words now. "She's taken in her sisters, manages two shops." He was sitting forward on the couch now, arms on his thighs, as he explained the benefits of his plan.

A woman, huh? Finally, and not his usual type, Reye thought. Joe always had women, but went nowhere near any that would maybe last past temporary. He never talked about them, and he wasn't talking about her much now, but this was huge for Joe.

"So you think it might work, that it's a good idea?" he asked her.

"It's worth a try," she responded, reaching for his hand.

"That's what I was thinking," he said, glancing around, watching for signs on her face that he'd given away his appreciation for Piper in his conversation. He squeezed her hand.

"She sounds like a nice woman," she said. "What does she look like?"

"Why?" he asked, now on the alert.

"Maybe I've seen her around. Austin's not that big, and I've hit most of the popular coffee places. I may have met her."

"She is about your height, hair long, curly, all around her face, light brown skin, athletically built," he said. Reye's eyebrows lifted at that description. It was more than she expected.

"Okay," she said. "Well let me know how it goes."

"I will," he said, sitting back like this had been a major decision for him. Reye smiled. Joe liked a woman. Her smile widened. No way was she telling him that, but inwardly she was so pleased. Oh, please, let him find someone to love. He deserved it. She didn't know about the whole of his childhood, what had brought him to this place where he loved his nephew fiercely, but guarded his heart like his life depended on it.

No one but the sturdy got through to Joe. She hoped this woman was sturdy enough to withstand Joe and the guard dogs surrounding his heart. What a catch he'd be for the one who could break through. A more loving, committed man she'd yet to meet. She had included him with Stephen, her brothers, and her dad—the gold standard for them all.

—⁊⁊⁊—

October

Saturday morning Piper stood behind the counter of her shop with the girls, surprised as she watched Joe and Shane walk through the door.

Shane waved at her before moving to his friends, who were dancing in front of the TV to a video game. Joe walked over to her with something in his hand. The look on his face was uncomfortable.

"Hi," he said, a little tentatively.

"Hey," she replied.

"Shane and I were out shopping today and we thought.... I mean we wanted to drop this off as a way of thanking you for the help last week. "

"It wasn't a problem. We don't mind helping if you need us," she said.

"Thanks again anyway," he said handing her a small square-shaped object wrapped in plain brown paper.

Piper opened it. It was a CD of zydeco music. She wasn't familiar with this artist.

"He's new on the scene," said Joe, watching her face. "You'll like him."

"Thanks, Joe, that was very thoughtful."

"Do you have time to talk for a second, maybe in your office?" he asked.

"Sure, let me call some help and we can head back."

She stuck her head into the kitchen and said something to someone. A few minutes later, Joe watched as a college student dressed in the coffee shop uniform came out and moved to the counter.

"Shane, Taylor, Ken," Piper called, waiting for the three heads to turn her way. "Joe and I will be in my office for a second."

"Sure," all three children replied in unison, happy to have more time with Shane.

He followed her in and over to the small couch where she sat down and looked at him expectantly as he joined her.

"What's up?" she asked.

"I have a proposition for you," Joe said, getting straight to the point, catching the interest as it flickered across her face. "I would like to hire you to pick up Shane after school on the days that I'm tied up. Picking up Shane has become a problem for me since I've accepted this new position. I thought I could manage it and Shane, and I haven't had much luck finding a long-term sitter I could count on. And believe me, I've tried. Shane really likes being around you and your sisters, and I need a reliable place for him to be."

"I offered, remember?"

"I know, but this could be more than occasionally."

"Still, it's not a problem. Shane's easy, my sisters love him, and he's a sweet kid." She turned to find his eyes on her, serious. She was finding out when it came to his nephew, he was always serious.

"I'll help, but you don't have to pay me," she said.

"Yeah, I do. It works better that way."

"Okay," she said, choosing not to argue the point. Just 'cause he gave it to her didn't mean she had to spend it.

"So how long would you need me?" she asked.

"For as long as you have the girls living with you. I wouldn't expect you to help if you didn't have your two," he said.

"Okay," she replied.

"There are some days each week that I'll run late, usually no more than two. I'll know as early as Monday which days they'll be. I can pick Shane up from the shop. Would you be willing to take him home with you if I'm later than 6:30?" he asked.

"Yes."

"So," he said.

"So," she replied, chuckling.

"I thought we could meet every Monday morning to cover our schedules, to confirm the times that I'll need you. I'll drop by the shop, if that's okay."

"Sure, if you want. You could just contact me by e-mail instead of coming here if that's easier for you."

"No, I stop somewhere for coffee most mornings anyway, it might as well be here. I would also like to list you as an emergency contact for those times when I can't get to Shane. There are also last-minute things that might come up. If I'm on call I might need your help, too. Most times I can work from anywhere, but there are occasions that I need to go in."

"Okay," she replied.

"Can you start next week? Thursday and Friday, to be exact. Can you take him with you from school both days?"

"Sure," she said.

"So what about the pay schedule?" he asked.

"What about it?"

"What do you want?"

"Whatever you pay the others is fine. You're more familiar with all of that than I am."

"Fine," he said and sat back, relaxed now. She could see the loosening of his body.

"Thanks then," he said, looking around her office. "Is your other shop similar to this one?" he asked.

"It's older, and a different crowd too, more college kids."

"It's impressive, what you've done."

"Not really. I've been lucky to have my dad to help," she said, catching his gaze. She had no idea what he was thinking.

"Well, if you need me, call me on my cell, and of course Shane has his own cell and can call me when he likes. I'll notify the school to add you permanently to the list of people who have my permission to pick up Shane," he said, standing up. "I'd better get going. Shane and I still have a few more errands to run."

He led the way back to the front and immediately called Shane, who said goodbye to the girls. They left just as unceremoniously as they'd entered. Interesting, she thought, her mind moving in so many directions; dissecting his visit, the gift, his request for help.

—⁂—

What time was it, Joe wondered, checking the clock on his nightstand. Two in the a.m., late Saturday night, or early Sunday morning was more like it. He'd hung out with Shane the rest of the day after he'd dropped that package off to Piper.

After his talk with Reye, he'd decided that Piper's taking care of Shane would be a great idea and was glad that she'd agreed to help him. The purchase of the gift had come from a different place; his spur-of-the-moment decision surprised him. He and Shane had been at one of those all-in-one music, video, and electronic stores. While Shane looked for a new video game, Joe had been browsing the music section. He found the CD and purchased it with her in mind.

Before he knew it, he'd had it wrapped, and didn't think to put it away before Shane had gotten an eyeful. Then the inquisition began, so he'd ended up explaining what an impulse purchase was to his nephew. Then, of course, he had to deliver it to her amid all his second thoughts and misgivings of what it meant.

He liked watching the delight on her face, and the pleasure reflected in her eyes at receiving it. A bit of something else was in her eyes, too, and he liked watching that part as well. He was glad he'd done it. He still felt weird, a little disconcerted by the whole of it.

So, he called up Sondra — red hair falling down her back, no-strings-attached Sondra, professional-by-day, wild at night Sondra. They'd gone to a movie and then come back here. He turned to find the space next to him in his bed empty and sighed. He hated when that happened, and it almost always happened. Woman on the roam in his home.

He sighed, sat up, pulled on his jeans, and walked out of his room, running his hand through his hair. There was a small light on in the kitchen. He headed toward it.

And yes, there was a nude woman, hand on the door, staring at the contents of his refrigerator. He stood quietly and watched Sondra move, admiring the female form before walking over to her to slap her softly on the part that was the closest to him, causing her to jump and giggle. She pushed herself into his body, seeking his lips, which he gave over quite willingly.

"Hey, sweet cakes," she said, smiling, and then lifted her head up to his again for more.

They stood there for a second, lost in the kiss, when Joe heard a sound and turned. Shane stood in the doorway, taking it all in, and Joe moved to put Sondra behind him.

"Didn't see your light on," he said to his nephew.

"I heard a noise," Shane said. "Sorry."

"No, nothing to apologize for," he said. "Head on back to bed. It was just me making noise. I'm sorry I woke you," he said.

He knew better, he thought. He was usually more careful, but it was two in the morning and Shane usually slept like a brick. Still, Joe silently admonished himself.

"Night, Uncle Joe," he said, turning and walking back toward his bedroom.

—⁂—

Shane stumbled back to bed. His Uncle Joe was something. Women loved his uncle. He'd noticed women checking his uncle out when he wasn't looking, even Piper, but she turned away before his uncle noticed.

And this wasn't the first time he'd seen women here. He hid sometimes when Joe had them over, and there was always something to see, if you hid in the right places.

He knew that his Uncle Joe, when it came to women, was the best. He hoped he'd be around to offer advice as Shane grew up. He seemed to know what to say, and sometimes, like tonight, he'd slap their butts, but not too hard. They must have liked it, because they always giggled.

Shane didn't quite understand how that was fun for them, but they always kissed his uncle after he did it. Shane had tried it on Taylor and she punched him in his stomach.

"You do that again, and I'll knock your tongue down your throat," Taylor had told him. Maybe she was too young. It must only work for older women, Shane thought as he drifted off to sleep.

Chapter 10

Friday of the following week found Piper sitting on the floor in the game room. Shane, Taylor, and Kennedy sat on the couch above her, lost in a movie. She'd seen this one before, a film about kids taking over the world. She didn't like to contemplate that possibility, even on the movie screen. Joe had called her earlier that evening; he'd been delayed leaving San Antonio and would arrive later than he'd anticipated.

It was the last week of September and her first full week of taking care of Shane. She'd had him three days this week. She couldn't believe how fast the year was moving. The kids and work had kept her busy.

McKenzie and Pepper jumped up, tails in the air, standing up from their spots on Taylor and Shane's laps. They jumped down, started barking, and ran like hell down the stairs. The kids, engrossed in the movie, didn't move. Piper stood and walked down the stairs, following the two banditos. She had gotten used to having them around. She could see Joe through her peephole. He looked tired.

McKenzie and Pepper kept up the barking until he entered. He was promptly sniffed and approved. Then the barking ceased—they knew this guy. The world was safe once again, and they trotted back upstairs to the game room.

"Playing dress up? Don't see you in a suit and tie much," she said, holding the door open for him. He gave her a distracted smile and pulled at the knot of his tie, loosening it from his neck.

"The kids are watching a movie upstairs that has about another thirty minutes or so before it's over. Do you mind waiting? I could call Shane if you want to leave now. I know how appealing home can be after a long day."

"No, I don't mind as long as I can sit and not answer any computer-related questions," he said, looking longingly at her L-shaped sectional sofa in the living room. It was cushy and large.

"Be my guest," she said and pointed toward the couch. He kicked off his shoes, his pair mixing in with the four other pairs in a pile. He'd recognized Shane's tennis shoes in the pile, along with a couple pairs of flip-flops.

He stepped into her living room. The carpet felt soft to his feet as he wiggled his sock-clad toes and stretched his arms above his head. He turned to find her gazing at him. He turned away, fighting not to respond to the desire he saw in her eyes. He needed female, he thought, and soon. He moved over to the couch, taking in more of the clutter he now knew was Piper.

Magazines lay on the sofa and books were stacked on the floor and on the large, chest-like coffee table. He walked over and picked up a book. "Creole Peoples of Color," he said, reading the title out loud. "Creoles?"

"My people, my mother's people, anyway, originally from Louisiana, migrated to an area north of Houston," she said.

"Oh," he said, setting it down and reading the titles of some other books. There were a couple of political science books along with a few romance novels. He fingered a couple.

"Creoles are still African-American?" he asked.

"Yes," she said. "Well, it depends…it's complicated."

Joe looked confused, but let it go.

"Do you want anything to drink while you wait?"

"How about some of whatever that is I smell," he asked, turning toward her, his nose in the air, sniffing. His stomach growled, loud in the silence between them. He placed the book back on the table.

"Hungry, huh?" she asked.

"Starving. Nothing since lunch," he said, giving her another tired smile.

"Well, I guess I could feed you," she said, turning and walking down the hall that led to the kitchen. He followed her, taking in her grey sweats pants, loosely hanging off her hips, New Orleans Jazz Festival t-shirt on her upper body, feet bare, yellow toenails with red and white stripes and hair in one huge puff resting on the top of her head. He'd always found her sexy, and still did, very much so. Music played softly from somewhere; he couldn't locate its source.

"You really like your music."

"Yes, the music of my childhood. The early part, anyway," she said, entering her kitchen.

"What's for dinner?" he asked, walking behind her to the stove, lifting the top from a pot, bending his head. His smile widened at the aroma. His stomach growled loudly again.

"Gumbo and rice, one of my favorites, and, lucky for you, a house specialty. Better lose the tie, though," she said.

He removed it from his neck and laid in on the table before sliding over to the sink where she stood, standing a little behind her.

"Need to wash my hands," he said, smiling, stepping to stand next to her, hitting her with his hip, bumping her out of the way. She'd bet he knew the effect he had on her. There was a small smile on his lips as she watched him soap and wash. She handed him a towel to dry.

"Thanks," he said, turning and moving back to the table.

"Your kitchen fits with the rest of your house; it's lived in," he said, taking a seat at the wooden kitchen table, round in shape, resting on a tiled floor. Wood cabinets hung on light green walls.

"I try. If you can't be comfortable at home, what's the point?" she said, reaching for a bowl from the cabinet. She filled it with rice, followed by a ladle full of gumbo. She placed it in front of him and gave him a spoon and a napkin. He smiled and began eating. She sliced some bread she'd made earlier and placed it on the table before him. Well, actually the bread machine made it, but she put the bread mix in.

"Thanks. This is good."

"Want something to drink?"

"Sure. What are my options?"

"Soda, wine, beer."

"I'll take a beer, if you'll sit with me."

"Okay." She grabbed a beer and then turned and pulled a wine glass from another cabinet. She poured a glass of wine for herself and took the seat next to him, pulling her legs into her chair. She took a sip from her glass. She smiled. He looked at her, his face studying hers.

"Piper Renee Knight," he said.

"That's my name. Don't wear it out."

He chuckled. "Piper's an unusual name," he said, putting another spoonful of gumbo into his mouth, closing his eyes at the taste. "That's really good."

"My mother's contribution," she replied.

He looked up, a question in his eye.

"The name. My name is my mother's clever idea. She met my father after a boxing match, hung around for a while, became his latest arm candy. After a time, as he did in those days, he moved on and left her with the ultimate gift. Me. My mother had to move back home to Raywood, Texas, near Houston, to give birth to me. Not what she'd had in mind," she added, watching as he took in another mouthful.

"Anyway, after I was born and after about a month of living with her parents she went in search of my father. She had named me Piper, as in 'it's time to pay the piper,' you know from the kid's story, the Pied Piper," she said.

He nodded.

"Anyway, my dad needed to step up and take care of his baby, but, more importantly, he needed to take care of his baby momma, which was more of what she had in mind."

He couldn't detect any rancor in her voice as she relayed that bit of history to him.

"You seem to be okay with the way it turned out," he said, taking in another spoonful, closing his eyes at the taste of her food. His eyes closed in pleasure. It was a nice look for him.

"What can you do? You get what you get in life and make the best of it, or not. It's a choice, always a choice," she said.

"Is that what you do, make the best of it or not? What you're doing with your sisters?" he asked, eyes opening to look at her.

"I guess so. I've been making the best of things as far back as I can remember. Plus, I know what it's like when adults don't have their shit together and the kids are in the middle of it. If I can help them, I will," she said.

"Where's your mother now?" he asked as his hand dropped the last of his bread into the bowl to sop up the remains.

"Like that, huh?" she said laughing softly, and watched as he smiled.

"Very good," he said, putting his napkin on the table while he reached for his beer.

"To answer your question, she lives in Paris, the City of Lights, married. No more children, though," she said.

"No anger?" he asked, looking at her.

"It is what it is, and anyway, what could I have done to change her? Why sweat what you can't fix?"

He nodded and watched her as he tilted his head back to take a long swig of his beer.

"That's one way to look at it," he said when he was done, catching her eyes on him. She turned away, embarrassed at being caught staring.

"It works for me," she said.

She was pretty tonight. He'd started to view her that way now. Not beautiful, no, but more appealing to him the more he learned of her. She sat next to him, one foot in her chair, twirling her wine glass in her hand, casual and easy. He'd found her easy to be around, uncomplicated, easy to work with, easy to laugh with. He was reluctantly developing a fondness for easy, and that was scary.

"I'm impressed at how well you are managing," he said.

"You do what you do, right? You know that. You've got Shane. I'm no different from you."

"Okay. So how'd you get into the coffee making business?" he asked, changing the subject.

"I went to college in Atlanta. I wanted to be away from my dad. I needed my space. I came back here for graduate school, received my MBA from the U of H. My dad's first wife lived in Houston," she said.

"How many wives did your father have?" he asked, curious now.

"Three, not including mine. He didn't marry my mother," she said, unable to read his expression. "Anyways, after graduate school I decided to work for my-self, but wasn't sure doing what. I was sitting in a cof-fee shop one day and it seemed so sterile, not like I would have done it at all.

"I went to my dad with a plan for the shop on Fifty-fifth Street. He helped with the financing. Next to box-ing, business was my dad's second love. He told me I should avoid banks, if I could. Easy for him to say. He was the big-time boxer, plus he saved. He'd always been fiscally sharp and frugal like you wouldn't be-lieve. Anyways, I'd saved some of my own money and we purchased the first shop together. I saved more and bought him out of the first one, with the help of my mother's guilt money, which I had no trouble using. I had to take out a loan for the second shop," she said.

They heard footsteps coming down the stairs. The dogs trotted into the room first, followed by an excited Shane, Taylor, and Ken.

"Hey, Uncle Joe. We had a blast today. The movie was great. Did you like the gumbo? We all pitched in—me, Piper, Taylor, and Ken. I can make it at home for dinner one night if you want," he said, talking a mile a minute.

"We will have to try it," Joe said, pushing back from the table, standing up and reaching for his tie. He placed it back around his neck.

"That was delicious. Thanks. Well, we'd better get going. You've got the shop in the morning, right?" he asked.

"Yes," she replied, standing up too, taking his bowl and putting it in the sink. She turned to walk them to the front door.

Ken, who had been rooting around in the pantry, now walked over to the table with a box of cookies in her hand. "Taylor, can you get me a glass of milk?" she asked.

"Nope."

Ken stood up, glaring at her sister as she grabbed a glass from the cabinet and milk from the refrigerator.

"Want some, Shane?" she asked, blatant in her attempt to ignore her sister and prolong her time with her new love.

"Maybe next time," Joe said, smiling at Ken, who winked back at him. He laughed.

"Okay, then, we'll be on our way."

"Okay, then," she said, walking them to the door.

She and Taylor watched as the males made their way to their car. Piper looked over to find Taylor staring at her, assessing her.

"Don't get a crush on him, Piper," she said, arms crossed, serious. "Shane says he has lots of girlfriends."

"Thanks, I'll keep that in mind," she said, moving to make sure the door was locked.

She was going to shoot the person who'd come up with the idea of children bringing their pets to school to be blessed. The Blessing of the Pets was an annual ceremony at the kids' school, a tribute to St. Francis of Assisi, the patron saint of the poor and animals. Today she was in charge of corralling McKenzie—not hard—and Pepper—the most difficult—and bringing them to school for the kids.

Of course, McKenzie cooperated. Pepper, on the other hand, had seen the other animals—dogs and this one cat—and had gone crazy in the car and wouldn't settle down for anything. So here she stood, McKenzie on his leash waiting patiently by her side, while Pepper had yet to settle down enough for Piper to get her leash on.

"Pepper, calm down. You can't go without your leash. Please?" Of course, Pepper wasn't listening.

"Need some help?" Joe asked, startling her. He stood beside her, laughter in his eyes, apparently having heard all of her dog talk. Piper glanced at his two animals, a dog currently sitting smartly at his feet, and something big and scaly in a cage he was holding in his hand.

"She won't cooperate enough for me to put her leash on," she said, looking at Pepper, who was barking furiously through the window at a cat held in a woman's arms.

"Let me try," Joe said, handing his cage over to her. Piper's eyes moved from the cage to Joe.

"What is it?" she asked.

"A gecko."

"Oh," she said. "It doesn't look like that talking gecko on that insurance commercial, the cute green one with the English accent." He smiled at that.

"He won't bite and he can't come through glass. Just hold the cage. I can't help you if you don't."

She took the cage from his hand and watched as he bent to the window.

"Pepper," he called out. The little dog turned, startled out of her barking by this new, yet familiar face. She ran across the back seat, sticking her head out the window, licking Joe's face, apparently pleased as punch to see him.

"Where's her leash?" he said, reaching out his hand toward Piper. She put the leash into it. She heard Joe snap it in place. He opened the door and Pepper scampered down, walking over to his dog, sniffing away, but not barking anymore.

"Can you wait with me for a second? I need to lock up my car. Can I set this down?" she asked, lifting up the cage with the lizard in it.

"Sure," he answered, bending down to reacquaint himself with his friend Pepper.

He absently rubbed the dog, but his eyes were fixed on Piper as he followed her ass as it swayed side to side in her jeans. Piper reached for her purse, trying to decide if she needed it. The two dogs and a purse were maybe more than she could handle. She pushed it down on the floorboard in the back seat, set her alarm, and walked back over to Joe.

"Thanks for helping me."

"You're welcome."

They led their animals into the school, taking the left that would bring them to Taylor and Shane's homeroom. She could have dropped off Pepper first, but she didn't want to leave Joe just yet.

"Thanks, Joe," Shane said, greeting his uncle at the door of their classroom. Taylor seemed equally excited as Piper handed McKenzie over to her.

The kids were talking amid a mix of fish, dogs, cats, and other things in cages. Was that a snake? Okay, so maybe it was time for her to leave. She gave one final glance at Joe on her way out of the room and found him in a conversation with Mr. Marshall. She needed to get Pepper to Ken before the ceremony started. She looked at her watch. She had fifteen minutes. She didn't want him to get the idea that maybe she was waiting for him. She felt oddly nervous around him now, that awkward moment when you like someone but you're not sure what to do with it yet.

She dropped Pepper off with Kennedy and, a few minutes later entered the gym, taking in the chairs that had been set up in rows for parents and guests. She decided to sit near the wall, on the left side. It was relatively empty there, and a few rows back from the animals.

A microphone had been set up in the front of the room for the speakers. Piper took her seat and relaxed. That hadn't been bad after all. This motherhood thing was working so far for her. She patted herself on the back for having successfully and safely handed the dogs off. She was interested in watching the proceedings of this, her first Blessing of the Pets ceremony.

Joe entered the gym and spotted Piper seated alone to his left. He glanced over to the other side of the room, his right, where mothers, fathers and some grandparents had taken seats, waiting for the show to start. He turned back to Piper, catching her eyes as she'd looked up and caught his, gave him a smile, tentative and interested.

He turned and walked over to her. "Lost all of your animals, too, I see," she said once he reached the chair and sat down next to her.

"Yep. The lizard is with a friend."

"I feel naked without kids. Who would have thought, huh?"

"It doesn't take long for them to become a part of you," he said, glancing around the room. The kids were entering the gym now. The younger grades were entering first. Piper turned to find Kennedy walking with Pepper by her side. She waved.

Dogs were barking at each other, pulling kids on leashes. Cats in cages were scared out of their wits. There were also all manner of lizards, small amphibians in cages, a few fish in small jars, and one stuffed animal on a leash being dragged behind a child. It was a strange sort of Noah's ark as the children strolled in, not two by two but class by class.

Piper hit Joe in the side with her elbow and pointed toward Shane with Charlie followed by Taylor with McKenzie, as the fifth grade began entering. Once the kids were seated, the principal stood up and approached the microphone.

"I would like to welcome you all to our annual Blessing of the Pets Ceremony. We've adopted St. Francis as one of our representatives of the school. As you know, he is the patron saint of animals and the poor. We've invited Reverend Salizar to conduct our ceremony today, so let's start by bowing our heads in prayer."

The ceremony went smoothly from there. The animals mostly cooperated, or at least as much as one could expect animals to behave stuffed in a gym with three hundred children, parents, and teachers. It was controlled chaos in here, Piper thought, taking it all in, amazed and impressed by the teachers and staff's calmness and air of confidence. That is, until the back door swung open, hitting the wall with a crack.

A horse stood in the middle of the door, regal in its bearing. A white spot was in the middle of its chest, the only mar in its otherwise black coat. He looks like he's wearing a tuxedo, Piper thought. A white top hat sat upon his head, completing the ensemble.

The reins were held by what looked to be a middle-school aged student who was standing beside him, also decked out in tuxedo shirt and white top hat. Everyone in the room turned at the sound, surprised into silence at the sudden appearance of this guest.

And then it was total and complete pandemonium. The dogs, in unison, began barking, while one small dachshund broke away from his child and took in an all-out pursuit of the horse like he'd been shot from a cannon. Two other small dogs escaped from their owners and gave chase to the dachshund.

The owners of the dogs, followed by a few parents, ran to catch their animals. Piper looked over and found that Joe had left his seat and was making his way toward the front of the gym. He and two other students, middle-school aged, she guessed, were moving quickly to try and recapture the dog and his companions. The dogs, however, had a different idea in mind. For them, this had turned into a classic game of chase. Things were heading south fast. Mrs. Foley stood and made a dash for the microphone.

"Children, please take your seats. Children! Teachers, please gain control of your classes," she said, her words ineffective. Bedlam reigned, and was moving speedily toward the point of no return.

Coach Stanton, the athletic director, walked to the front of the room. He blew his whistle. Loud. She didn't know it could be that loud, but it cut into the noise and everything stopped, like a game of Mother May I.

Piper laughed, watching as the horse disappeared from the door and the dogs were recaptured. Joe held the main culprit, the dachshund, in his arms. A child stood next to him, a dog in his arms, too. Piper watched as Joe gave the kid a high five, a smile on his face as he handed his dog off to his owner.

He walked back to his chair and sat down, trying to contain his laughter. He turned to look at Piper. Why did he do that? She made a face and he started laughing. She joined in, sharing the moment, before it changed. He saw something more in her eyes, a match for what he felt inside.

It was still loud in the gym, but more settled now. The atmosphere returned to a more normal state for this type of ceremony. Reverend Salizar was sprinkling water over the room, finally giving the animals their blessing.

She turned to look at Joe again, but his eyes were turned forward. Okay, she wanted more. A hookup, but more if she could get it. If not, she'd work with that for starters. This Joe was someone she could see herself with. They sat in silence until the program ended. The children filed out first, followed by the teachers and the parents.

Piper and Joe went to pick up their respective animals. She went to Ken's room first to pick up Pepper, and then to Taylor's. She must have missed Joe. Shane stood next to Taylor, minus both his animals.

With both of the dogs and their leashes in hand, she made her way to her car. She opened the doors to let both schnauzers in when she felt someone at her side. She turned to find Joe there.

He couldn't leave well enough alone, it seemed. He'd seen that look of longing in her eyes, and it had pulled him in. He'd left Charlie and the lizard near the front door with a parent who liked him. He told her he'd forgotten something in the gym and would be back in a second.

"You got your dogs all in?" he asked.

"Yep," she said, closing the door, turning to face him. He walked closer to her, moving still closer until his body lined up with hers, touching hers. In her heels she was the same height as he, and he leaned into her, watching her widening eyes. He took in her hair blowing around her face, and moved it from her eyes. Then his eyes moved to her mouth, and he moved in close and kissed her softly on the lips. The feel of her was as old and as fresh as yesterday.

Her hand had moved downward to his waist. He remembered this. They played at each other's mouth for a good minute or two before Joe straightened and pulled back from her.

Joe, Joe, Joe, he inwardly admonished himself. So much for keeping a distance, as he continued to gaze into her eyes.

Why in the world did I say no to him? Piper wondered.

They looked at each other's mouths for a good two or three seconds more, remembering, before he pulled back further. He didn't say a word, just pulled back, and she had no idea what he was thinking then.

"See you later," he said.

"Sure," she said, watching as he turned and walked away. She pushed her hair from around her eyes, catching her breath, trying to calm down, looking over her shoulder at his departure. What the hell, she thought again and got into her car, checking on McKenzie and Pepper moving from one window to the other, scanning the streets for prey.

"What do you think?" she asked them. McKenzie scampered over and licked her hand. Pepper wasn't interested. Her eyes remained glued to something going on down the street.

"What to do?" she asked McKenzie, who was looking at her like he understood her dilemma. Piper turned again, catching Joe as he disappeared around the corner of the building. She started her car, and pulled out of the parking lot.

Chapter 11

"Okay, now move your feet this way," Piper said, grimacing as Shane stepped on her toes again. She should have put on some shoes, but she avoided wearing them at home. They were in the kitchen, zydeco music turned up loud. She was trying to teach the kids a simple two-step.

Kennedy was the most adept of the group. Shane, however, was willing in spirit, even if his feet weren't. Her feet, however, were paying the price for his willingness. Taylor had gotten angry, decided to sit the whole exercise out.

"Piper, why do you like this music so much?" Ken asked, doing her own dance in the corner of the room, picking up McKenzie's two front paws and moving him around with her.

Piper laughed at them, then grimaced as Shane stepped on her toes again.

"I grew up with it, listened to it on the radio all the time," she said. "My grandparents played it all the time. I like it. I like the instruments, the sounds the rub board makes along with the sounds from the guitars, violin, drums, and accordion."

"What's a rub board?" Kennedy asked.

"It looks like a washboard," Piper replied.

"What's a washboard?" Kennedy asked.

"Forget it, and that's enough dancing tonight," she said.

"Don't forget to ask Joe if Shane can come with us tomorrow night," Taylor reminded her again. "He might agree if you ask him. He likes you. You can invite him to come, too."

"I won't forget," Piper said. Saturday was the next zydeco night event at her shop, and the girls had invited Shane. She had planned on asking Joe to attend, even before the kids had made the suggestion. She remembered the way he moved on the dance floor, the way he'd moved into her, welcoming any opportunity to be near him again. That recent kiss was just fuel to the fire. All he had to do was ask her again. She'd say yes.

—⁓—

Piper stood in the utility room an hour later, after stuffing her last load of laundry into the washing machine. She closed the door, shutting off the sounds emanating from the washer and dryer, and heard for the first time McKenzie and Pepper barking near the front door.

Joe must have arrived. She removed the scarf from her head, ran her hands through her hair, and walked to the door. Joe stood on the other side. He seemed tired, more so than usual for the end of the week.

"Hey," he said.

"What's up?"

"Nothing much. How are the kids?" he asked, walking in.

"Fine. Hey, before I forget, tomorrow is zydeco night at the shop. Thought you and Shane might like to come. The girls made me promise to invite the two of you, and Shane's hounded me since he's been here. So you've been officially invited," she said, offering him one of her more enticing smiles.

"If I'm not on call," he said. Hell yes was his internal answer; he had given up on his attempt to put distance between them. He was back to the hookup question. He'd figured out how to prevent it from morphing into more. The kids' schedules they could work around.

He watched as she turned and headed up the stairs, taking them two at a time. What a nice stride, what energy. He stepped into the foyer, picking up Shane's backpack from the floor near the door.

He stood there waiting while she rounded up Shane. In less than five minutes, all four were heading down the steps, kids and dogs in front, Piper bringing up the rear.

"Good night," Shane said to his friends and he and Joe left, waving goodbye a final time as they drove away.

"Did you ask him?" Taylor asked.

"Yes, I invited them," Piper said.

"What did he say?"

"If he's not working."

"That's means no," Taylor said.

"Not necessarily," Piper said.

—∽—

Joe pulled up to Lights Out the next night. He was free, not on call, and energized. He was one big knot of anticipation, probably more than what was healthy. But so what? The extraordinary pull he felt from Piper convinced him to try the hook-up again.

He parked. Shane had gone in, hopping out before Joe had a chance to put the car in park. He'd seen Taylor standing at the window, peeking out, her baseball cap's brim pushed against the glass, watching and waiting for her buddy.

Joe peered through the windows, amazed at the size of the large crowd. He entered, his eyes scanning the crowd immediately for her. There she was, low-riding jean shorts clinging tightly to beautiful and shapely thighs. A tight Lights Out polo tucked into them, showing off a slim waist and breasts he knew fit perfectly in his hands. His favorite Ropers were on her feet, and her hair was in curly ringlets surrounding her head. As she smiled she showed those lips he longed to taste again. She stood behind the counter, working, talking to some African-American dude, not bad looking, who was smiling back at her.

Piper had spotted him, tall and fine, walking toward the back of the shop, toward Shane and Taylor. She didn't know how she'd missed his entrance; she had been on the lookout for him. Piper started toward the back, too, wanting to say hello, kind of eager to see him. They arrived at the kids' area at the same time.

"Hey, Joe, glad you could you make it," she said, giving him a smile, her eyes roaming and cataloging his body, which was packaged splendidly tonight.

"Me, too," he said, his eyes smoky, doing a little up close roaming of his own, hoping she might need some help in her storage room again.

Shane and Taylor walked over and stood in front of them.

"Taylor, you know where the food is if you get hungry. Just show Shane, and keep an eye out for your sister, okay?" she said.

"Where's Ken?" Shane asked, scanning the room for signs of her.

"In the office playing on the computer," Piper answered, ruffling his hair and giving him a wink. "Have a good time, Joe. I'll see you later," she said with much invitation in her eyes.

So far, so good, he thought.

Joe walked over and found a table near the counter, close, where he could watch her. He felt someone near his arm and looked up to find Sondra—off-and-on Sondra, the appeasement of late-night-appetites Sondra—staring at him with a knowing smile in place. She was dressed in a red figure-hugging dress. She slid in the booth beside him, a lot closer than was his preference. He scooted over to make space.

"Hey, stranger, you've haven't called me lately."

"Been busy," he said, wondering what to do now.

"That's okay. I'm here now," she said, scooting closer. "How long do you have your sitter? We could go back to my place."

"Actually, my nephew's here with me tonight, so I can't."

"That's okay, too. We can enjoy each other here, or maybe sneak out back later."

He smiled. "No, I'd better stick close," he said.

"Okay, we can do that, too," she said, smiling, slipping her arms through his.

He groaned. His night had turned sour. Fuck me, he thought, meeting Piper's eyes across the room. She gave him a small smile, her eyes no longer twinkling. He sighed and sat back. He wanted to tell her that Sondra didn't mean anything, she was just a hookup, not like what he'd wanted from Piper…which was, okay, another hookup, but different somehow.

Right, Joe.

—m—

Later on that night, Taylor stood in front of Piper.

"It's okay, really, Piper. Shane has already asked his Uncle Joe. His uncle says if it's okay with you, it's okay with him," Taylor said in earnest, a pleading look on her face—a staple of life with kids, Piper had learned. They were always pleading for something.

"Can Shane come home with us tonight?" Taylor asked again.

Piper had been busy tonight, and hadn't had much time to look up, much less keep an eye out for Shane's uncle, who was holed up with the redhead anyway. Piper recognized her from before; probably just another hookup, not like she herself would have been. She laughed out loud at that. She'd caught his expression from time to time, but it was unreadable.

"Sure," she said absentmindedly. She focused her attention on serving a beer to the woman standing in front of her. A few minutes later she looked up into Joe's eyes.

"What can I get for you?" she asked, smiling, putting everything she had into that smile. She refused to let him know she was bothered.

"One Shiner Bock and one glass of wine," he said, digging into his pocket for money. "So Shane is going home with you tonight?" he asked, handing money over to her, waiting for her to look at him.

"I believe so," she said, taking his money, and pulling change out of the drawer, not making eye contact.

"He didn't bring anything with him. Do you mind stopping by our house? Or I could bring something over."

"I don't know when we'll be leaving, so let me just drive by. Write down your address," she said, bending to retrieve a bottle of wine and a wine glass. She started pouring.

"Shane has a key and I'll be home," he said, taking the glass of wine from her hand.

"Okay," she said, handing him his bottle of beer. "Thanks for bringing him tonight. Taylor is having a great time. It helps that she has a friend. And you have yourself a good evening." She smiled winsomely, clearly startling him with her attitude.

"Thanks," he said, turning and walking back to his table.

He walked away, not sure what Piper was feeling. He could have kicked Sondra and her timing. He had tried everything in his arsenal tonight to get rid of her, and she hadn't budged.

—⁓—

Two hours later Joe stood in Shane's room, packing a bag for him to take over to Piper's. He was aggravated and disappointed. He'd finally gotten rid of Sondra. His last-ditch effort had been to just leave, way earlier than he'd wanted to. It was okay. He could pack up for Shane, and maybe he could convince Piper to come in if it wasn't too late.

The doorbell rang. He walked toward it, a smile on his face at the prospect of seeing Piper. He opened the door.

"Hey, I'd made it all the way home after leaving Lights Out and was sitting on my couch thinking of you being here alone. Heard you tell that woman at the counter that Shane was going home with her, so I thought you might be lonesome and we couldn't have that," Sondra said as she squeezed between him and the door and entered his home.

His heart sank. Fuck me, he thought again for the second time tonight.

—⁂—

Piper pulled up in front of Shane's home a little after midnight and saw Joe standing at the door. So this was his home. It was nice and neat in appearance. It was dark out so she couldn't see it all that well. Joe stepped out on the porch. He must have been waiting for them. He waved, and she waved back.

"It will only take a second," Shane said, hopping out of the car and heading to the front door at a dead run.

"Maybe I should go in and help," Taylor said.

"Nope, he'll be back in a second. We don't want to bother Joe too much."

Probably keeping him from something other than sleep, Piper thought, taking in the second car parked in his drive with the round pink breast cancer awareness sticker on the back window. *Feel your boobies*, it read. She assumed the car belonged to that woman, Sondra.

She watched as Shane disappeared inside. A few seconds later, Joe and Shane walked over to her car. She lowered her window.

"Thanks for making the stop."

"No problem. Got company?" she said, her eyes moving to the car parked next to her.

"Yep, didn't expect her. She was just about to leave."

"No explanation needed," she said, cutting him off. "Well, see you tomorrow. I'll drop him off in the afternoon. Will that work?"

"Yes."

"Okay, see you then," she said, pushing the button to close her window.

He stepped away and started back to his front door. He was wearing sweats, and a t-shirt. He was delectable, but not for her. Someone else would be dining on him tonight. She didn't believe that BS he'd given her about the woman leaving for a minute.

"You guys ready? Seat belts on?" she asked, glancing over at Shane, who was busy checking his bag, and then into Taylor's eyes, which reflected something else. She'd been watching her sister and Joe for a while.

"Yes, seat belts on," Kennedy said from the back.

"Thanks, Piper, for letting me sleep over," Shane said.

"No problem. We like having you around. Hope we didn't bother your uncle too much."

"No, he has a friend over tonight, too," he said.

Well good for him, Piper thought. They arrived at her home about ten minutes later, parked in the garage, and entered the door. Fifteen minutes later they were all tucked in bed, and she lay in hers trying to talk to herself again about Joe. Seeing Joe with that Sondra had startled her, making her rethink the whole hookup question. Yes, her feelings had gotten themselves twisted tonight, and she hadn't even done anything yet. She reminded herself of the hazards of hooking up, which was her reason for stopping this in the first place. Now what to do? She punched her pillow and closed her eyes.

---—๛—---

October

Piper was finished putting away groceries for the week. Her dad was in town and had stopped by yesterday, Saturday night, and picked up her sisters. He was taking them with him to his apartment, spending more time with them. She approved. He was trying to change. Go figure.

Kids loved their parents in spite of most things; she knew that first-hand. She still loved her mom, and was reconciled to her flaws. Mac was bringing them back today, Sunday, hopefully not too late since they had school tomorrow. The dogs took off toward the front door, a clear sign of company coming to call, barking loudly.

"Hey, McKenzie and Pepper," Piper heard Kennedy say. Then she and Taylor called out to her, both on their way up to the second floor, dogs bounding up with them. Piper heard their feet on the steps, then above her head. A set of feet were headed toward her kitchen, heavy footfalls. Her dad came into view, as always a commanding presence.

"Hey, Pops," she said.

"Hey, Renee," he said, walking over to kiss her.

"Have a good time?" she asked.

"Yes. We went to the movies today."

"Homework?" she asked.

"Done," he said, a smile on his lips. "This isn't my first time in the ring."

"I know, but usually you have a wife around to help. I'm just checking. It's a new habit of mine," she said, adding water to her pot for coffee. "Want some pie? I made it myself."

"What kind?" he asked, pulling out a chair and taking a seat.

"Apple. Your favorite," she said, pulling out two plates, "So…. how is Christina?"

"I'm thinking about going to see her."

"Going to see her where? In Vietnam?" she asked, surprised.

"Yes."

"Seriously? Huh. Okay, does she know about this?"

"We've been talking—well, she has—and I've been listening."

Piper lifted her eyebrows at that. He smiled.

"She doesn't think I love her. Thinks I want other women. I don't."

He frowned at Piper's expression of disbelief.

"I know my past, but I've been faithful to Christina," he said.

She was surprised at that, too.

"I'm getting old, Renee. Old enough to know a good woman when I have one," he said, taking the plate with his slice of pie from her. She handed him a cup of coffee and sat down in the chair in front of him.

"I'm surprised. Have you told Christina?" she asked.

"Yes."

"And…"

"And she wants to start a career when she returns. That's the other reason why she left. Wants me to play house-husband and let her lead for a while. I'm not the type," he said, placing a forkful of pie into his mouth.

"Is that so bad?" she asked.

He sighed and didn't respond for a few seconds as he chewed. "I'm getting old, too old. Can't teach an old dog new tricks," he said.

"Don't know if that response will work for you," Piper said.

He looked at her. "I know, I know, but, believe it or not, I'm giving it some thought. Not the complete house-husband thing, but maybe being around here more, giving her some room to figure out what she wants to do, helping out more with the girls. I'm willing to try, and hopefully going back will also help her see that I want to try. I do realize that I married her young, didn't know, and hadn't thought that she might miss her mother. The self-centeredness thing again," he said with a sheepish smile. "I love her in my own way. Never been or going to be demonstrative, just not, but I can maybe find a way to do enough for her to realize that I want her here, that we can work through the rest."

"That's a start," Piper said and reached for her dad's hand.

"It's always been me at the center of my universe. Boxing, winning, building a business empire required huge amounts of confidence and time," he said, a little hint of a smile on his lips, "so I'm going back to get her, to meet her mother, to hopefully show her that I care, if it's not too late."

"Don't know about the empire-building part," she said, smiling. Then she laughed. He gave her a mock glare, squeezing her hand, hers small in his larger one.

"So if you go, how long will you be gone? What about the girls? The holidays are coming up. What do you need me to do?" she asked.

"You're a beautiful woman, Renee," he said. "Do you know that?"

"Thanks, Dad."

"I mean it. It's not just looks that makes a woman beautiful. You know that, although I think you're beautiful in that way, too. I would be crazy if you hadn't been here to help me," he said.

"You're welcome."

"So, let's see. You'll have your sisters through Thanksgiving and Christmas."

"Yes."

"What do you need?" he asked, and they began to discuss money and what would need to be done to ensure the girls had a good holiday.

—⁂—

Joe stopped by the shop to review next week's schedule. It was Monday morning.

"She's in the back," the girl at the counter said. She knew he was here to see Piper, but gave him an I'm interested smile anyway. He didn't even notice. He immediately turned and walked back to Piper's office.

The door stood slightly ajar. He could see in. She was changing into the shop's uniform polo; it lay on the desk in front of her. She was standing in a sports bra and reaching for the polo. He watched her pull it over her head and felt his blood warm, his pulse quicken. He was disappointed by the way Saturday night had turned out. He knocked.

"Just a second," she said, pulling all of that hair into a ponytail. He stepped back as she opened the door fully.

"Hey. Calendar alignment time already?" she asked, reaching over the desk to pull her purse from a side drawer. She started digging though it for her BlackBerry. "What does our week look like?" she said, finding it, waiting for him to sit.

"Monday and Thursday this week," he replied.

"Great. That works for me. Duly noted," she said, fingers flying over her BlackBerry as she made note of the days. "Thanks for bringing Shane to zydeco night. He and the girls had a great time. Looks like you may have had one, too," she said, teasing and watching the discomfort in his eyes. "Should I expect any more poetry?" She chuckled.

He smiled. "I didn't invite her to zydeco night or back to my house. Her visit was not planned, at least not by me. She left soon after you did," he said, his eyes on hers.

"Good to know," she said, inwardly pleased that he'd wanted her to know that.

"Basketball season is approaching. Are you signing Taylor up to play?" he asked.

"Don't know. Probably, but I'll ask her," she said.

"Okay then, see you later," he said. He felt better now that he'd cleared that up.

Chapter 12

Halloween night found Piper standing in the volunteer's booth in costume. She dressed as a boxer, courtesy of her father's gym. She was here to check in and find the location of the dunking booth, tonight's volunteer assignment. She was part of the second group of dunkers, those that belonged to the parents' group, who were designated to give the teachers and coaches—the real headliners—a break from the water.

Piper had left her sisters near the entrance—Ken in a cheerleader's costume and Taylor dressed to represent Team Edward, whatever that meant.

"We'll find you later," they'd said. They didn't want their older sister following them around. The alarm on her cell chimed, interrupting her from her wanderings, a reminder to get to the dunking booth on time. She'd worn her swimsuit under her costume, so it was now or never.

Next to the dunking booth stood Joe, a nice coincidence that he was scheduled for the same time as she was. She secretly hoped they would be working together tonight, especially in light of his semi-explanation/apology the other day.

"Hi," he said, watching her walk toward the booth. "You volunteered to help here tonight?"

"I did," she said, stopping next to him. "For the next hour. You?"

"The same," he said.

They stood together, eyeing the teacher currently sitting in the booth, not quite sure who he was. They stood and watched as a boy missed his final shot.

"So are you two working the next hour?" the woman standing behind the table asked, looking them over.

"Yes," Piper said.

"Yes," Joe replied.

"Good. Since you're both here, let me explain what's required of each of you tonight." Piper and Joe listened attentively to her explanation.

"Who's going to be first in the booth?" she asked, looking between the two of them after she stopped talking.

"I don't mind going first," Joe replied.

Joe walked over to the booth and began to disrobe. She watched as he kicked off his shoes and pulled his t-shirt over his head. He owned a nice upper body, developed and lean, and touched by the sun; it was a really nice match to the hair that brushed his shoulders. He climbed up the ladder, walked across the seat or ledge or whatever it was called, and took a seat. He lifted his arms over his head in a stretch, shook his head, and placed his hands on either side of his body. He was relaxed on the seat—ready, cool, waiting for their first customer.

"Uncle Joe," Shane called out, running toward them full-out. "Come on, Taylor, he's here." Both children ran headlong toward the booth, skidding to a stop in front of Piper and looking over at Joe, big-ass grins on their faces, tickets in hand.

"Hey, Uncle Joe!" Shane said, waving to him. "You're going down, dude!" Shane handed over his tickets to Piper. She handed him three balls in exchange.

Shane threw. The first ball missed wide, followed by his second, which was too high.

"Is that the best you can do?" Joe asked.

"Watch this," Shane said, throwing his final ball, putting all his effort into it, watching it swing left.

Joe laughed. "Dude, you're letting our family down," he said, smiling.

"Piper, can I have another try?" He dug into his pocket for more tickets, handing them to her, and going to stand back at the line. Joe yawned, making a big production of it as he laughed while Shane missed again, again, and again.

"Dude, you throw like a girl," Joe teased.

Taylor was next in line. She threw her first ball—truly like a girl—and it knocked Joe into the water. Shane and Taylor whooped it up like they'd won the World Series.

"Bet you can't do it again," Joe said, lifting himself out of the water, his awesome upper body strength on display, muscles straining, water rushing over hard surfaces as he resumed his seat on the bench.

Taylor threw her second ball and it hit. Joe fell again, blond hair moving across the surface of the water, shorts ballooning out around him as he dropped like a torpedo, hitting the bottom with his feet and pushing up, breaking the surface with a huge smile on his face.

Be still my heart, Piper thought. Taylor and Shane went crazy then, dancing around, laughing. Joe laughed with them this time and pulled himself up again, pushing his hair away from his face.

"One more time, Piper," Taylor said.

"One more time," Piper said, and watched as Taylor threw her final ball. And wouldn't you know it, Joe went down for the third time in a row. He came up, treading water, laughing.

"Good job, Taylor. You've got some arm," he said and pulled himself up again.

The remainder of his time was spent falling and getting out of the water, as Shane and Taylor were determined to throw as many times as they could. Although other kids purchased tickets and took their chances, too, none were as successful as Taylor. Shane finally hit the mark, too. Thankfully, Joe's thirty minutes were over.

She was up next. Taylor and Shane wouldn't leave, and more of their friends were milling about now, waiting for their chance to dunk her. Joe had climbed down and was standing next to the tank, in the process of drying off. She had gotten in a peek but quickly turned away, not wanting to get caught staring. She waited until he was dressed and back at the booth, where he took over as ticket-taker.

"Your turn," he said and watched as she removed her robe and shimmied out of those boxing shorts, revealing a bold pink full-bodied swimsuit. It wasn't a bikini—there was nothing skimpy about it—but it fit her like a second skin. He stared at her for a moment, perusing her from head to toe, before he caught himself. Enough, Joe. He had a job to do, and it wasn't to stand here and gawk.

"Could I play?" one of Shane's friends asked, pulling him from his study of Piper.

"Sure," he said, taking the kid's ticket and handing him three balls. Piper had kicked off her shoes and was now climbing the stairs, her back to them, her legs and butt moving nicely up the stairs and over to the bench above the water where she took her seat.

"Ready," he called out, and she smiled. He smiled back, too, unscripted, just giving in to the pleasure of watching a lovely woman smile at him. He liked her, and liked being around her. He still wanted her— hadn't really ever stopped.

The kid threw the first ball, and it hit. She went under and he watched as her arms propelled her back up to the surface. She laughed and started to pull herself up. He watched that, too, that little part of her swimsuit bottom that had risen just a little bit, offering a glimpse of a well-toned ass.

She pulled herself up, resumed her position, and was hit again. He laughed this time, and he spent the remainder of her time in the booth encouraging the kids to hit her, teasing her, and smiling at her.

She watched him with the kids, laughing as he helped some of the young ones throw balls. Except for that one time, their pitches went wide. He laughed and talked with the other adults too, and if she thought him sexy before, he was in woman-killing form now.

She was back to the way she'd wanted him in the beginning. So what if he had other women? She could be one, for a night or two. She wanted to, and had agreed to it before the girls came. She would have a talk with her feelings and come to some type of truce with them about Joe. He was too good to pass up. She would work around her sisters and ask him for the hookup this time. It's what she wanted, anyway. There was no use pretending.

She sat through the remaining minutes, her decision solidifying in her mind. No worry as to whether he'd be on board; of that she had no doubt. She might as well ask tonight if she got the chance.

Coach Stanton, the next dunkee, had arrived, bringing with him a truckload of students willing to pay a price to dunk the coach. He was preparing to sit in, the headliner for the next hour, and the line of kids was twice as long as theirs had been. She dried off, put her clothes on, and walked over to the table to count tickets. Joe was waiting for her, smiling.

They worked in silence for a while, each counting their stacks of tickets. She was aware of him, standing next to her. Here goes nothing, she thought.

"You're headed home after this?" she asked.

"Not sure," he said, head bent, his eyes on his hands as they moved tickets from one pile to another, counting. "You?" he asked.

"I'm sticking around. Shane's coming home with me, remember?" she said.

"I know, not that he'd let me forget," he said. Done with his counting, he looked at her eyes, which were focused on the tickets in front of her. Her lips moved as she counted aloud. She was a study in concentration, like she was employed by a major accounting firm. Everything was organized and efficient with Piper. He waited until she was done.

"Thirty-six," he said and gave his stack to her. She combined it with hers before placing all of them in the clear plastic baggie. She wrote the number with a black marker on the front. He watched as she bent over and placed it under the table in the larger envelope, and then watched her rise and smile at him.

"Want to hang out for a while?" he asked.

"Sure," she said, offering up a surprised and unscripted smile. "Where to first?"

"Feed me," he said, and she laughed, grabbed his hand, and headed toward the food booth.

—m—

Piper was up early Sunday morning in spite of getting home near midnight. The Halloween carnival ended at eleven and hadn't gone according to her plan, at all, again. There was a plot afoot in the universe to keep her and Joe apart; at this rate, they'd never get together.

Mr. Marshall had a crush on her. Ugh. He was a nice man and all, but not her type. He had spent more than enough time with her and Joe last night, and her plans were thwarted again. She'd given every possible hint at her disposal to get him to move along. No such luck. After about an hour or more, Joe had given up, too. He left before she'd gotten the chance to ask him. Mr. Marshall was her very own version of Sondra, and a not-so-perfect ending to her evening.

It was quiet this morning. The kids were sleeping, and it was the first quiet she'd had in a while. She showered and headed toward the kitchen, in the mood for pancakes. She opened Ken's door. Yep, sound asleep. Pepper stood up and trotted out. Next she checked on Taylor, who was in the top bunk. Piper couldn't see her face. Shane slept snuggled into the lower bunk, moving around a little as she peered in. Piper and the dogs made their way downstairs and to the kitchen. Piper opened the back door and they scampered out.

She turned the coffee maker on, walked over to the sink, and looked out the window above it that faced her back yard. She watched as McKenzie and Pepper made the backyard rounds, searching for early morning prey. She poured herself a cup and walked over to the door, letting the dogs in. They both trotted upstairs and took their usual sleeping places outside the girls' doors.

She turned and walked over to the dishwasher. Of course it needed to be emptied. She opened the dishwasher door, preparing to put the dishes away. She walked over to the CD player and selected a nice, slow zydeco tune to start the day. She turned the volume to low and went back to work removing dishes from the dishwasher.

She didn't hear Shane enter; just felt the sting of someone hitting her butt and the shock had her standing up quickly, too quickly. Her head caught the corner of the cabinet—hard.

WTF was her only thought before everything went black. Piper fell like a tree into Shane, knocking him down underneath her. Shane had been standing there in shock at what he'd done. He'd been pretending he was his uncle, doing what had worked so well for Joe. Piper had fallen into him and they'd both barely missed Ken, who had followed Shane down the stairs to the kitchen.

"You've killed my sister!" Kennedy shouted at the top of her lungs, watching as blood leaked from Piper's head.

"Go get Taylor," Shane said urgently, his hands shaking, trying to slide from underneath Piper without hurting her more.

"Go get Taylor!" he said again, louder this time, as he slid free of Piper's body. "Now, Ken!" Ken took off. He could hear her feet on the steps. He looked at Piper's head. There was a deep cut; blood was seeping out of it, starting to run to the floor. What to do?

Think, Shane. Stop the bleeding. He remembered that first aid class he'd taken with his uncle. He needed to apply pressure, needed a towel. He looked around the room for one. Where was a clean towel? Be calm and think. Don't panic.

He stood up, dashed to the counter, and grabbed several towels just as Taylor slid into the kitchen, baseball cap on. She slept in that thing, he now knew. Kennedy entered a second behind her.

"What happened?"

"She hit her head. It knocked her out."

"Call 911," Shane said, applying the towel to Piper's head where blood still escaped. Taylor reached for the phone, dialed 911, and squatted down next to Shane.

"Do you think she's dead?" Taylor asked, voice shaky.

"No, she's breathing," Shane said, his voice wavering. "Look, her chest is moving." Taylor bent her head down to Piper's nose, nodding in confirmation.

"911. Do you need police, fire, or an ambulance?" the person on the line asked.

"My sister hit her head and knocked herself out," Taylor said, hands shaking. Ken had started to cry.

"Stay on the line and let me get you to EMS."

Then a different voice came on the line. "What is the address of the emergency?"

"It's 1753 Saddleback Street. My sister's head is bleeding," Taylor said.

"Is there an adult in the home?"

"My sister, but she's the one who hit her head. It's just me and my little sister and a friend."

"What is your telephone number?"

"It's 767-3465. My sister is not waking up. You've got to come quick."

"We are. The ambulance is on the way now. I need you to answer a few more questions. Someone is on their way, okay?"

"Okay."

"What's your name?"

"Taylor Knight."

"Is your sister conscious?"

"No."

"Is she breathing?"

"Yes."

"Is she bleeding?"

"Yes, but my friend has a towel over the cut. He say's it'll keep her from bleeding so much," Taylor said.

"Good. Stay on the line. That was fast thinking on your friend's part. Do you have any pets?"

"Yes. Two dogs."

"I need you to put them away. The ambulance will be there soon."

Taylor turned to her sister. "Kennedy, stop crying and go make sure McKenzie and Pepper are locked away." She watched as Kennedy left the room.

"My little sister is going to put them up now."

"You're doing good, sweetheart," the operator said.

"The ambulance is close to your home now. In a few minutes you'll hear them knocking on the door. I want you to let them in. Is this a cordless phone?"

"Yes," Taylor answered as Kennedy arrived in the door, out of breath.

"The dogs are in my room and the door is closed," Kennedy said.

"The dogs are locked away," Taylor told the operator.

"Good. Take the phone with you when you answer the door."

"Okay."

"How old are you?"

"Twelve, and my sister is ten. My friend is twelve, too."

Taylor and Shane looked up at the sound of knocking on the door.

"I hear them knocking," Taylor said.

"Okay. Go answer the door. Stay on the line. Take the phone with you."

"Okay," she said, walking to the front door.

"You're doing a good job. Let me know when you open the door," the operator said, as Taylor opened the door.

"They're inside," Taylor said.

"Okay, sweetheart. I'm hanging up now."

"Okay, thank you."

"You're welcome."

"My sister is this way," she said, leading two EMTs toward the kitchen. One was an African-American woman, and the other a short, bald-headed young Hispanic with glasses. They entered the kitchen.

Piper still lay in the same spot, Shane holding the bloodied towel to her head as if his life depended on it, his face marked by anxiety.

"Hello. My name is Earline, and I'm a paramedic. I've come to help your sister. Would you please stand over there with your friend," she said to Shane as she bent down at Piper's side. Shane moved to stand near the door with Taylor and Kennedy.

I need to call Joe, Shane thought. He slipped out the door, hitting the stairs two at a time, and ran down the hall to Taylor's room. He found his phone in his backpack. He punched in Joe's cell number and waited. It was early, so Joe was probably still asleep.

"Hey buddy. You're up early," Joe said, answering the phone on the first ring. He'd gotten up early and was sitting on the couch drinking coffee and watching the sports recap.

"You have to come quick, I hurt Piper. She hit her head and now the ambulance is here," Shane said and started to cry.

"Hey, dude, calm down," Joe said, standing up and walking to his room. He dressed quickly and headed toward his garage door, scooping up his keys as he listened to Shane continue crying.

"Come on, Shane, it'll be okay. I'm on the way. Where are you now?" Joe asked, walking to his car, getting in, and pulling out of the garage a few seconds later.

"Upstairs. I had to call you," Shane said.

"Good buddy, take a deep breath, you're okay. You've got to stop crying, though. I need you to talk to me. Tell me what's going on. Can you do that?" he asked, turning the corner of his street. Thankfully Piper lived close to him, less than five minutes away.

"Yes," he answered, taking a deep breath.

"Now keep the phone with you and walk back downstairs to check on Piper. I'll be there in less than three minutes. Okay?"

"Okay," Shane said. He had stopped crying. Joe turned off his street and sped onto the major thoroughfare that would take him to Piper's, hoping his luck would hold and he wouldn't encounter any police.

"Piper is still on the ground," Shane said, breathless now and back in the kitchen. "They are looking in her eyes now with a light."

"She's waking up," he told Joe as Piper's eyes fluttered and then opened.

"Good. I'm hanging up. I'm on Piper's street now. I'll see you in a minute," Joe said, the lights of the ambulance coming into view. He pulled in and parked in the drive next to it. He was out of his car in a flash. The front door was unlocked. He could hear conversation as he made his way into the kitchen. He stepped inside to find Piper being loaded and strapped onto the gurney.

"Is there anyone to help you with the children?" the female EMT asked Piper.

"I can," Joe said, looking at her.

"Okay. Is that okay, Ms. Knight?" she asked, and accepted Piper's nod of confirmation. Piper gave a weak smile to Joe.

"Sir, we are going to have to transport her to the hospital. She needs stitches. If you'd like to meet us there, we'll be taking her to Seton on Thirty-eighth. Are you familiar with that hospital?"

"Yes."

"We are leaving now," the female EMT said, rolling Piper through the kitchen doorway and down the hall to the front door.

"Shane, how about you, Taylor, and Kennedy put some clothes on and we'll follow Piper to the hospital," he said. "That way we can bring her home when she's done." He squeezed Shane's shoulder.

They headed to their rooms while he followed the EMTs out into the early morning sunshine. He glanced over at Piper, who gave him another weak smile. He smiled back and squeezed her hand, then stood aside and watched as she was loaded into the ambulance. The doors closed. He watched the ambulance back out and pull away and then turned to go inside. He found Shane, Kennedy, and Taylor at the door, ready to go.

"Dogs?" he asked.

"In their crates," they replied on unison.

"She'll be okay," he said, making sure the door was locked before joining them in his car. He backed out of the drive. He looked in the rear view mirror, taking in apprehension and worry on all three faces, now quiet. "The EMTs told me what a good job the three of you had done in making sure Piper received help."

"I did just like we learned in class," Shane said.

"So tell me what happened," he said, looking back at the road, listening to Shane recount the story through his tears. He hadn't had that kind of scare since he was a kid, but it could have been so much worse.

He pulled up into the parking lot reserved for emergency room patients, and all four walked through the automatic doors. They made their way to the emergency room waiting area. It was empty. Joe marched to the admitting desk. An older Hispanic woman with her hair pulled back into a bun sat behind a window.

"May I help you?"

"Yes, a friend of mine just arrived by ambulance. We are here to drive her home."

"Her name?"

"Piper Knight."

"And you are?"

"Joe Sandborne," he said.

"Well, thank you, I'll make note of it," she said.

Joe strode over to the kids, their faces forlorn and anxious.

"She will be all right," he said again, taking the seat next to Shane.

Joe looked at his watch. 8:30 a.m. They'd been waiting for thirty minutes now. The waiting room was still empty. Shane sat next to him, looking totally dejected. Kennedy sat next to him, her arm on Shane's, offering comfort, and Taylor next to her, baseball cap pulled low on her head. He couldn't tell what she was thinking.

Joe looked over at Shane and caught his eye. "Do you guys want anything to eat? Maybe we could find a snack machine."

"Yes. But could I go to the restroom first?" Taylor asked.

"Sure, let's find one," Joe said, standing. "There is one over there." Taylor and Kennedy headed off in that direction, and Joe turned to Shane, glad for the opportunity to talk to him alone.

"Shane, what were you thinking?" he asked. He had been given all the details as to what had happened on the drive over. He just needed the why from Shane.

Shane was quiet, his eyes looking forward. "You'll get angry," he said.

"I won't get angry. Just tell me why."

"I've seen you do it a thousand times. The girls like it when you do it," he said.

"Do what?"

"You know, in the mornings or sometimes late at night. Sometimes they're in the kitchen with you, looking through our refrigerator or making coffee, and you pop them sometimes on their butts. They always laugh, not hit their heads and almost die."

"She didn't almost die," he said, his hand moving to rest on Shane's head.

He was at a loss for words. He'd thought that Shane had been asleep during those nights, racking his brain and finally remembering that one time—but that was just one time, or so he'd thought.

"I only remember one time."

"It was more, but you didn't see me…I like the way the girls like you and I thought I could try it out on Piper."

"But she's an adult," he said gently, saddened by his nephew's forlorn expression.

"I guess I forgot…but she likes me," he said. They stopped talking when the girls returned.

"Let's ask the nurse at the counter if there a place to eat."

"Just the vending machine down the hall," had been her response. He reached into his pocket and pulled out his wallet.

"Think you three can handle it? I'll stay here and wait for Piper," he said.

"Sure," they said in unison, taking the money and walking away.

This was his fault somehow. Shane had been watching him. He stood there, more than a little stunned by Shane's explanation. Some example you've been setting here, Joe.

"Where are the kids?" Piper asked, coming up from behind him. He turned, taking in the bandage on her head and blood on her shirt. In a way, he was responsible for it.

"What?" she said, looking at his face. "What's wrong?"

"Shane told me what happened. I'm sorry," he said.

"Let's talk about it later," she said, her eyes moving behind him as he heard the kids' footsteps approaching.

"Piper, are you okay?" Taylor said, walking over to wrap her arms around her sister in a hug. Kennedy followed suit while Shane stood back watching.

"I don't get a hug?" Piper asked him.

"I almost killed you," he said, fighting back tears.

"Nope. See? Fine," she said, holding her arms outstretched, smile in place.

"I'm sorry," he said.

"I know, dude," she said. "Give me a hug." He went to her, hugging her tightly.

—⁓—

It was later that morning. Piper hadn't made pancakes after all. She just sat at the table while Joe prepared omelets—his specialty, according to Shane. The kids seemed to be fine after a million questions over brunch and had just headed upstairs to play video games. Seems video games were the antidote to any troubles in the world. Joe was helping her put her dishes away. She stood near the counter, more watching him than working.

Piper talked and laughed, recounting the events of this morning from her perspective, waking up finding the EMTs over her. She hadn't known where she was at first, thought she had been in her dad's boxing gym and gotten knocked out. She had experienced that one time when her mouth had surpassed her boxing proficiency and she'd challenged some guy to a bout. She had awakened to her dad's concerned face standing over her, more embarrassed than hurt.

"It took years off of my life, driving over here, worried, not knowing what I'd find," he said, his smile turning serious. "I'm sorry. It seems that Shane was attempting to follow in his Uncle Joe's footsteps, and not the ones worth following. He'd apparently seen me do something similar at home before with some of my female friends."

"I see," she replied, laughing again. He stood there, watching her laugh at what could have been a serious injury.

"What has Shane seen, exactly?" she asked, a teasing glint in her eye, wicked smile at her lips.

"None of your business," he said, turning around and removing the last of the dishes from the top portion of her dishwasher.

"Come on, you can tell me. We're friends, right?" she said, walking closer to him.

"Nope. What happens in Vegas, stays in Vegas," he said.

"That bad, huh?" she said.

"Not going to say either way," he said. It was quiet as he looked through her cabinets, searching for what went where. She took a seat behind him.

"Joe," she said.

"What?" he said absentmindedly as he searched through her cabinets. Was this where the plates belonged? Nope. Glasses. How many glasses does one woman need? he wondered, closing it and opening another. Okay, plates belonged here.

"We're friends, right?"

"Last I checked, but maybe not since my nephew tried to kill you," he said, laughing, starting to stack the plates into the cabinet.

"I've been thinking," she said.

"That can't be good," he said, and laughed again, this time dodging her foot.

"Well, how about instead of having those…women over all the time, at your house in front of Shane, you could just have me," she said, her words rushed now. "It could just be me, us, just like you asked for at the beginning," she said, watching him slow down in his placement, going back to the dishwasher. "I could take care of those needs occasionally, and you take care of mine."

He turned to her. "What did you say?"

"You heard me," she said, her eyes locked on his, taking in his startled expression. She forged ahead. "You know I have needs, too. With the girls living with me those needs are never met. Not that they were met before they'd moved in, but then at least there was the possibility. Not so much now. Unlike you, I just don't have people throwing themselves at me. Plus, I know you. You're a good guy. You know me. We're friends, so why can't we…sort of like killing two birds with one stone."

He'd never heard it described quite that way before.

"Tell me you hadn't thought of it again?"

"I had," he said.

"See, great minds think alike. It's a perfect idea. Now I'm used to the girls. They're on a schedule, at school most of the day. We know each other's schedules, the kids' schedules. We can work around them. We meet on Mondays to plan the week, right? We don't always have to meet at the coffee shop. Sometimes you don't have to be in to work early. There is ample time. What do you think?"

He sighed. Hell, yeah, it's what he always wanted, so why the reservations now?

"How about we take some time to think it over?"

"What's there to think about?" she asked. She felt as if she'd just had the wind kicked out of her.

"Don't get me wrong. I want to, you know that, and after last night watching you in the swimsuit I was going to ask you to reconsider the hookup question again, Mr. Marshall got in the way," he said, glancing over at her, finding surprise on her face at that comment.

"But now that the option is placed before me, I find I have reservations. Well, more like a reservation."

"What?" she asked.

"I don't want to ruin our friendship," he said, and smiled at the surprise that registered on her face. "I know. I've come to rely on you. You've come to mean a lot to Shane, plus I value your friendship, too. I like you. Sex, I can have with anyone. Friendships haven't been so easy for me to find. I don't have many. My choice, I know, but I do value yours." He was as sincere as she had ever seen him.

Ahhhhhh, she thought internally, pushing forward now that there was a little daylight showing through the fog. "It doesn't have to alter our friendship. I mean, FWB is the way the world works nowadays, right? I can handle it if you can."

He was silent for a second or two. "Occasional, huh?" he said, looking at her, one eyebrow lifting, sly smile at his lips.

He turned away, back to removing the last of her dishes. What am I doing? She was offering him what he wanted, and he was hesitating.

"So do you want to give it a try?" she asked.

"I need you to promise me one thing," he said, turning to her again.

"What?"

"You have to always be honest with me," he said, gazing into her eyes, intense and focused on her. "If this becomes too much for you, your emotions get too involved, you let me know. This isn't going to turn into a long-term thing for me. You need to know that up front. I value you too much to have you think otherwise."

It was quiet for a second as she processed his words. Okay, she hadn't thought he was in for the long term anyway, but that could change. The dreamy-eyed optimist within her always kept hope alive.

"Okay then," she replied, looking around, suddenly nervous.

"One more thing. I should warn you that I'm demanding when it comes to sex. If this is to be an exclusive relationship, I think you need to know what you're signing up for," he said, lifting an eyebrow in question.

"And how demanding is demanding?"

"Demanding," he said, and gave her a look that could boil water.

She cleared her throat. "I can do demanding," she said. She hoped so, anyway. "Demanding, like in everyday demanding?" Her eyebrows lifted in question, seeking confirmation. "Like what? Not whips and chains kind of demanding," she said.

"Nope. No whips or chains, unless you want to," he said and laughed at her expression. "But maybe other things."

"Other things, huh? Nothing painful," she said, seriously biting into her bottom lip.

He fought against smiling.

"Not painful, but often," he said.

"Often can be painful," she replied, her eyes glued to his now. "So how often is often?" she asked.

"Enough," he said, watching her face. She was not a very good poker player. "So are you sure about this? Is this what you're signing up for, what you had in mind?"

"Uh…" she said, looking around, not so sure anymore. She stood quiet for a second, took a deep breath and found his eyes again. "I'm sure."

He shrugged. "Here's an out. We'll give it a try and if it's too much for you, just say so and we'll stop."

She nodded, a small movement, her eyes turned inward, considering.

"Okay, it's a deal," she said.

"When do we start? Do you want to go out first?" Joe asked.

"No, that's not necessary. I'd have to find a sitter and so would you. I don't need all that wining and dining stuff, don't have time for it, anyway. So how about we just do what comes natural, you know, just let nature take its course," she said, proud of herself for her pragmatism.

"Do what comes natural," he said, mulling that over in his mind. And when was that, exactly? He rubbed his hand across his forehead. "Is there a time-frame for when things come naturally?"

"No, whenever you feel like it's natural," she said.

He turned back to the counter and finished with her dishes, closing the cabinet doors as she started to talk about the Thanksgiving trip. He half listened, his mind on their new agreement.

Chapter 13

The following Sunday found Piper at home enjoying the peace and quiet, a reminder of her life before kids. The girls were at a birthday party, not due home for another five hours. It was one of those six-hour thingies, held at one of those all-in-one places that included a movie, bowling, laser tag, video arcade, and food. She'd dropped Taylor and Kennedy off about an hour ago. Joe had been in charge of getting Shane there. A parent who lived nearby was bringing all three to her home—returning a favor—and Joe would pick Shane up from here.

"What are we doing here, Cowboys?" she asked the TV as she sat on the couch, reading a book, and half listening to the football game. Her feet were up, a glass of wine on the table in front of her.

The doorbell rang and she groaned. The dogs started in with their barking while she debated whether or not she should answer it. She looked over at McKenzie and Pepper standing in front of it, searching their tails for clues. Friend or foe? The duo barked regardless, but tail wagging in earnest meant friend, not stiff and pointed, the sign of the enemy.

Piper sat up, pushed herself up from the sofa and moseyed over to door. Her breath hitched after she recognized Joe standing on the other side. He wasn't due here for another five hours, not unless he was coming for…Remain calm, she told herself and opened the door. He looked good, dressed casually in jeans and a t-shirt.

"Hey," she said. "You're early."

"I had some errands to run after I dropped off Shane. They took less time than I thought so instead of going home I decided I'd stop by and see what you were up to," he said, peering over her shoulder. "Am I interrupting anything?"

"No, just reading and watching the game. Come on in," she said, stepping aside and letting him enter. As she closed the door behind him he squatted down to scratch the neck of two of his favorite friends.

"What game?" he asked.

"Cowboys at Arizona," she said, walking back into the living room and taking her place back on the sofa.

"Make yourself at home," she said, watching him as he walked over and settled on the other portion of her couch. Guess not today, either. She'd thought he'd jump right on her request, but no, he'd proceeded as normal, hadn't mentioned it again or made any moves toward her. It had been a week since they agreed to more.

"Want anything to drink?" she asked.

"Nope. I'll just watch the game for a while," he said.

"Here's the remote. I'm not tied to this game, doing more reading than watching," she said, handing the remote over to him. He flipped through channels and watched her out of the corner of his eye. He watched as her head fell back to her book.

He glanced again, taking in her feet stretched out before her—nice toes painted blue with white stripes, shorts cut high, t-shirt snug over her breasts. He went back to flipping channels and ended up back where he'd started.

"So, Piper," he said, watching her eyes finish reading before she looked at him. "I was thinking that now might be that natural time you'd talked about. What do you think?"

"Natural," she repeated. Her eyes had moved from the book to the TV. She was now preoccupied with a commercial advertising a sale of shoes, confusion marking her face. A few seconds later it cleared. "Natural, oh, that kind of natural?" She looked over at him. "Right now?"

"Yep," he said, all relaxed like, spread out on her sofa. She skimmed his body from head to toe and back.

"Now," she said again.

"Well you did say that you didn't want any wining and dining, and the kids are gone for," he checked his watch, "five more hours. And someone else is dropping them off here, right?"

"Yes."

"Okay, why not right now?" he said, watching her face and the feelings that passed over them like the wind—recognition, shock, acceptance, interest, and, finally, apprehension.

"Okay…where? Here on the couch?"

Here works, he thought. "Where would you like to go?"

"My room?" she asked.

"Your room it is," he said and stood up. Now that she was on board, he was so there.

He watched her stand. She ran a hand through her hair, turned, and eyed the stairs. Come on, Piper, this is what you said you wanted. Let's go, she thought and headed for the steps. He followed, and she could feel him at her back, his eyes glued to the sway of her hips, cheeks curvy and full, his hands held in his pockets to keep from reaching for them.

He followed her up the stairs and down the hall to her room. He hadn't been here before. They reached her room and she entered first and turned to face him, her hands together behind her back. He closed the door behind them and looked around, taking in the clutter that was so her. It wasn't so bad that it prevented you from walking, but was far from his neat-as-a-pin housekeeping.

He turned to face her, watching her. He could tell she was nervous. Her teeth were tugging at her bottom lip.

He took a step toward her, so ready, hard like you wouldn't believe. He had so looked forward to this, since the beginning. He hadn't pressed her until now. For some reason he wanted to make sure she was truly sure.

They stood for a second, eyes glued to each other. He reached for the bottom of his t-shirt and pulled it over his head, dropping it to the floor. She stood, watching, her mouth parting slightly, eyes growing large. He grew harder if that were possible, watching her staring like this, hunger mixed in with a little bit of shyness. She was even startled, like it was her first gander at a man's chest.

"You know what? Maybe on second thought…" she said, her hands brushing the hair from around her face, thinking now about the demanding part. Was she up for this? She wasn't anywhere near the sexual athlete that she'd bet her life he was. "Maybe I would like the wining and dining option, now that we're here. Maybe we should get to know each other more, in a more relaxed setting, you know. This seems so sudden," she said, backing up closer to the bed.

"It's not that sudden," he said, kicking off his shoes. His hands went to the snap of his jeans, and he unzipped and opened them. "And you know me," he said, letting them fall to the floor. All that remained were his boxers, with a noticeable dent in them now. She swallowed hard and watched as he took another slow step toward her. He started to push his boxers slowly down his lean hips. He watched her eyes fixated on his hands as his boxers moved downward. Her eyes then went to his body, taking in the nice V of a man who was in great shape. He smiled when her eyes landed on his erection, his boxers at his feet now, and heard her sharp intake of air. Her eyes found his, alarm in them now.

He smiled again, took two more steps, and stood in front of her.

"I don't know, Joe," she said.

"Sure you do," he responded, and reached for her, his arms moving around her waist, pulling her close. He bent his head to the curve of her neck and he kissed her lightly there.

"I..." she said again, abruptly quiet as his hands lifted her top and pulled it over her head. Just as quickly he reached for the snap of her bra and removed it, pulling it outward from her arms. He moved those wonderful hands to cup her breasts while his mouth was just under her chin again, moving tantalizingly slowly toward her lips.

He felt so good, so strong, so everything. His hands were cupping her breasts, softly moving over them. Was she even still breathing?

"Is this okay?" he said, his mouth at the corner of hers now. "Just trying to do what comes naturally." His hair softly touched her shoulders. She nodded, her eyes locked onto his, mesmerized by the strength, humor, and the certainty she found in them. She couldn't think with his hand moving over her so. He went back to kissing that spot underneath her ear.

"Relax. This was a really good idea," he added, his mouth making its way along the ridge of her jaw toward her mouth. She stood still, trapped like a deer, until his mouth found hers.

Damn, he was good. She opened her mouth at the request of his tongue, which was probing the seam of her lips. She moaned, and he chuckled and kissed her slowly, exploring her mouth with his tongue, getting the feel for her, marking her. He probably had no idea of the impact he was having on her, but she didn't think she would ever be the same.

He was moving her now, or at least she thought she was moving. Her mind struggled to keep up, to just take in and process his hands teasing her breasts while his tongue teased her there, too. She wasn't sure she could handle anything else.

He walked her over to the bed. She knew she was there because her knees hit the mattress and he stopped, his hands moving to her shorts. Her hands joining up with his, helping him unsnap them and slide the zipper down. He laughed against her mouth.

She was so ready and so on board now. "Condoms?" he asked, stepping back to pull her shorts down her hips. He kissed the junction of her thighs, causing her to sit hard on her bed, her legs no longer able to hold her up. He laughed while finishing his task of removing her remaining clothing before standing to look down at her on her bed, nude, those long legs slightly parted, hair loose and wild about her head, eyes closed, her face a mix of want and serenity, just like he'd imagined.

"Condoms?" he asked again. She pointed to her nightstand. He reached over and grabbed a few. "Extra large," he said, reviewing the package he held in his hands. "Thanks, I think."

She opened her eyes and smiled at him, a big ole giant smile, slow and sexy, and he felt a flutter in his chest.

"Gimmee," she said, slowing sitting up on her elbows. She extended one arm, pointing to the condom in his hand and wiggling her fingers for it. This opportunity was too good to waste. She hoped that he was as demanding tonight as he'd said he could be. He smiled and placed the package in her hand.

"This was a good idea, wasn't it?" she said, looking at him from beneath her lashes, a sexy expression on her face as she tore the package with her teeth. They both laughed, and then it was all pleasure.

—∞—

"What about this problem?" Kennedy asked, waiving her fingers in front of Piper's face the next day. They were seated at a table in the coffee shop. Piper was supposed to be helping her with her homework, but so far all she had done was stare out of the front window.

"Piper," Kennedy called again.

"I'm sorry. Did you finish that problem? Let me check it," she said pulling Kennedy's paper in front of her to review. It was quiet for a few seconds as Piper did the math. "Great," she said, sliding the paper back over to Kennedy. "Two more and you're done for the night," she said, her head turning back toward the window. She stared out, not seeing anything outside, her mind reentering the world of Joe, lost in yesterday with him, their first time together. Wow, was all she could think. She'd replayed that afternoon in her mind twenty times if not once since then.

What an inspired idea for them to combine their forces, literally, although she would have to shore up her game to keep up with him. He was certainly on top of his. He did warn her he would be demanding, and now she knew exactly what that meant. She might not be totally up for all of his demands, but she was willing to try most of them.

She turned and looked over at her sister, Kennedy, whose head was bent over her work, pencil moving intently as she worked through her nemesis, division. Taylor and Shane had finished their homework, and they were playing another of their favorite video games. Piper turned back to her thoughts again.

She would never ever look at her middle name in quite the same manner again.

Renee. A simple name for her friends and family's use, mostly; those who were close to her called her that. Piper was what most other people called her, and in spite of her mother's reasoning for giving that name to her, she liked the name—preferred it, actually—until she heard her middle name fall from Joe's lips.

When he said her middle name it became poetry. Renee, the only name he'd called her when he'd made love to her, like she was a different woman there with him. Just thinking about it warmed her blood, conjured up images of sweat and want and need.

She sighed, and Kennedy looked up, a question in her eyes.

"You okay, Pipe?" she asked.

"Yes, I am," she said, blowing out a breath before sitting up straighter in her chair and returning her attention to math.

—⁓—

Later on that evening Piper stood in the kitchen, putting dishes in the washer, when she heard the dogs barking at the front door. She dried off her hands and headed toward them. It was Joe letting himself in. They had exchanged keys a while ago in case Shane left something at home and Joe wasn't able to get back. She'd given him a key, too, pretending that it represented more between them, heading toward permanence. It made her feel special. She knew she was fooling herself, but she'd decided she could fool herself if she wanted to.

He bent to rub the dogs who, as always, were lapping at his hands, licking his chin. They looked at her before turning and heading back upstairs. Joe smiled, stood up, and met her halfway.

"Where's everybody?" he asked.

"Upstairs," she said, watching as he walked back to the bottom of the stairs and looked up, his head turned as if he were listening for something. Apparently satisfied, he turned and walked toward her, a glint in his eye that had her body going soft. He grabbed her hand and towed her along behind him to the kitchen. Looking around, he spotted the pantry, pulled her in, and closed the door behind them.

It was dark. The light was on the outside of the door, but apparently it didn't matter. He pushed her against the door. His lips met hers in a kiss hot enough to burn rubber. Good Lord, this man knew his way around a woman's body. His hand found her breast and his lower body found its match in hers. He pushed inward. She groaned, and he continued his assault, his hand moving to her ass, pulling her closer. He lifted her while one hand reached for his belt buckle.

The dogs were barking again, breaking through the fog in her brain. She pushed him away, pulled her mouth away, one reluctant lip at a time.

"Joe," she said, panting.

"Yeah, I know," he said, stepping back.

He opened the door and pushed her through, and she was blinded for a second by the light. The dogs were at the back door, wanting to go out. A squirrel or bird was calling their names. She ran her hands through her hair and opened the door. The air from outside was doing her good, somewhat clearing the lust from her brain.

Joe stepped out of the pantry, calmer except for his eyes. They gave him away. He wanted what she wanted, and had been thinking about since the first time.

"I'm in town tomorrow. Can you swing lunch?" he asked.

"Sure." This was a first. "Where?"

"Here," he said.

"Oh…here…" she said, eyebrows raised. "Okay… that kind of lunch. Sure, lunch here works. What time?"

"Noon, but I'll call you to make sure," he said.

"Okay, see you then."

He took a deep breath, walked over, and kissed her, hard and quick, before going toward the front door. "I'd better get Shane," he said, heading up the stairs.

"Sure," she said, following along behind him, overjoyed about the prospects that lunch might bring.

—⁂—

Hurry up, Piper thought, watching the hands of her watch move. He was due to arrive at eleven-thirty. He'd called her ten minutes ago, told her he was on his way and that he would meet her at her house.

Yes, she was so on board with that, with him. What to do now? Should she get undressed and wait for him upstairs, like some seductive vamp of old—long satiny lingerie covering her body—or she could come up with something creative to surprise him? She could be inventive, too. Who was she kidding? She had a long hill to climb to match Joe in creativity.

Unable to come to a decision, she sat here on her bottom step, dressed in her Lights Out gear, waiting for him to arrive. She who hadn't had sex in years was champing at the bit now…but what a bit to champ on, she thought, and giggled. I'm really losing it here, she said to herself.

If there was a silver lining, he seemed just as needy as she, as ready for another time as she was. She could hear it in his voice, see it in his eyes. She loved his eyes. She heard a car pull up, pulling her from her thoughts, and heard the door close. Feet were moving toward the front door. She opened it before he could knock. He smiled. Oh, Jesus, what that man could do with a smile. He was apparently impatient, too, because he entered the house and started up the steps before turning around and making a beeline for the couch. He pulled her to her feet.

"I just need a few times, quick," he said, sitting down, pulling her over to him, tugging at the belt on his slacks, unzipping his pants. He looked at her and gave her a get your ass in gear look.

"Come on, Renee."

There he went with her name again, in the way that only he could say it. It just about turned her to butter. It sounded decadent, and his smile was decadent, too—a shot in the arm. What are you waiting for?

First things first. She kicked off her shoes and wiggled out of her jeans and underwear, eyes glued to him the whole time; he was undressing quickly, too.

Bottoms gone, she pulled her shirt over her head, removed her bra, and pulled the scrunchy from her hair. She shook it loose and looked at him, a smile at his lips giving way to laughter at how fast she'd gotten undressed.

"What is with this urgency?" he asked, his face puzzled for a second as he pulled out his wallet, grabbed several condoms from it, and put one on. He pushed his hips outward to the edge of the sofa, making sure she had room on either side of them. He pulled her to straddle him, knees on either side of his thighs.

He leaned up, his eyes fixed on her, serious now. He cupped her face with his hand and pulled her in for a kiss, so soft, tongue entering immediately. "Renee," he whispered softly against her lips, his hands moving to her breasts, cupping them, squeezing them before moving downward to her hips, where he lifted her and held her above him, anticipating. He held her still for a few seconds, gazing into her eyes, which reflected his need and want.

He pushed her hips downward and pushed into her body slowly. Don't hurry, he thought. How was it possible to feel this good? He thrust into her again, harder this time. A moan escaped his mouth and he pulled her head forward, seeking her mouth.

"Fuck…" she said into his mouth, and felt him smile.

"Renee," he groaned, as he continued to lift and lower her over him, his hips pushing in hard as he pulled her down to take more of him into her body. She moaned against his mouth, her forehead falling to his as she just let herself feel the power of him smoothly moving in and out of her body.

"Renee…please…I'm…" And he came with more force than he was used to. He really was not prepared for the intensity, and he ground his teeth and held her hips down on his as he went with the power of his release. He just let it run through him, and let out another groan as his head fell to rest against hers.

Her eyes popped open and she smiled, hair springy and bushy around her head, eyes twinkling.

"Don't laugh," he said.

"I won't," she said, laughing. She leaned in, found his lips and kissed him, making love to his mouth just as he'd just done for her. Well, not quite for her, but she knew he wouldn't leave her hanging so she just made love to his wonderful mouth until he was ready for seconds. She knew he was ready now, could feel him in her, ready.

"More," he said in that commanding way of his. Hell, yeah, she thought.

He stood and she locked her legs around his waist to hold on. He took a few steps away from the couch, found an empty spot on her floor, and laid her there.

"Give me a second," he said, before leaving her and walking to the small bathroom located downstairs. He returned a few seconds later and covered her body with his from soup to nuts before kissing her and rolling over onto his back.

"I'm not quite there yet, but this one should be somewhat longer. I'm still walking along that edge."

"I think I'm starting to get the demanding part," she said.

"Not really, but we're breaking you in slowly," he said.

She lifted herself on her arms and looked down at him and started to move her body around him. His hand found her hips and helped her along, going to the spot where their bodies met. He didn't want to leave her behind this time. She was different, he'd give her that. Once she decided a course of action, she was all in, and he admired that particular brand of courage. He watched as she put all her effort into moving upward and then down, speeding up, sharp and fast, in some kind of hurry, so he just held on this time, his hands moving to clasp her breasts firmly in his hands, moving his hips striving to keep up with her pace.

"Joe, oh God..." he heard her say, and a few minutes later he watched her come, head thrown back, face beautiful, and he followed.

He waited until her breathing slowed and she looked down at him through pleasure-filled and satisfied eyes. Was that a bit of mischief lurking in there, too, as she watched him from above.

"Edges all smooth yet?" she asked. He grinned.

"You have no idea," he said, pulling her head forward for a kiss.

"Now I can take my time," he said, smiling and sitting up, clasping her legs around his back, his arms going around her waist.

"You are kidding, right?" she said, watching him smile.

"Nope," he said, grinning. "I did try to warn you. Want to back out?"

"Hell, no," she said.

"So you can hang with me a while longer?"

"Yes, I guess so," she said and laughed as he attempted to lift her from the floor, almost breaking his and her necks in the process. It seemed like all they could do was laugh about it.

After they'd managed to get themselves upright, his arms went around her waist and she swung her legs around his back. He took a few steps backward, pretending to groan under her weight. She pinched him.

"I'm not that heavy," she said as he proceeded to carry her up the stairs, stopping to kiss every few steps.

He entered her room, walked them over to the bed, and laid her down. He found her stack of condoms, disposed of his old one and sheathed himself before he turned her on to her side, facing away from him. He settled in behind her, spoon-style, pulling the covers over them. He kissed her shoulders, wiggling his right arm under her head until it formed a pillow for hers, while his other hand began its travel over her body, caressing.

"So now that we're getting to know each other, tell me what kinds of things do you like to do," he said as his hand found her breasts.

"I like what we just did," she said, her hips moving, pushing back into his. His breathing changed, but his hands continued their play at her breasts.

"So do you ever do anything out of the ordinary?" he whispered into her ear. She closed her eyes. And here she'd been thinking that they'd just done out of the ordinary.

"What's out of the ordinary?" she asked instead.

"I don't know. You could dress up, try a little role play, maybe, or I could tie you up. If you're okay with it. Or, if not, I could introduce you to some of the things I like to do, slowly of course," he said softly in that sexy voice of his. All the while his hand moved over her body, creating this need to have him again. His hand moved downward to the juncture of her thighs. He heard her sigh when he reached his destination. Her hips moved backward toward his, seeking, pushing into him, asking for more.

He pushed one of his legs to slide in between hers, and taking himself in hand, helped guide himself into her. She groaned. He loved that sound from her, all pleasure, and he began to move, so slowly, in and out, a slow smooth glide. He pushed her upper body away from his, so that she lay in the doggie position on her side. He gripped her hips with both hands now to hold her steady.

He'd stopped talking and just moved within her, edges all gone. Now he would take his time and enjoy the feel of her body surrounding him. When was the last time he'd been this relaxed?

He was deliberate and patient, as he'd been looking forward to this since the first time. Slowly he moved in her, bringing her almost to a climax, waiting until she calmed only to start over. He was thorough, and after two more times of bringing her to the brink, sweat-drenched and weak, she came, calling out his name, pulling him along with her, he feeling the power of his release down to his toes. What the hell? he thought, pulling her into his chest to hold her while they regrouped.

After they'd showered and prepared to leave her room, he stopped at her bedroom door and turned to her.

"You didn't answer my question," he said, his gorgeous smile in place, a kick to her system.

Her forehead furrowed as she looked up. "What question?"

213

"What do you like to do?"

She smiled. "I'm pretty plain, I guess, old school and simple. But if you're willing to show me the merits of other things, I guess I might be willing to try them. Except I'll have to think about the tying up thing," she said, walking over to stand in front of him, moving in to kiss his mouth. He kissed her back softly and she pulled a few inches away and stood there, her eyes closed, her face filled with pleasure.

"You're good. You know that, don't you?" she said, her eyes open now, looking up seriously into his.

He reached for her curls, filled his fist with them, and used them to pull her back into him for another kiss. "I enjoyed it, too. Until next time?" He walked out the door, looking back at her, his eyes indecipherable.

"Until next time," she said, following him down the stairs.

Chapter 14

The following Monday Piper was in her office waiting for Joe to arrive. He was running late for their Monday morning alignment of calendars.

She looked forward to having him here. The past week with him had been one for her memory books.

If only Joe would share more of himself. Joe kept all things personal under lock and key, and no amount of sharing from her seemed to impact his guard. She knew from growing up with her dad and the other males that dominated her father's gym that men weren't the greatest communicators of feelings.

She was determined, however, to give it her best effort. Maybe she'd somehow get Joe to talk more. She wanted to be the one he would share with, the one for whom he would lower his defenses. She was after that part of him more than anything. Good thing for him she was tough, in her own way. Dealing with her dad had taught Piper the benefits of persistence.

She looked up at the knock at her door and smiled, watching him enter. He was dressed casually in slacks and a shirt. Gorgeous Joe. Her heart skipped, and then settled.

"Sorry I'm late," he said.

"No problem," she said, pulling out her Black-Berry. "Basketball practice starts this week. Taylor is playing. Shane?"

"Shane will be playing, too," he said, pulling out his BlackBerry and taking a seat on her couch.

"Practice is on Monday, Wednesday, and Thurs-day, right after school until five thirty. What days are late nights for you this week?" she asked, standing up, coming around her desk to sit on the couch next to him.

"Wednesday and Thursday," he said, looking over at her as she sat.

"You on call?"

"Nope. Next week," he said, watching her type, head bent, hair falling forward and obscuring her face. He loved the wildness of her hair.

"I've got to train employees this week. Any days you could pick them up and drop them off at my home would be greatly appreciated. I don't usually need help, but I've got to train someone on closing. There's always turnover. The trouble with college students," she said.

"What days?" he asked. His eyes moved back to his schedule.

"Today and tomorrow."

"I can pick them up for you."

"You sure?" she said, looking up at him, surprised.

"Sure. No problem. You help me all the time. You know what? I'll take them home with me, feed them, and you can pick them up when you're done train-ing," he said.

216

"Really? Are you sure?" she asked again.

"Sure. It's not a problem, really. You don't trust me?" he said, giving her a don't ask me that again look, his hands moving, typing it in.

"I don't know. Thought you only knew how to cook omelets," she said.

"I got this," he said, smiling at her jab at his cooking.

"Coach is supposed to hand out the basketball schedules for the season at the end of the week, and I'll add them to the calendar," she said, changing the subject.

"That works," he said, looking over at her. "You okay?" he asked. She'd appeared worried, thoughtful today.

"Working on finalizing Thanksgiving plans," she said.

He tilted his head to the side but didn't say anything.

"I'd hoped to take the girls to visit my grandparents. Remember? I've told you about them," Piper said.

He vaguely recalled a conversation about her sisters. Actually, Piper's stories had merged into one lump in his brain. She'd told him so much in such a short time. It was hard to keep up with it all.

"What's the problem?" he asked.

She shrugged. "I want my sisters to join me, and I don't think they are going to be able to. Margarite called this morning. Samantha and Blair might not be able to make it down. I really wanted us all to be there as a group. I'm just a little bummed about it," she said.

"Margarite is your dad's first wife?" he asked, trying to keep her family, extended family, and shop family straight. He knew that family was a big deal for her.

"Yes," she said, surprised he'd remembered. He really had been listening.

"What about you? What are you and Shane doing?" she asked, changing the subject. He grew leery and his body tensed up a little. She could tell; anything too personal sent Joe into lockdown.

"I'll struggle alone, cook dinner for us," he said, smiling, trying to make a joke of it.

"Why don't you let Shane come with me and the girls? It's a couple of weeks away, so think about it. I mean, if you don't mind him not being here with you, and if he wants to come with us, of course. I won't mention it to Shane or the girls until you give me an answer. It would be fun. My grandparents live out on the prairie as I grew up calling it, kind of a farm, not many animals—a few chickens, maybe. Still lots of land on which to roam. He is more than welcome to join us if you need a break," she said. Since he didn't respond, she kept on talking.

"You could come if you wanted," she said. Too soon, she thought immediately. His eyes changed and his smile became more fixed.

"I'll think about it, and I'll talk to Shane about it, too," he said, standing up, putting his BlackBerry in his hip holster. "Thanks again for all of this, and for helping me with Shane and thinking to include him with you and your sisters."

"It's nothing. We like you. We like Shane."

"We like you, too," he said, walking out of her door.

But not as much as I like you, she thought, feeling thirteen again and hoping she hadn't scared him away.

———※———

Joe unlocked his front door and stepped aside to let Shane, Taylor, and Ken pass. Ken was turning into a miniature version of her older sister with her hair in a version of afro puffs today. It didn't quite work because her hair texture was different from Piper's. She gave him a wink and a smile on her way in. Piper's dad was going to have his hands full with that one, Joe thought.

Joe followed them in and dumped his gear on the floor.

"Homework first," he said.

"Ah, Joe, I was just going to show Taylor my animals," Shane said.

"Ten minutes, tops. Then to the kitchen table, all of you," he said.

"Okay," they said in unison and headed to Shane's room.

Joe had purchased this home two years ago. Shane had been the impetus, but he realized soon after that the sense of permanence had been good for him, too.

It was not a big home; the front door opened into one room, a living room on one side, a dining room on the other, which led to a hallway. If you took a right you were in the kitchen. A left took you to the three bedrooms—one of which he used as a study—and two baths.

He walked to his bedroom, changed his clothes, and walked back to the kitchen. He needed to cook. He wanted to show Piper that he was just as adept at the childcare business as she was. Okay, maybe not. She was one organized woman. And why did he need to show her anything, he asked himself.

He walked over to the refrigerator and found some chicken to grill, as well as rice and veggies. He was good to go.

Ten minutes later all three kids entered, walked over to the table, and put their backpacks on the floor, each pulling out a chair around the table. They sat down and started pulling out books.

"I hate math," Ken said.

"Let me see. Fourth grade, multiplication and division?" Joe asked over his shoulder.

"Yep. I hate division," she said.

"I'll look at it with you. Give me a few minutes," he said and went back to cooking.

After he got dinner started, he pulled up a chair next to Ken. "Let's see what you got," he said. He pulled his chair closer. "Which problems are you assigned?"

"This entire page."

"All that, huh? Seems like a lot, but you're smart, right? We can figure it out. Let me see you try and work the first one," he said and watched her, figuring out where her problem lay.

He spent the evening helping Ken with her problems, keeping an eye on Shane and Taylor, both who seemed to know what was required and had gotten right to it. He monitored Ken as she worked through several other problems, slowly getting the hang of it.

"You finish up here and I'll check your answers when you're done. Call me if you need more help, okay?" he asked.

"Okay, and thanks, Joe," she said, reaching out and cupping her hand to his cheek. "You're a nice guy," she said, smiling, dipping her head down, suddenly shy.

"So are you," he said, once again thinking she would be a handful for MacArthur Knight. Good thing her dad was an ex-boxer.

"That smells good, Joe," Kennedy said later. She was done, he guessed. She walked over to his side as he pulled the chicken from the grill.

"We'll see what it tastes like," he said, looking over his shoulder at Taylor and Shane.

They all sat down to eat, complimenting Joe in turn on his cooking skills. After dinner Taylor and Shane had reading to do. They wanted to read in Shane's room and promised that they wouldn't goof off. Growing tired of their begging, he eventually gave in.

He cleaned up the kitchen and walked down the hall to check on the threesome, peeking into Shane's room, always shocked by the loud blue of his room and the clutter. Shane was seated at his desk, head in his book, Taylor on the floor next to him, Charlie, their lab, lying at her feet on his side while she absently rubbed his belly.

Ken was lying on Shane's bed reading, too. They all looked up when he peeked in. He smiled and walked back into the living room to check it over and make sure it was clean.

What did it matter, anyway? Piper was more like Shane in the clutter department. Clean she did, but she was nowhere near as neat.

She wanted more from him. The invitation to meet her grandparents had thrown him. He'd been clueless, had thought she was satisfied with the addition of the sex component. It was as he'd thought it would be, but more, if he were honest.

He walked over to the front door, picked up his bag, and found a spot on the couch. After turning on the TV and muting it with the remote, he booted up his laptop. There was always work to be done.

—⁂—

Around eight Piper pulled into Joe's drive. It was a nice home, at least from its outward appearance. It was nothing extravagant—it fit in with the other homes on his street.

She walked over to the front door and rang the doorbell.

"Hey," he said, stepping back to allow her to enter. She took a deep breath of air; she always felt like she needed fortification when she was around him, especially now. This need to touch him was always present, growing the more time she spent around him. He followed her eyes as they moved over him.

"Hey," she said, stepping in. "Thanks for taking the kids for me. You have no idea how much I appreciate it." She was acting all first-date nervous, stuffing her hands into the pockets of her jeans. Her hands had to work hard to find space in those pockets. He smiled at that.

"Nice to be able to return the favor," he said as she walked in.

"Where are the kids?" she asked, her eyes moving around the house, checking out his home. She hoped he wouldn't notice. He did. It wasn't what she expected. It was clean and mostly white with some beige and touches of brown thrown in. Seriously masculine.

The pictures were all of Shane. In many he was playing soccer or with their dog, but there were a couple of Joe and Shane together. A big-ass TV was mounted on the wall in front of the couch. Prints covered two of the walls. They were fairly large prints of landscapes, snow on the ground, a few barren trees. Okay, she wasn't even going to guess what that said about Joe.

"How was training?" he asked.

"Not too bad. The usual college students—some good, some not, only time will tell. Nice place," she said.

"Thanks."

"Guess I should get the girls," she said.

"They're in Shane's room. Right this way," he said, leading her down the hall. She followed. More white walls and wood flooring. Wow, she thought, Shane's room didn't belong to this house. It was the opposite from the rest of it. Navy blue walls greeted her, a shock to her system given the whiteness of the rest of his home.

"You go, Shane," she whispered under her breath.

Two large bookshelves stood against the wall adjacent to his bed. Blue and red covers were pushed to the foot of the bed and lay next to a desk where Shane sat, head over his book. Books lay stacked on the floor. Some collection he had.

Three heads looked up at her as she entered the room.

"All of our homework is done. I know that's what you're going to ask," said Ken, getting up from her reclining position on the bed. Charlie got up, too, walked over to Piper, waiting for a rub, taking a sniff. She rubbed him underneath his chin, watching Taylor stand and start to gather her books, putting them in her backpack.

"Thanks for picking them up," Piper said.

"Yes, thanks Joe," both girls said.

"Didn't mind at all," he said from his perch by the door, where he leaned against the frame and watched her.

"Thanks, Shane, for having them over," Piper said.

"It was fun, and they're coming over again tomorrow after school, right?" he said, looking between Piper and Joe.

"Yes," she said, turning to Joe for confirmation.

"Yes."

Joe, Shane, and Charlie followed Piper and her sisters out of the room. They walked them to the door, followed them to the car, watched them load up, and waved as they drove away.

"I like them," Shane said.

"Me, too," Joe added. Both males and Charlie turned and walked back inside their home.

—ฑ—

"So how did it go?" Piper asked, driving them home.

"Fine," Taylor said, not giving up much information. It was Kennedy she could depend on to talk. Kennedy gave full descriptions on just about any subject.

"Did you guys eat?" Piper asked, hoping to inspire Kennedy to talk.

"Yes. First Joe helped me with my homework, my math. He's pretty good at explaining. Then he fed us. He can cook, too," Kennedy replied.

"That's good," Piper said.

"I like him, Piper. He's cute like Shane. They both have long hair. I like long hair on boys," she said. Taylor rolled her eyes and Piper laughed.

Chapter 15

What was I thinking? Piper asked herself. She owned two coffee shops, was responsible for the temporary care of two girls, and had two dogs to manage, and she'd somehow felt it was necessary to sign up to help with a field trip. Well, she'd actually signed up to drive, but driving had somehow morphed into actually planning the trip, calling the Humane Society, securing a list of items one could donate, reserving a place in a nearby local park to have a picnic following the trip, sending e-mails out to the parents, and, finally, gathering said donations in one place. Not too hard, just a little time-consuming, and more work than she'd anticipated.

She was currently standing outside of Taylor's classroom, waiting on the arrival of the other four parents who'd signed up to drive today. People assumed most private schools were raking in the Benjamins; maybe some were, but not this one.

"Hi, Piper. Thanks for setting all this up," Trudy said as she marched over to meet Piper. Trudy was Isaac's mother. She was short and stocky, blonde hair cut short, and dressed for a day outdoors. Isaac actually had two mothers, Trudy and Sheila. Isaac had been with them since birth.

"No problem," Piper replied.

"Do we have enough drivers?" Trudy asked.

"I think so. We need five. You and me are the first to arrive." A few minutes later, two other parents joined them. Piper thanked them for volunteering and left to notify Mr. Marshall.

"How many do we have?" Mr. Marshall asked over the din of the kids in his classroom, who were sitting not so quietly while they waited for their car assignments.

Piper looked back over the group of parent drivers. Joe was here. He hadn't been on her list at all. He smiled at her as he walked up to stand over with the other parent drivers.

"You driving?" she shouted, pointing to him.

"Yes."

She turned back to Mr. Marshall. "We have five drivers." She said, swallowing her surprise and delight at seeing him.

"Great. I'll send out students in groups of five. I'll ride with you if that's okay," Mr. Marshall said.

"Sure. No problem," she said, groaning under her breath as she walked back to the parents to relay his instructions.

"Hey," she said to Joe as she walked up to stand beside him. She'd mentioned the field trip to him at the beginning of the week when they'd gone over their schedules, but no way had she expected him to show up and help.

"I wasn't sure I'd be able to get away, and didn't want to commit in case something came up."

Five minutes later Piper pulled into the parking lot of the Humane Society. She had been the last of the caravan to arrive. All of the other cars with their parents and students had parked and were now emptying, moving toward the entrance, their hands stuffed with goods for the animals. Some had formed a line in front of the door, waiting for Mr. Marshall to lead them in.

It took them about thirty minutes to tour the front half of the facility, where the cats were kept, and another thirty to visit the dogs. An hour later they were back in their cars, headed to the park located ten minutes from the school.

Joe tried to hear his own thoughts over the noise in his car, looking in the rearview mirror at Shane, Taylor, and three others as they tried to outtalk each other. He was glad he managed to drive today, reliving the moment when Shane had seen him outside in the hallway. It was priceless. The pleasure and surprise on his nephew's face had been a sucker punch to his heart. He loved that kid.

He looked in his rearview mirror at Piper trailing him in her car. He hadn't seen much of her so far today. She'd been at the back of the tour, busy being the leader, organizing her world. He and Shane were now a part of her world, organized along with everything else, or as much as he'd allowed her to organize them. She thought she was being subtle in her attempts to take care of him and Shane. Feeding them when he'd stopped to pick up Shane after work, talk, talk, and more talk, coffee ready and waiting when he dropped in most mornings, helping Shane with homework, treating him like he belonged to her, just like her sisters.

They arrived at their destination and children spilled out from their cars, some running and screaming like banshees toward the table of food that had been set up ahead of time while others headed toward the swings.

The kids spent the next thirty minutes plowing through pizza before moving off to play. Some had taken off toward the basketball hoops behind the picnic tables. Shane and Joe stood near the soccer goal, a soccer ball at their feet. Other children, Taylor included, were moving toward the two. Joe looked the part. He looked like a big kid; hair loosely tucked under a baseball cap, loose-fitting t-shirt, shorts, tennis shoes on his feet. It was good to see him relaxed.

Piper watched as Joe organized the kids into teams. He looked to be a pretty good player, but what did she know? Soccer wasn't a sport she'd followed.

A few minutes later the soccer game was in full swing with about eight kids on one side and six with Joe on the other; a handicap, she guessed. Taylor had just scored and was now running around Joe, taunting him, doing some kind of dance. She was shy unless she was in a game of some type, then she became this whole other girl. Joe was laughing, a picture worth a thousand words.

Ten minutes later she caught Trudy and Heather starting to clean up. She stood up and walked over to join them and clean up the remains. Fifteen minutes later, cleaning done, they loaded up for the return trip to school. It was about twenty minutes before school let out so she opted to wait in her car, maybe even close her eyes for a second.

She'd just lowered her seat when she heard someone knocking on the window. It was Joe standing outside her car's passenger door. She unlocked the door and he slid into the seat beside her.

"Haven't had a chance to talk to you today," he said.

"Nope," she said, taking in Joe's sexy, windblown look.

"So you are raiser of children, coffee shop owner, and organizer of events," he said, smiling at her.

She yawned.

"And tired," he added.

"A little," she said, sitting up, not as tired as she thought.

"Today was nice," he said, a few minutes later.

"Glad you enjoyed it. Shane appreciated your being here," she said.

They were both quiet for a second. Joe looked out the front window and then at her, laying back, seat lowered to the reclining position, shorts on, t-shirt pulled tightly over her body, hair pulled back.

"What happened to Shane's mother?" she asked, looking over at him. He didn't look at her, but instead turned his eyes to stare out the front window.

"I don't know. She took off almost two years ago. We haven't heard from her since."

"Do you think she's okay?"

"Don't know, Piper," he said, his words a little clipped. It was silent again. "You know, I don't really want to talk about Shane," he said, turning now to look at her, his face serious, and with more than a little challenge mixed in it.

"Sorry. Didn't mean to pry. You don't have to get angry. It was just a question, Joe. Not asking to read your diary," she said, angry suddenly. How long had she known him? How long had she been taking care of Shane? Talk about trust issues, she thought, turning to look out the window.

"Sorry," he said after a minute, touching her on her arm. "It was a hard period for me and one I don't like to revisit if I can help it. But, to answer your question, my sister has left him twice—once when he was younger, and again two years ago, which is why I have Shane with me now." His words were still on the curt side, like he was being tortured, raked over the coals for that bit of information. He went back to staring at the space in front of her car. "I don't like to talk about it."

"Sure." She could do clipped, too. Her eyes returned to the view outside her window. She looked down at her watch. "The bell's about to ring. We'd better head in," she said, opening her car door and stepping out. He watched her, noting her anger. He was frustrated with himself, and with her for asking those questions.

—⁂—

Later on that night, Joe called Piper. He didn't owe her any apology that he could see, but he wanted to offer one anyway. She had been good to and for Shane, had been good to and for him, and he'd acted today like she'd wanted the key to his heart or something larger when all she'd asked were questions regarding Shane. He'd clammed up. It's what he did when he was probed. He hated being probed, so maybe he'd gotten a little bit short with her.

She'd just asked a simple personal question, something anyone would want to know, especially if they were responsible for the care of that person.

"Hello," she answered in a cool voice.

"Hey," he replied, pausing for a second. "So, in case you're angry at me, I wanted to apologize to you for today. I don't talk about Shane much, but I'd be willing to for you if you have any more questions that you'd like to have answered."

"Now?" she said.

"Now."

It was quiet on the phone for a few moments. "Nope, I'm okay. I know how much you value your privacy Joe. I just thought we were becoming friends and I know you've noticed I've been telling you my life story. You probably know more than you want to know about me," she said, laughing, hoping to lighten the moment. Silence still reigned. "I kind of hoped you'd feel comfortable enough to tell me yours at some point."

Silence again.

"It's okay, though, it's your business. I'm okay with that. You don't need to tell me anything. Just promise to tell me if there's anything I need to know for Shane's safety and protection. The rest you can keep to yourself," she said, a little hurt. It was quiet for another minute.

"It works better for me this way, Piper. I've found that it's just better to keep personal things to myself. I'm sorry if that offends you. It's not my intention to hurt your feelings."

"No problem," she said, and it was quiet again.

"So we're good?"

"Yes, we are good," she said, working to make her voice sound upbeat.

"You've got Shane tomorrow?"

"Yes, I do."

"See you then," he said.

"Yep. See you then," she replied and hung up.

—᚜—

Third week in November

Later on that week Piper walked into the front doors of the school headed in the direction of Kennedy's classroom. She had gotten here early at the request of Mrs. Samson, Ken's teacher, who wanted to talk to her about something.

She usually made the right to Kennedy's class without thinking, but today she glanced left and saw Shane standing outside in the hall, his face a mask of contrition as Mr. Marshall was speaking to him. About what?

she wondered. She stood there, partially out of view, and waited until he and Mr. Marshall were finished and they re-entered the classroom.

Okay, I wonder what was going on with that?

Pressed for time, she turned and continued on her way to Ken's classroom, hoping it wouldn't take long.

Twenty minutes later—longer than Piper had anticipated—she was free and she and Kennedy were making their way toward the front office. She debated whether or not to seek out Mr. Marshall to find out what happened with Shane. He wasn't her child, but she wanted to know and didn't want to wait for Joe to tell her, either. She was not in the mood for tight-lipped Joe today.

Lucky for her—and proof that the stars aligned sometimes—Mr. Marshall was headed toward the front of the school, same as she. He looked up and caught her eye. She smiled.

"Ms. Knight, do you have a moment?" he asked, stepping over to one side of the hall.

"I do," she said, coming to stand next to him. "Ken, will you wait for me by the couch?"

"Sure," Ken replied and walked away, stopping to talk with some other child, apparently always happy to talk to her friends.

"I just spoke with Shane. He's been bothered by one of the newer students in another class. He exchanged words with the student. They were having difficulty communicating. I was listening to his side of things earlier. I saw you standing there," he said gravely. "I also know that you're close to his uncle. Taylor and

Shane are good friends and I understand that you're responsible for Shane sometimes."

"Yes, I am."

"I left Joe a message to call me tonight. I wanted to talk to him about it. Would you remind him? He's busy, I know, but make sure he returns my call tonight," he said.

"Sure," Piper responded, and tracked his departure as he turned and walked back toward his classroom.

She and Ken did their normal wait for Shane-and-Taylor drill, and they all headed back to the coffee shop. Piper found out the details of what happened to Shane as she listened to Taylor drill Shane about what happened today between him and the new kid.

About an hour later Piper walked into the kitchen at her shop, groaning at the stack of boxes she encountered. A delivery was waiting for her to dispose of. She left Shane and Taylor in her office on her computer, working on some paper or project they'd been assigned. It was due in two weeks, they'd told her. Ken was in her office, too, sprawled on the couch, killing two birds with one stone—completing her homework and keeping an eye on Shane, still her number one crush.

—⁓—

Joe entered the shop near six, which was early for him. He looked around the shop for Piper and the kids.

"She's in the kitchen," Estelle said, smiling at him. She always gave him that I've got a secret smile, which always left him wondering if he'd missed something.

"Hello, Estelle," he said, passing by her on his way to the kitchen.

"You're early," Piper said, glancing back at him from her place near the door of her storage closet. He walked over to stand in the doorway. She was on the floor, on her knees, stacking paper towel rolls on the bottom shelf.

"Delivery today. Putting away supplies," she said. He could tell; several dismantled boxes lay in a stack nearby.

"My lucky day, I guess," he said, looking at her as she bent over, admiring the view. Jesus, she was something. "This is a good look for you," he said, laughing.

"Cut it out," she replied and threw a roll of paper towels his way, which he caught smoothly.

She hadn't changed her behavior around him. He'd worried for nothing after their discussion about Shane's mother the other night. He thought maybe she might have called it quits and told him to find someone other than her to take care of Shane; at the very least, he expected her to be distant. But nope, it was Piper as usual, back in her normal form.

"I want to talk to you about something," she said, getting up off the floor, pushing him out of her way as she marched past him out of the storage room and into the kitchen. She made her way over to close the door leading from the kitchen to the shop, peeking out first to make sure it was free of children. She walked back over to him, stopping right in front, now all up close and personal with him, her eyes at his nose level. She looked up, serious. He looked back, serious too, after watching her secure the door like they were expecting big trouble.

"What?" he asked.

"Mr. Marshall wants you to call him about Shane. I saw him out in the hall today after school talking to Shane. He says a kid at school was giving Shane trouble. Taylor says it's more like being bullied. I did a little information-gathering on my own. What are you going to do about it?" she asked.

"Do about what?"

"About Shane being bullied?"

"Call Mr. Marshall, like he requested," he answered, gazing at her now, arms crossed at her chest.

"That's it?" she said. "Talk to the teacher is all you're going to do?"

"Talk to the parents…" he said, looking at her sideways, trying to figure out what she wanted him to say "Talk to the principal?" Apparently, talking to the parents was not the answer she'd been looking for either.

She stood before him, arms crossed again, one foot tapping a new and lively tune. He looked down at her foot, in that boot, tapping away. He was either really sick or really, really needed to get laid because that was working for him, his body was responding to her foot in that boot. It was sad that it took so little to move him.

His eyes were headed back up to her face, but stopped for a quick peek at her chest; it moving in time to her breathing, making her perky breasts even more noticeable. He loved her breasts.

"I've been thinking," she said, turning and walking away from him to the other side of the kitchen. His eyes moved to her ass.

She stopped pacing and stood there watching him. He could tell she was impatient with his response. What did he miss? She was staring at him with disappointment in her eyes.

"As I was saying, my dad has a few boxing gyms here in the city. Lights Out Boxing Gyms. You've heard of them, right?"

He had and nodded. "Yes." Who hadn't?

"I could take Shane over after school once a week. You know, teach him how to protect himself. I learned when I was young—right after I moved in with my father—and so have my sisters. Shane needs to learn, too," she said.

"What?" he asked, his face watching hers. "You want to teach Shane to box?"

"Sure." Her expression was earnest, sincere, and concerned. "He needs to learn to protect himself."

Piper, he was finding, had this uncanny ability to surprise him. It had happened from the first time he walked into her shop. She and her sex-tinged banter had taken him by surprise. The appearance of her sisters was another surprise; then there was the care she gave to Shane, a child that wasn't even her blood. Now this.

"It's okay, Piper, I've spoken with Mr. Marshall before. Today wasn't the first time," he said, pulling his mind back to the conversation.

"So what are you doing about it this time?" she asked.

"I'll give Mr. Marshall a call tonight. I'll talk it over with Shane, too," he added.

"Sometimes you have to knock some heads together," she said, pushing her hands together in demonstration. "Push back when people push you. Sometimes talking doesn't always work."

"I know, but talking will always be my first choice. I grew up with fighting, standing my ground. It's not always the answer," he said.

"Sometimes, though, a good punch in the lip can create a whole lot of make nice," she said.

He laughed. Couldn't help himself.

"What's so funny?" she said.

"Nothing. You are. I didn't know you had this violent side," he said.

"I'm not violent. I just know how to protect myself."

"This is new, this kick-ass Piper," he said, arms folded, leaning back on the counter, smiling.

"I'm tough," she said, crossing her arms, too.

"Sure you are."

"What do you mean by that?"

"You don't have to pay me for keeping Shane. It's on the house. You give free coffee to that homeless guy. I've seen the neighborhood kids come in and take money out of the tip jar for smoothies or whatever."

"Yeah, so what?" she said, defensive now. "No one should have to go hungry."

"I didn't say they should; just that you're more soft than you are tough."

She ignored him and started pacing again. "You know we don't have to sign him up with my dad. I know enough, I could teach him," she said, and he watched as she demonstrated, taking a fighter's stance, arms up, on the balls of her feet, punching into the air surrounding her. He couldn't help it this time. He started laughing.

She just looked at him, bent over in laughter, refusing to join in. She'd been serious about anyone messing with hers, and Shane was included in that group now. He continued to laugh. A few minutes later he slowly stopped, winding down to a few chuckles.

"You done?" He could see he'd offended her.

"I'm sorry. I didn't mean to make light of it, or of you," he said, closing the distance between them. He reached for her, bringing her into his body, her chest against his, his arms going around her waist. He found her mouth and kissed her before he'd even recognized what he'd done. It was so unplanned, so instinctive. He went with it, though, his mouth moving over hers, forcing her to open, letting himself go, hoping to convey his appreciation of who she was, hands moving over her body, one he'd started to know like his own.

"Does this door close?" he asked, moving her toward the storage room.

"What? The kids," she said.

241

"I know, but give me a minute," he said. "I'll stop. I promise." He moved her inside and closed the door behind them. He backed against the door and went back to taste her again.

Her hands moved to the zipper of his slacks and worked their way into his boxers. She found and stroked him once, twice, while her mouth gave over to the onslaught from his. He found her hand a few seconds later, stopping its movement, and removed it to hold in his, as he ended the kiss, resting his forehead against hers until his breathing slowed.

"Soon," he said.

"Soon," she replied. He stepped away from the door and opened it. The coast was clear. She walked out. He followed a few seconds later, grinning.

"What?" she asked, gazing at his smile.

"Nothing," he said, laughing now at them and their urgency. "I know who to take with me if I'm ever in a fight," he said, going back to their earlier discussion.

"I'm not helping you. You can talk your way out of it, Dr. King, the new man of non-violence," she said, walking back over to finish putting the supplies away, looking back over her shoulder at him.

"Shane is okay, really?" she asked, serious now.

"Yes, he is," he said, watching her. "Thank you for caring about him," he said, serious now too.

"Just doing my job," she said, startled. That whole smoldering thing was in his eyes again.

"Where are they, by the way?"

"Who?"

"The kids," he said, laughing.

"He and Taylor are on the computer, working on a project in my office."

He stood up. "I'll go see if they're done and head on home."

"I'll come with you," she said, putting the boxes left to empty away, under the counter in the middle of the kitchen, and wiping her hands on her pants. His eyes followed her movements. She walked through the kitchen door and he followed behind.

—◆◆◆—

Later on that night Joe removed the stopper from the sink, grabbed his beer, turned and leaned back against the counter. Having finished the after-dinner cleanup, his thoughts turned to Piper. He was glad she'd become his friend, and more. He'd been moved by her passion and commitment on Shane's behalf today. As someone who had faced his problems alone for much of his life, he was awed by it.

Chapter 16

Joe stood outside of Piper's home thirty minutes later, watching as her sisters lugged out their bags for the trip to her grandparents' home. Piper was excited; her other two sisters were meeting her there along with her step-mother Margarite.

And exactly how many months was the Thanksgiving holiday, he wondered, examining the sizes of their suitcases. Ken's was the worst, followed by Shane's. Taylor had the smallest suitcase; it was probably just filled with baseball caps and video games, he thought.

He'd helped them load the suitcases and now stood waiting for the trips to the bathrooms to end. Piper had insisted.

Shane walked out first. "Thanks, Uncle Joe, for letting me go. Are you going to be okay by yourself?" he asked.

"I'll manage. I'll have McKenzie and Pepper with me, and Charlie will help keep me company, too," he said, looking at the two dogs next to his feet, packed into their cages, ready to go and surprisingly quiet.

"Just invite some of those girls you like over. You'll have the whole house to yourself. They can giggle and laugh as loud as they want," Shane said, giving him a wink. And it was a guy wink, an I know the deal kind of wink. Joe looked around, making sure Piper was nowhere near.

Out came Taylor with her usual baseball cap on.

"I want to sit next to Shane," Kennedy said, following Taylor out of the front door, dressed impeccably in her lovely brown frock with matching boots and tights.

"He's my friend. He doesn't have time to hang out with fourth-graders," Taylor said, walking to the back to push in some extra Xbox games she'd forgotten to pack.

Last out the door was Piper, also in a baseball cap—puffy pony tail peeking from the hole in the back—and jeans and t-shirt that clung nicely to her body.

"So are we ready, gang?" she asked, walking toward Joe and stopping. They both watched as the kids loaded themselves into the car. Shane had claimed the seat by one door and Ken had squirmed her way in the middle. No amount of pleading from Taylor could persuade her to move.

"Piper? Can't you make her move?" Taylor asked.

"How about you let her ride until we make a stop and then you two can switch? It won't kill you," she said. Taylor glared at her but got in.

"That was clearly not the answer she was looking for," Piper said to Joe, smiling as she looked up into his face.

He was quiet, caught up in her smile. It was a kick to his system. He watched the smile leave her face, replaced by desire that matched his.

He moved closer to her. She seemed startled. His head lowered, looking at her mouth.

"Joe?" she asked, breaking this from-out-of-nowhere pull. What was he thinking?

"Sorry," he said, a little embarrassed, and stepped back. "You guys call when you get there. Have a good time, and remember, I'll be here all by my lonesome," he said.

"Sure, I'll call," she said.

He watched her get into her car and pull away.

―⁓―

Nothing had changed much in Raywood, Texas, since the last time she'd been there. She drove slowly through town, examining it for any changes in the landscape. Nope, none; it was the same as the last time she'd driven through.

She turned left onto the mile-long dust-covered road that dead ended at her grandparents' property. If all went well, she would arrive without having to get out of her car to shoo away any cows that had wandered onto the road. And why did they always stand in the middle of it, and not on the side? That would have been too easy. She could have driven around them, but no, it was always a get your ass off the road confrontation with them.

She looked over her grandparents' land, noting the changes that had been made to it.

There it was. The old homestead was coming into view, conjuring up so many good memories of comfort and safety and freedom. Her grandparents' home sat right smack dab in the middle of the land, about a half mile from the entry gate.

The house was just as she remembered it; a rectangular white wood farm house, trimmed in navy, with a carport extending from the right with room enough for one car to be parked underneath it.

"We're here," she said to the three heads asleep in the back seat. They had conked out just outside of Houston. Ken was first, followed by Shane and then Taylor, whose baseball-cap-covered head was propped up by the window now. Kennedy lay across the back seat, her head in her sister's lap, her feet in Shane's. That couldn't have been comfortable. She watched as they all sat up, exploring their surroundings through the window as they came fully awake.

"Is this the prairie?" Taylor asked, stretching her arms out and unbuckling her seat bcat.

"It is," Piper said, opening her car door and standing up, needing a stretch, too.

"Hey, Nanny," she said, walking over to her grandmother, who had walked out of the side door of the house. She smiled brightly at Piper. Her hair was grey and curly. She reached to Piper's armpit. Piper had grown tall quickly like her dad, passing up her Nanny when she was in the fifth grade.

Piper turned into that hug. It always had the power to make her feel at home, cared for, and loved. She surrendered to her Nanny's kisses, bending down to receive them.

"I'm so glad to see you," Nanny said stepping back, but keeping her hands locked in Piper's, turning as the kids reached them, standing now at her side.

"Nanny, this is Taylor and Kennedy, my sisters, and Shane, a good friend of ours," she said, pointing to each of them in turn.

"Well, hello," Nanny said, walking to hug them each in turn, like she'd known them forever. "I bet you all are hungry. Have they eaten anything, Piper?" she asked, turning and walking to the side door of the house. "I've got some pork chops, rice, and gravy on the stove. Y'all come on in, wash up, and I'll heat you up some dinner," she said, holding the door open for all three to walk through.

"You look good, Piper," she said, following them into a small room that had once been one large room but was now divided into two. The right half was used as a den. It held a small TV and a couch. To the left of the den sat the kitchen table, an old wooden one that had been around as long as Piper, six chairs, the room separated from the kitchen by a small half bar.

"Piper, show them where the guest bathroom is," Nanny said, passing Piper and moving to the kitchen, reaching for the apron hanging from the knob on the wall.

"The bathroom is at the end of the hall," Piper said to the three children, pointing. She watched as Taylor led the way back into the house. "Where's Papa?" Piper asked as she followed Nanny into the kitchen.

"He went into town," Nanny said, heating up the food and pulling out plates from the cabinet. Her Nanny was in perpetual ready-to-feed mode.

Piper took a moment to look around, familiarizing herself with everything. Nothing had changed here, either. There were the same pictures, the same knick-knacks in the same places. She walked through the kitchen into the door's opening that led to the formal living and dining areas.

"Can we get our stuff out of the car?" Taylor asked, approaching Piper from the back of the house.

"Sure, then we'll eat and I'll show you around the prairie," she offered, looking at her Nanny.

"Okay," Taylor said, first to head back outside to retrieve her bags. Piper followed her out, taking a moment to call Joe.

He answered on the first ring.

"You're there?" he said.

"Yep, about fifteen minutes ago."

"Good drive?"

"Yes, the kids slept most of the way," she said.

"That can be a positive thing," he said, chuckling

"It's not so bad. No arguing between siblings. You know how that can be," she said, but did he? She had no idea.

"I'll call you later, after we get settled. I've got to go eat. Nanny's cooked enough to feed a small army," she said, laughing.

He smiled and hung up, glad that she'd called.

—⁂—

Dinner done, she and her grandfather walked slowly behind the kids, who'd wanted a tour of the farm.

"So…how've you been?" her grandfather asked.

"Fine. The girls and the shops are keeping me occupied."

"You like it. I can tell. How are their parents?"

"Getting their marriage back on track," she said. "I don't understand how it got off track in the first place."

"Spoken from someone who's never been married," he said, and she laughed.

"Yeah, but still."

"How about you? Any men in your life?" he asked.

"No, not really," she said.

"Why not?"

"Don't know. Busy. Hard to find someone that lives up to you," she said.

"Don't fool yourself, Renee. I'm no prince. Just ask your Nanny," he said, laughing. "She could tell you some stories."

"I know. We all have our skeletons, but I was holding out for someone that wants a family as much as I do," she said.

"Well, I'm going to have to come up to Austin and look around for myself," he said, smiling.

"It's not as easy as it looks," she said.

"Nothing worth having ever is," he said, squeezing her into his body. They continued to talk, catching up with the kids, who had gone into the barn and back out and were now headed to the old stables.

—∞—

It was near ten when Piper took her cell phone back out to sit on the step. It was quiet and crisp out here, the sky clear, the stars visible and bright, and it was dark as tar, except for the light above the carport. But the reception was better out here. She called Joe.

"Hey," he said.

"Hi," she said. It was quiet for a second or two.

"So…" he said

"So…what?"

"So how was your day?" he asked, surprising her. He'd never asked her that question. She had been the one that always posed it to him on the nights he stopped by to pick up Shane, usually while he ate her food.

"Good. The kids met my grandparents and they liked each other. My grandfather gave them a tour of the prairie," she said. "It looks the same, smaller, but still in good shape. He wouldn't have it any other way. There are a few oil rigs that weren't here before, but other than that, nothing's changed much. I'm glad I came. I always am," she said.

"Your grandparents mean a lot to you."

"Yep. They took care of me when my mother decided child rearing wasn't for her. They have been the biggest blessing of my life so far, but I've told you my history before. You don't have to hear it again," she said.

"I don't mind. Not everyone is as lucky as you were to have someone to fall in and help," he said. She noticed there was no anger in that statement. It was the first time he'd ever mentioned anything remotely about himself.

"We're talking about you?" she asked.

"We are," he said.

"Your mom and dad?"

"Alcoholics," he said. It was quiet for a minute. "So what's on tap for tomorrow?"

"Friends and some family will come over for dinner. My sisters from Houston and Margarite should be here by noon, then dancing tomorrow night. My favorite," she said.

"I haven't seen you dance," he said.

"I can hold my own. Or, at a minimum, I can hang with you. I've seen you dance."

"You sure about that?"

"I'm sure," she said, detecting a change in his tone.

"Can we get together when I get back?" she asked, her answer to the change in tone of their conversation.

"As soon as you get back," he said, in his firm and commanding way.

"Whew, I'm so with you there," she said, and they both laughed. They talked a few minutes more before hanging up.

She stood up and entered the back door, locked it, and made her way to the bedroom she was sharing with her sisters. She looked in on Shane before finding her own bed, squeezed into the side, pushing Kennedy over to the middle. She dozed off, thoughts of Joe in her mind, wondering about his childhood, what he hadn't said to her about it. She vowed to be patient with him, and then her dreams of Joe drifted into much more pleasurable territory.

—⁓—

She sat in the bedroom with all of her sisters surrounding her—all various shades of brown, all different, but the same. Samantha and Blair had arrived before dinner, but this was the first time they could be alone, just the five of them. She'd finished cleaning up the kitchen with her Nanny and her aunts while Margarite was sitting on the porch talking with her grandfather.

Taylor was pleased. Piper knew her sister well enough to tell. And Kennedy was in heaven. Finally, big sisters that dressed in the style she was accustomed to.

"So, did Taylor tell you that she plays a mean game of basketball?" Piper asked.

"No, she didn't. You must have gotten your athletic abilities from me," Blair said. "I made the varsity team my freshman year. Not that I'm bragging or anything," she added, smiling.

"You did?" Taylor asked, now awestruck.

"I did. Maybe before I leave I'll show you some moves."

"When are you guys leaving?" Kennedy asked.

"This evening. Someone has to get back to see their boyfriend," Blair said, teasing, looking over at Samantha.

"Whatever. No one looks at her, so it doesn't matter," Samantha said.

Kennedy and Taylor were taking it all in, happy to know that they weren't the only sisters that bickered.

"To have a sister, or any sibling, for that matter, is to argue," Samantha said, reading their minds. "You like us now, but just wait until I start riding your butt. Then see if it's so great to have another older sister."

"So, Piper, how are the shops of yours? Are we going to be rich soon?" Blair asked. They spent the next hour or so bringing each other up to date on their lives. They retrieved Piper's laptop and spent another hour on Facebook setting up a group for the Knight girls' private use, so that they could remain in touch privately.

Piper left them an hour later. Blair and Taylor were searching for a basketball to shoot hoops into the old rickety goal near the barn. Good luck with that, she thought. Kennedy was walking Samantha through her suitcase; clothing was always a subject open for discussion. Piper went in search of Shane.

She found him and her grandfather in the carport, zydeco music blaring, her grandfather dancing, with Shane laughing at his moves. She smiled. "What are you two doing?" she asked.

"I'm trying to teach this boy here some moves," he said, shaking his head as if it was a lost cause, his eyes twinkling. "We are taking the girls out tonight, and he has to…What is it that word your age group says?" he asked, looking at Piper. She shrugged her shoulders.

"We have to represent?" Shane answered.

"Yes, that's it. Shane has to represent himself tonight."

"It's just represent, Papa, not represent himself," Piper said. She and Shane smiled.

—⚬—

Piper's feet hurt. They had gotten stepped on by Shane most of the night, as she had turned out to be his dancing partner of choice for the evening.

The kids were in bed now, and she was making her way to the back step to talk to Joe after debating whether it was too late to call. It was twelve. She was calling. She dialed and waited through three rings. Maybe she should have called in the morning.

"Hello." He'd been asleep, she could tell. Crap. She so wished she was there with that smoky voice, low and way sexy.

"Sorry, it's me. Didn't mean to wake you," she said, rushing the words out. "I'll talk to you tomorrow."

"No, it's okay. What's up?"

"Nothing. We went dancing tonight, thought you might like to hear about it."

"I would," he said.

"You should have seen Shane. Didn't think he'd ever stop dancing. I believe his shoe tread is still visible on my feet. God, they hurt," she said and he chuckled, that low and sexy thing again.

"We're just getting back," she said, and continued to fill him in on the events of her day, about finding her sisters sitting around talking to each other, what

255

it had meant to her, what she could see it meant to Taylor and Kennedy. And he listened.

"So, your turn. What'd you do today?" she asked, having wound down the kid talk.

"Nothing much. Stayed here and watched the games," he said.

"Not too lonely."

"Nope. Not lonely at all."

"Are your mother and dad still alive?" she asked, prepared to be met with silence.

"My mother is. My father died before high school," he said.

"Any grandparents?" she asked.

"None that stepped in," he said.

Stepped into what, she wondered. It was quiet for a second. "Tough, huh," she said, more statement than question.

"Yep," he said quietly. "So when are you all heading back?" he asked.

"I hope to leave early, but I don't usually get out of here till late. I'll call when we get to my house. If it's too late, you can pick Shane up Sunday morning."

"That works."

"Good night," she said.

"Yeah. You, too."

—⟋⟍—

Joe's car was parked in her drive waiting for them as Piper pulled into her driveway. It was near midnight.

Talk about surprised. This was the last place she'd thought he would be, yet here he was.

The front porch light was on. Piper pulled into the garage and Joe stood in the door leading from the garage into her home, his look sexy and serious.

"Hey," she said, smiling in pleasure as she got out of her car. He walked over to meet her.

"Hey," he replied, smiling at her. "Need some help?"

"Sure."

Both looked through the window at the three heads slumped over in slumber.

Joe carried in all three kids, all knocked out, deciding to let Shane spend the night. He put him into the bottom bunk in Taylor's room.

Piper followed, putting the necessary luggage into each child's room before she and Joe headed back downstairs and over to the couch. She yawned and leaned her head back against the couch.

"Long drive?" he asked.

"Yep, didn't leave early like I should have," she said. She yawned again.

"I'd better get home, let you get some sleep," he said. He kissed her forehead and walked to the front door.

"Don't get up, I'll lock up," he said, glancing at her one final time. "Really glad you're back," he said, before he turned and walked out the door.

Chapter 17

It was the Friday before Christmas break and the last day of school before the two-week holiday. Piper had made arrangements for gift buying with her dad and Christine two weeks ago. They communicated daily concerning the girls, and she, Mac, and Christina made use of the school's on-line service to check on grades and other school-related stuff. And they, like she and Joe, discussed and planned for them weekly.

Piper stood in the gym waiting for basketball practice to end.

"Hey, Joe," she heard someone say and turned to see him enter. He saw her and smiled. Her heart skipped a beat.

He stopped to talk with another parent before making his way over to her. She lifted her face to his and caught herself. What was she doing? She smiled to cover that lapse, blaming it on the intimacy that they shared.

"Been here long?" he asked.

"Nope, about ten minutes before you arrived," she said, admiring him up close. "I'm looking forward to the Christmas holidays."

"Me, too."

"What do you and Shane have planned?" she asked.

"Nothing much. The usual opening gifts on Christmas day, followed by my cooking dinner."

"Want to hang out with us?" she asked.

"When?"

"Whenever, no set schedule. I'm going to relax these next two weeks, work at the shop, do whatever the girls want to do each day. Kind of go with the flow."

"Sure. Hanging out sounds good," he said, eyes moving around the gym.

"You're working next week, right?" she asked.

"Yes, and you've got Shane," he said, looking at her for confirmation.

"Yep."

"Have you finished your Christmas shopping?" he asked.

"Yes. Only have a little bit left," she said, pausing a minute. "Friday night after Christmas is zydeco night at the shop. I've moved the date back to include it in the holidays. Want to come?"

He smiled. "You might be able to talk me into it," he said, wanting to kiss her right now. That wasn't possible, so he settled for pulling her to him in a short hug, which surprised her. She punched him, laughing.

"You," she said.

"What?" he replied. "But since you've brought that up, when can we get together again? I'm behind in my list of things to introduce you to," he said, all humor gone, his eyes smoldering.

"Hey, you're the one that promised me demanding, and I got to tell you, so far…" she said, looking at him, "…I'm not so sure you're holding up your end."

He laughed, ending with a wolf-sized grin and a nod of his head. He moved close to her side, close enough for her ears only.

"Joe…oh, Joe…yes…whatever you say, Joe, yes… right there, Joe," he said, mimicking her. She gave him a quick, hard jab into his side, and he laughed. "What?" he said, watching as she turned away, hips swinging.

—ᴍ—

"Thanks for coming and for helping me," she said to Joe as he sat on a stool next to the counter. Piper stood behind it passing out drinks, meeting and greeting the families that came to what she called Zydeco Christmas. It was definitely family night today, even more so as locals brought their family members along that were in for the holidays. Everyone was dancing, clearly in the mood for celebrating.

Taylor, Kennedy, and Shane were holed up in the corner on a video game, four of them at a time, playing, fighting or whatever the game of choice involved. It was near midnight.

Piper loved having people here; it always brought her back to her childhood days. She looked over at Joe, who sat engaging in a little people watching of his own. She'd caught his eyes on her often, pleased and hopeful…just a little hopeful, anyway.

"You love this," he said, and she smiled.

"Yes, I do. Always. The shops help me feel connected," she said, looking around the room before turning back to him. "I'm glad you're here, you and Shane," she added in case that was too much for him. He smiled but didn't say anything.

She was glad he'd attended, and that he'd stayed. They'd danced earlier, and, of course he could keep up with her. Joe of the many surprises—dancing, a good uncle, good friend, great and way more creative in bed than she'd known a person could be. Who came up with all those positions?

"What?" he said, catching that look in her eye.

"Nothing."

"Sure, nothing," he said, but he let it go and gave her one of his killer smiles. She shook her head.

He continued to sit at the makeshift bar, watching her as she laughed and talked with her customers. She was one talkative woman. She could talk to just about anyone. He'd known that, but watching her in her element was a learning experience. He only talked when he had to, kept to himself mostly, cordial for work, but nowhere near her on the social scale.

Had he ever been that free and unguarded? It had become second nature to keep his feelings to himself. But it hadn't always been that way, had it? There were times he remembered from his childhood, good times; every now and then he'd catch a glimpse of them, some old forgotten memory of life before drink ruled their home. There were some happy times after he moved in with his foster family. They had given him a

slice of what a family could be, but he'd stopped looking for that long ago.

He had spent a lot of time with her this week, she
and her sisters, him and Shane, a make-shift hodge-
podge of a family. They'd taken in a few movies, gone
skating, bowling, just about anything the kids could
come up with. He found himself relaxing this week.
The fact that Piper was a friend lessened the pressure
of having to entertain her. He could just be himself
and not have to worry about keeping it simple, fending
off the inevitable questions about taking this relationship further.

"Joe." He heard his name and turned to find her
smiling at him. "Want to help me find something in
the back?" Her grin let him know that there was something special to be found back there.

This was fine for him now. He didn't need more or
want more.

—⁂—

January

It was the last Monday in January. Where had the
time gone? Piper lay in her bed, waiting for Joe. They
were meeting at her home this morning instead of at
the coffee shop.

It was a convenience for them both, a superb tactic
to accommodate their appetites for sex. No more long
stretches of time in between; neither seemed able to
do that anymore.

She heard the front door open, followed by his footsteps in the hall, moving closer to her room until he was there, standing in her door. Her heart did a double take. Him and that sexy-ass smile, cocksure and confident. He deserved it to be confident; he had earned all of his strut and swagger, at least as far as she was concerned.

"I like it when you're here, waiting for me," he said, smiling, kicking off his shoes, slipping out of his jeans and ditching his t-shirt as he sauntered over to the bed, slowly removing his boxers.

Her eyes roamed over him and he smiled. He pulled back the covers, immediately sliding in and situating himself on top of her, loving the way she felt underneath him.

"So what are you up for today?" she asked as he lowered his head, taking her lips in a kiss.

He didn't respond, caught up in the pleasure of his mouth on hers, hot, moist, and mesmerizing. He'd think about tying her up later. Right now he just wanted in; he pushed her legs apart and moaned into her mouth as he entered her.

—⁓—

"What's that?" she said, turning on her side about thirty minutes later, looking over to a package he'd dropped by the door when he'd entered earlier.

"That's for you. Or at least I had you in mind when I purchased it," he said, and watched as she stood up and walked toward it. He stared, transfixed by the sight of her nude form. He watched her from his perch on the bed, on his back, pushing up to his elbows as she stood there and opened his package.

Her mouth fell open after she'd removed the packaging. "What am I supposed to do with this?" she asked, holding it up in her hand.

"Wear it."

"Not much of it to wear. It's just an apron. Is there something missing?" She tried the apron around her waist. "A French maid? Really, Joe? Where's the rest of it? I know there's supposed to be a dress with it."

"Don't forget the cap. Those were the only pieces I wanted," he said. His eyes started to smolder again.

"You are one strange man," she said, putting on the cap and walking back toward the bed.

"You've led a sheltered life, Renee, if you think that's strange," he said, observing her as she strolled over to him.

"Where are those boots I like so much?" he said, smiling, his eyes becoming darker now, a smoky grey.

She laughed and straddled him, pushing him back on the bed.

"No boots. And I'll show you sheltered," she said, laughing.

—⁓—

Later on that morning, Joe waited for Piper to come back to bed. She'd gone downstairs to retrieve cups of coffee for them both. He was now hanging over the side, nude still, on his stomach, his BlackBerry in hand, waiting for her to return. They needed to cover the week's events.

He heard her feet in the hall outside and looked up as she entered, smiling at her. She was a pretty woman. He hadn't thought so at first, and couldn't tell you when he began to see her that way. He'd always loved her body and would have thought he'd gotten used to seeing it, but it continually had the power to arouse him. He liked that she didn't seem overly concerned with her looks, didn't make a fuss over herself.

She strolled over, sat two cups of coffee down on the nightstand, and laid down next to him. They were both crossways on her bed now, on their stomachs, BlackBerries in their hands, legs stretched out behind them.

"Okay, what does your week look like?"

"Training off-site, most of it starting tomorrow, strictly eight to five, so I should be able to pick Shane up from school after basketball practice this week."

"Friday the kids are out all day—parent teacher conferences," she said. "Have you signed up for yours yet?"

"Yep. I'm scheduled for 9:30. You?"

"Afternoon," she said.

"I'll drop Shane off here Friday morning before I go in?"

"Sure," she said, mind focused on entering information. "Can you pick up the kids on Thursday?"

It was quiet while he looked over that day's calendar.

"Yep."

"Training at the shop?" he asked.

"No, covering for someone."

"Anything else?" he asked, looking over at her, reaching for the coffee cup and taking a sip.

"Nope. It's all good."

"It looks like I have a few more minutes before I need to get moving," he said, taking another sip from his cup before setting it back down on the nightstand. "Was there anything else in that package?"

"Yes, but we're not using it," she replied, turning to face him, her look skeptical. "Duct tape, Joe? Really? I don't even want to know." She watched as he set his BlackBerry on her nightstand, reaching for hers and placing it next to his.

"Hey, it's pink," he said, grinning.

"I don't care if it's gold-plated and covered in diamonds."

"Fine. Too soon. I understand. We'll have to figure something else out, then," he said, reaching for her again, laughing, pulling her in as she pretended to resist.

—✺—

Valentine's Day

Joe stood by the punch bowl in the small gym at Shane's school. His assigned task was to pour drinks for the participants and to act as a chaperone. Easy. Taylor and Shane's class was having an old-fashioned Valentine's Day dance, which meant dancing with air and daylight between two bodies.

The kids were now paired up, dancing their version of the waltz, trying to avoid looking at each other, except the girls that were into boys.

"Taking a break from the cake-cutting?" Joe said to Hassan, another parent.

"Yes. I was just filling in for my wife, who was running late. Thankfully she's here," he said, reaching for a cup of punch for himself.

"Where is your wife?" Hassan asked him.

"My wife?" Joe said, startled. "I'm not married."

"You aren't? I thought you and Piper…" Hassan said, his voice trailing off at the look on Joe's face. "I'm sorry. I just assumed. I see you two together so much, I just thought…"

"No. I'm not married. She's a good friend of mine. Her sisters are good friends of Shane's," he explained.

"Oh, I see. Sorry. I didn't mean to offend."

"I'm not offended."

Piper walked over to the table dressed in a sexy black and red dress, some kind of print, her hair pulled up, feet in some pretty red shoes, toes painted red with small hearts. When had oddly-painted toes become a turn-on for him?

"Hey, Hassan. Joe," she said, smiling at them both.

"Hello," Hassan said, looking over at Joe again. "I'd better go back and help my wife," he said, turning and walking away.

"What's up with him?" she asked.

"Nothing," Joe said, shrugging. "He thought you were my wife. Isn't that funny?" He smiled, like that was the best joke of the day.

"Yep. Pretty funny," she replied, her tone neutral, her face blank.

"The room turned out great. Good work on the decorations," he said, looking around again.

"Thanks," she said, watching the kids. They'd stopped dancing and were now headed toward the food and punch tables. "You're about to get busy," she said, handing him an empty cup to fill. "The kids are headed this way."

He took the cup from her hand and filled it with punch, then reached for another one. He'd filled a few already, so he had a head start on the rush.

"Hey, Trudy," Piper said, handing a drink over to her as she walked up.

"Things turned out really nice. You look great. Doesn't she look nice, Joe?" Trudy asked, looking over at him.

"Yes, she does," he said, running his eyes over Piper as he took another empty cup from her hand.

"You two make a really attractive couple," Trudy added.

"We're not a couple, and we are not married," Joe said with a little more force than he'd intended.

"Oh, okay. I'm sorry," Trudy said, taking in Piper's uncomfortable silence. "Sorry. I'd better go check on the children," Trudy said and quickly walked away.

The kids kept coming over for drinks. Heather and Stan walked up to their table a few moments later, reaching for a drink. Most of the kids had gone back to dancing by then.

"Hey, you two," Stan called out in greeting.

"We're not married," Piper said, pleasantly, with a smile.

"Okay…" Stan said, looking between the two of them and then over at his wife, confused.

Joe turned to look at Piper, taking in the stone-like set of her face. Why the anger? What did he say that was so wrong? They weren't married. Just friends, last time he'd checked. Mr. Marshall walked to them, dressed in a nice suit and tie.

"You look awe inspiring," he said to Piper. "Oh, hello, Joe. Didn't see you standing there," he added, continuing to smile at Piper.

Sure you didn't, Joe thought, viewing the appreciation on the teacher's face.

"I'm not married," Piper said, and Mr. Marshall laughed. She joined in.

"Would you like to dance then, single woman?" he said.

"Love to," she said, putting her hand in his.

Joe watched them walk away, noting the disappointed glances from Heather and Stan before they joined Piper and Mr. Marshall on the dance floor. Okay, that hadn't been his finest hour. He sighed. Piper didn't come back to the table after that, so he didn't get his chance to apologize. She was avoiding him now. He could tell, and it was so unlike her. He was smart enough to recognize that he overreacted to the marriage question.

He'd guessed from the outside it might appear that they were connected, maybe even married or living together. Their lives had become intertwined. He'd come to depend on her, and he loved the physical aspect of their relationship.

He hadn't been aware of when it started, before Thanksgiving maybe, the whole sense of family he'd felt when all of them were together. Christmas had been nice, too. All five of them. But it wasn't marriage, or a true family. Her sisters would be leaving at some point, anyway. Would what they had last?

He liked her; admired her, really. She was the closest he'd gotten to anyone other than Reye, not since he had given his heart long ago. And that had so not worked out. Would that be so bad, Joe? he asked himself then, forcing himself to give some thought to the question of marriage.

He was surprised that the idea didn't elicit the red flags that it used to. He hadn't given any thought to anyone seriously since Amy.

Amy. He thought back to his high school days. It felt like ages ago; hell, it was ages ago. He'd wanted to marry her. She'd gotten pregnant. He thought she wanted home and hearth. He was ready to skip college, work, make a life for them, but nope, it wasn't his kid. She'd wanted home and hearth with someone else.

Piper was not Amy, but this was still uncharted territory and he didn't know the answer to what he'd wanted ultimately with her. Seven months ago, the answer would have been an emphatic no, but he didn't know what he wanted now. Was this love?

—◊—

Joe parked in front in Piper's drive. He'd returned from delivering all three kids to a party, fulfilling a promise he'd made to her before their dance dispute, before she'd gotten her feelings hurt, before she'd started with the terse answers to all of his questions. He'd stopped by an hour ago for the pick-up and she'd been cool when he and Shane reached her front door.

He'd tried the teasing route. "We're not married," he'd said, chuckling, thinking he was funny. Not a good idea. She didn't appreciate his attempt at humor. At all. The go to hell look she gave him was proof.

So here he was, back at her home, tramping back to her front door. In two hours he'd have to head back to pick up the children. He rang the doorbell, which set off McKenzie and Pepper. He could see her stalking toward the door. She opened it and stood there, looking at him, a question in her eyes, a frown on her face.

"Forget something?" she asked.

"Can I come in?"

"Sure," she said, turning and walking back to the kitchen. Music was playing. It wouldn't be Piper's if music wasn't playing. She wore one of those long, floor-length skirts in some soft material, a wife beater on top, with the blue Lights Out logo stitched on the front of it.

He caught her before she entered the kitchen and forced her to turn around.

"I'm sorry," he said. Her head tilted back to look into his eyes. "I'm sorry for hurting your feelings. I was surprised, caught off guard, that's all. It's not that I

271

don't want to marry you. It's that I don't want to marry anyone, at least not now, and I thought we'd agreed to be friends, anyway. Did something change here and I missed it?"

"No. Nothing's changed. It just bothered me that you were so adamant in your denials. Is it such a stretch that you could be married to me?"

"No, it's not a stretch at all. You're a great woman. You're going to make someone a great wife. Anyone would want to marry you."

"But not you?"

"I don't know," he said and sighed. "Honestly, this is the first I've given it any thought. A few months ago it would have been no for sure. I'm still no, but not as absolute."

"Ouch," she said.

"I'm sorry, just trying to be honest here. We agreed to be friends. We are, and sex with you is amazing, but I didn't sign up for more. Told you that at the beginning, remember," he said.

"Ouch again," she said, quiet for a moment. "You're right," she added, looking away from him. He was still holding on to her arms.

"So are we okay with where we are? If it's too much, we can find another alternative," he said, giving her a small shake, bringing her eyes back to him. "I like you, Piper. I like what we have here. I like that Shane loves being here. But if it's getting to be more than we can handle, just say so. We can find another alternative."

Well, can you handle it? she asked herself.

"No, I'm cool with this," she said.

"You sure?" he asked.

"Yes, I'm sure."

"Good then. Come here," he said and he pulled her to him.

Chapter 18

Last week of February

Piper was standing in the kitchen at her shop when her phone rang.

"Hey, Margarite," she said.

"Hello, dear. Did I catch you at a bad time?"

"No, I'm at the shop, standing in the kitchen, trying to decide on my next chore. How are you and the girls getting along?" Piper asked.

"Blair's heavy into basketball, school, and clubs, and Samantha appears to be getting serious with that boyfriend of hers—much as I wish she'd take her time. Tell me about you. How are the girls?"

"They're doing well. Christina and Mac are together again. I'm glad for them. Her mother is in the final stages. They don't expect her to be around much longer."

"I'm sorry to hear that. I'm glad she was able to see her mother. Sometimes we don't have the chance to tell those that mean the most to us how we feel about them."

"I agree. So in case I forget, I love you, Margarite." They both laughed.

"So…tell me about Joe," Margarite said.

"Joe?"

"There are no secrets between the Knight sisters. Your Taylor told Samantha that she suspects you and Joe have a 'hook-up' thing working."

Piper laughed to cover her horror at her suspected love life being batted about on Facebook, even if it was within the confines of their private group. And what did Taylor know about hook-ups anyway?

"Oh."

"Is this serious?"

"No, not at all. We're friends," she said.

"Could it be?"

"Probably not."

"Do you want it to be?"

"I wouldn't mind, but he would," she said, giving a small laugh, hoping to camouflage her feelings.

"I see…if you want to talk, I'm still a good listener," she said.

"I know. You've listened to my boyfriend problems before. He's a nice guy. It's taken a while to get to know him, but he's a keeper. He's a great uncle, takes care of his nephew, helps me and the girls. I'm okay with where we are, and yes, I do want more, but you know men. They don't move where they don't want to go," she said, glad to get that out, to be able to say that to someone else.

"So what do you want to do?"

"Be here," she said.

"And you know what that might bring for you?"

Piper laughed. "You mean heartache, hurt feelings, loneliness? Yes, I understand," she said, giving in to laughter so as not to cry.

"You never know unless you try, and yes, the outcome may not be what you want, but what if it is?"

"I know, and we'll see. So what did we decide to do for spring break?"

"The usual. Going to the beach, I think," Margarite said.

They talked a few minutes more about their lives.

Piper stood in the spot for a few seconds thinking after she hung up with Margarite, appreciative of her stepmother's call, glad for someone to talk to about Joe. She'd pretended with Joe that she was okay with them, that it didn't matter, but it did.

—⚬—

Meghan Johnson, formerly Meghan Sandborne, sat with her husband of one year in the church's office. It was lunch. She'd come over to talk to him. He was always a calming influence on her. Aaron Johnson was tall with skin the color of coal. He was thin to the point of being skeletal, but he had seen her at her weakest, had stayed with her, helped her work the program, and listened more than he talked as she took back her life one day at a time. And then he married her.

"What brings you by?" he said, sitting at his desk. He was working on Sunday's sermon.

"Just wanted to talk. Feeling anxious," she said.

"About?"

"Shane. Joe. Wondering if I should contact a lawyer? You know, discuss my chances for getting custody of Shane."

"I thought you were going to talk to Joe first."

"But I know Joe. He won't believe me. He won't forgive. I know him," she said, taking the seat in front of the desk and reaching for his hands. He rose from his desk and walked around to take the seat next to her, knowing that he needed to listen.

She sighed. "I'm scared," she said, her eyes filling with tears. "What if it turns into a battle?"

"You can't control any of that," he said, squeezing her hand in assurance.

She sighed again. "No," she said. "I can't."

"He may surprise you. Give it over to God. We aren't in control of it anyway. What is the third step?"

"Make a decision to turn our will and our lives over to a higher being."

"Why don't we call Joe?"

"Now?"

"Do you want to wait?"

"No, now is fine," she said, pulling out her cell. She'd programmed the number in long ago, right after she'd returned to Austin, not sure when she'd be ready for this. Now worked. It was as good a time as any.

—⁓—

Joe checked his schedule, overjoyed that his plans for the day had changed. Some time had been freed up, just in time for lunch. He was glad that he and Piper had finally moved beyond the whole love question. He'd been worried there for a while, not sure what to do about her, recognizing that she'd come to mean more than he'd acknowledged. He was still working to figure it all out. He was glad she'd returned to normal in her behavior toward him. He punched in her cell number. It had been a while. He had been unreasonably busy, and beyond their nightly groping in the pantry when he'd come to pick up Shane he hadn't had time for much else.

"So what are you doing for lunch?" he asked her, laughter in his voice.

"What are you doing for lunch?' she repeated his question, laughter in hers, too, a sound he loved to hear.

"I was thinking about taking you for lunch," he said, and again he was rewarded with her laughter.

"Where would you be taking me?"

"Your home, of course."

"I'm not really all that hungry," she said.

He laughed again. "Yeah, you are."

"So sure, are you?"

"Yes. Where are you now?" he asked.

"Home, actually. And now I guess I'm waiting for my lunch to be delivered," she said.

"Well, today is your lucky day. It's on the way. See you in a few," he said and hung up, checking his phone. Someone had called but he hadn't clicked over.

He didn't recognize the number, but hit the button to listen to the voicemail message. The air left his body. His stomach sank.

"Hey, Joe," she said, her voice soft and upbeat. "It's Meghan, your sister." Her voice became more tentative now. "I would like to talk to you, to see you. I got your number from Franklin Jones, your old foster parent. I'm sorry I didn't know his wife passed. That must have been hard for you. I'm living here now, in Austin, married, even…and clean. He could hear her a take a fortifying breath before her next sentence. "I want to talk to you, Joe…about me and about Shane. You can reach me at this number," she said, pausing again. "Hope to hear from you soon." Then it went quiet.

Joe was at a loss. It doesn't mean anything, he told himself. She probably just wants to check in, see how her kid is getting on, no more no less. Don't read anything into it. He'd think about calling her back, but not now. Later. He'd think about it later. He moved to his car, going to Piper's, refusing to think about Meghan.

But he was unsettled. His chest felt tight. He should have gotten permanent custody of Shane. What had he been waiting on? His mind began spinning in numerous directions as he made his way to Piper's.

—∞—

Piper had arrived home thirty minutes before Joe had called so she could let the dogs out. The surprise of having him call had left her feeling festive and playful. So she'd stripped down to her bare bones and now she stood waiting behind the front door for him, naked as the day she was born. What a nice surprise for him, she thought, wishing he'd hurry up because she was getting cold. She wondered if she had time to dash upstairs for her robe.

She heard a car pull up. Nope, no time. She heard the car door close and footsteps approaching her door. A key went into the lock. She held her breath and the door opened, blocking his view of her as she stood behind it. He closing the door and turned around to find her standing there. He almost jumped out of his skin. She shifted her body from one leg to the other, one hand wrapped around her breast, silently watching and waiting, the other hand over her mouth to keep quiet.

She couldn't help it. Once he'd seen her, she gave in to her laughter because his expression was priceless. His eyes roamed over her, standing there in the nude. A bark of a laugh popped out of his mouth and his eyes widened and then narrowed. His smile changed from shocked to sexy, and his eyes did that smoldering burning thing. Another good idea, Piper, she told herself, still laughing as he stuck his hand out and reached for her, pulling her to him, his other arm moving around her waist.

She couldn't stop laughing and neither could he now. He had to let her go so they could both give into huge guffaws.

"It's cold," she said, her laughter winding down to giggles.

"Come here," he said, reaching for her, securing her wrist as he pulled her along behind him up the stairs. He pulled her into his arms as he reached the landing, feeling better already. He was glad he'd come, shoving thoughts of Meghan and what her call would mean for him and Shane to the back of his mind.

He kissed her, mouth open over hers, soft and hot. His tongue found hers and played. She was butter in his hands. She laughed as he started to dance with her, your basic two-step, in time to music he began to hum.

She smiled, getting into the spirit of it, following his lead, two-stepping between kisses as he moved her backwards to her room, one arm around her waist.

Please, please, please, can I have this one? I won't ask for anything more, she silently prayed. She was in heaven. They danced their way into her room, his mouth moving over hers, humming against her lips, before skimming the undersides of her chin.

His lips left hers then, only for a second, as she helped him pull the shirt over his head, dropping it to the floor. She unzipped his pants and pushed downward toward the floor. He stepped out of them, ditching his shoes and boxers.

"What a nice surprise," he said, turning them so he stood next to the bed. He sat, then laid back, pulling her to sit on him, not moving except to kiss and run his hands along her golden brown skin, releasing his thoughts of Meghan and what her reappearance could mean.

"It was, wasn't it," she said, and gave herself over to him.

—⁓—

Second week of March

Meghan had called twice over the past week. He would have to talk to her soon. It didn't seem like she was going away. He hadn't mentioned it to Shane or Piper. He'd called and made an appointment with his attorney, however. He stood now outside of Reye's, needing to talk it over with someone, sidestepping the issue that it should have been with Piper.

He walked up to the door, knocked and Reye opened it.

"This is a nice surprise," she said, letting him enter.

"Hey," he said, stepping into her hug. He stood there for a second, longer than before. He looked up to see Stephen standing in the doorway, a strange look passing over his face.

"Hey, Joe," Stephen said, walking toward them.

Joe gave him a nod. "Stopped by to talk to Reye," Joe said.

"Me, too," he said, bending over to kiss his wife, his hand going to her head to hold her in place. He kissed her longer than normal for a going-back-to-work peck, mouth opening over hers, surprising her with its intensity.

"See you later, Joe," Stephen said, looking at Joe, all trace of friendliness gone.

Joe laughed. They were back to that again. "She's safe," he said to Stephen.

"I know," Stephen said, and smiled, not the wicked one, reserved for her, but its meaner version.

Joe laughed again. For some reason he felt better already, more relaxed; nothing like a good fight to release some stress.

Reye shook her head. Men, she thought. She smiled at Stephen before he walked out the front door.

"So what brings you here?" she asked as he walked over to the couch and sat down.

"My sister's back," he said.

"Back where?" she asked, walking over to sit next to him. "When?"

"Two weeks ago. She called. Wants to see Shane," he said, glad to have someone to talk to. Someone who knew his history, someone who he didn't have to bring up to speed, someone who had been there when he was struggling to hold it together. Reye reached for his hand, giving it a squeeze.

"You have to talk to her," she said.

"I know, but I'm talking to that family lawyer first," he said.

She nodded at that. "You know I'm here for you and Shane," she said, squeezing his hand again.

"I know," he said.

"Have you talked to Piper about this?" she asked. He turned his head sharply to look at her.

"No."

"Why not?"

He shrugged. "I like her, I do. I dated someone a long time ago, thought it could have been more. Marriage. But it didn't turn out. Don't know if I want to do that again."

Reye didn't say a word for a minute, floored that he'd finally mentioned something about his past. Joe never discussed his life, at least not the personal part. She probably wouldn't have known about Shane had she not been around when his sister left him the second time.

"It says loads that you're considering her in that way. You know that, right?"

He didn't reply. "What if she wants him back, Reye?" he said, voicing the question that had been plaguing him since Meghan's call. "What should I do?"

"I think talking to the attorney is good, but you're going to have to talk to her, sooner rather than later. And what if she's gotten her life together? Really together. Then what? Doesn't she deserve a second chance?"

"I don't really want to hear that, Reye. Not now, anyway," he said.

"I know."

He was quiet again.

"How's Shane?" she asked.

They spent an hour bringing each other up to date with their lives. Reye didn't bring up Piper again, and neither did he.

—⚌—

Piper lay in bed, wondering if Joe had spring break plans for Shane. They could hang out again like they'd done at Christmas, pretending to be a family.

She hadn't seen or talked to him today. He'd picked Shane up from school, circumventing her. He was starting to do that more often. He'd seemed distant lately, preoccupied, a million miles away. Okay, he'd always kept his personal stuff under wraps, but something was up with him and she had no clue as to what.

The sex was still good. He was always present and accounted for there.

Her cell rang, breaking into her thoughts. It was her dad.

"Hey, Pops. What's up?"

"Hey, Renee. I wanted to let you know that Christina lost her mother today," he said.

"I'm sorry. How is she?"

"She's doing well. Grateful for her time with her mother."

"How are you?"

"I'm good. Thankful, too, that she had the chance to come and see her mother. I shouldn't have stood in her way. I should have listened to her more," he said. His obvious sincerity surprised Piper.

"I've had five children, and the thought of one of you dying without me having the chance to say good-bye would be heartbreaking for me."

"It's okay, Dad. Christina did have her chance," she said. "Any idea when you'll return?"

"I'll be there in about two weeks. Christina is going to be here a while longer with her father and her brother. Then she'll head on back, somewhere around the end of April, first of May," he said.

Piper was quiet.

"You all right?"

"Yeah. It's just that I'd gotten used to having the girls here. It will be hard to see them go."

"They'll be in the city. Christina and I plan to live at the apartment in Austin until school lets out, and then we'll head back to San Antonio."

"That's good."

"So what's bothering you?" he asked.

"I want my own girls and boys and a husband."

Hopefully not in that order, he thought. "Have to have a boyfriend first," he said, chuckling a little.

"Don't I know it."

"Heard that you're seeing someone. Joe is his name, right? The girls mention him often in their e-mails to us. He's the uncle to that little boy you help with, right? Anything to that?" he asked.

"Just friends."

"I see…Friends, huh? I could talk to him," he offered. She laughed, remembering other conversations he'd had with her boyfriends. He'd scared more than a few away.

"Hell, no," she said, and he laughed.

"I'd better get back to Christina. I'll call you soon with flight details," he said.

"Okay," she replied.

"Talk to you soon," he said, hanging up.

She lay on her bed for a second, considering. She and the girls had an end date now—the end of the month. She would miss them. She called Joe.

"Hey," he said in that way of his. At night it was usually sexy and sometimes sleepy, a combination that made for a more potent Joe.

"My dad is coming back in two weeks," she said, getting right to the heart of the matter. "He just called. The girls are going home to their parents. They're going to live here in Austin in my dad's apartment until school's out," she said, the words rushing from her mouth.

Joe was silent. "That's good, right? Good that their parents have worked it out, going to be around, especially your dad. You've said so yourself," he said.

It was quiet. "Yeah, I know. Going to miss them, though."

"But you can see them whenever you want until the summer?"

"Yes."

"But…" he asked.

"But why does that idea bother me so? I mean, I should be happy and celebrating. I'll have my home back. No kids, and no kid commitments. Free to do whatever I want. That used to sound great. Now it just sounds empty," she said.

"It was your life before your sisters."

"I know, but now it's different. I want someone who loves me, wants kids, and wants me, too. I want my grandfather, and maybe even my dad, now that he realizes the importance of family," she said, her voice quivering. Was she crying? "Nothing to say?"

"It may happen," he said.

But not with you, she thought. "So how are you? Didn't see you and Shane much this week," she asked, wiping her tears away with her hands.

"Fine. Work has been easing up for me lately."

"How's Shane?"

"Fine. You have him Friday?" he confirmed.

"I know…see you then. I'd better get some sleep and let you get back to yours. Thanks for listening." She hung up.

What did you think would happen, Piper? she thought, mentally kicking herself. What had she hoped he'd say? "It's okay. I'm on my way over. We can make two babies to replace your sisters. You can marry me. It'll be our two plus Shane, right, Piper?"

She turned off her light and lay there in the dark, wishing for things to turn out differently.

—*w*—

Monday afternoon Joe entered Lights Out Coffee, driven by a desire to check on Piper. She'd told him about having to pick up her dad from the airport this morning, and she'd seemed a little sad the last two weeks, her mourning process, which he understood. He had his, although he didn't like to think about Meghan much. But that didn't mean it wasn't there, hovering in his mind, robbing him of his peace.

He scanned the room and spotted her sitting at one of the back tables next to a woman. The woman looked familiar, blonde and tall, almost as tall as him. He scanned the rest of the room before they returned to Piper and that woman. He knew her. He had grown up with her most of his life. He'd taken care of her when his parents hadn't. Meghan. What is she doing here talking to Piper? How long had they known each other?

Piper spotted him, stood up, and walked over to meet him.

"Joe," she said.

"What are you doing, Piper?" His expression was tense and angry.

"What?" she said, confused by his tone.

"Talking to her," he said, his head nodding in Meghan's direction. Piper turned to look back.

"Meghan? I just met her. She stopped by for coffee, says she knew you from when she was young, said she grew up with you. I was coming to bring you over to her."

"It's not necessary," he said, turning and leaving, moving toward the front door.

"Wait. Where are you going? We haven't gone over the schedule for this week. When do I pick up Shane?" she said, taken aback by his abrupt behavior.

He turned and walked back to her, getting right up in her face. He was angry, a look she couldn't remember seeing on his face. He glanced over her shoulder toward the back of the room.

"What, Joe?" she asked, staring into his eyes.

"She is my sister. Shane's mother. She's been calling for the last month, trying to worm her way back into Shane's life, to disrupt it again. That's not going to happen," he said. His voice was firm.

"The last month?" she asked, glancing back at Meghan.

"Yes."

"Were you even going to tell me?" she asked.

"It wasn't your concern," he said.

"Not my concern," she said.

"No, not your business," he said again in case she'd missed it the first time. "I don't appreciate you going behind my back, Piper."

"I didn't know she was your sister."

"I'll get Shane today," he said, stepping back from her. "I'll call you if I need your help," he added before walking through the door.

Piper stood at the window, watching him get into his car, totally perplexed by the news and by his behavior. This was Joe's sister? She turned to look back across the room and met the woman's eyes. They were sad. Piper sighed and walked back over to her.

"I'm sorry. I shouldn't have come. I thought you could help, but I can see he hasn't talked to you," she said, standing up and reaching for her purse, making Piper feel superfluous.

She shook her head. "No, he hasn't."

"It's okay. Same old Joe, I see," she said, her voice disappointed. "Sorry to put you in this position. Joe and I need to talk."

"Can I help?" Piper said.

"No, it's Joe that I need to talk with. I haven't forced anything. Thought I should go slow, but maybe that wasn't the best course."

"Maybe not," Piper said, her eyes on Meghan.

"Again, I'm sorry. Maybe I'll see you again," she said, shouldering her purse and walking toward the exit to the shop. She knew it would be unlikely Joe would forgive, especially if he was as quick to judge as he used to be.

Piper watched her leave. Her emotions were all over the place. She was turmoil personified, and she didn't know where to begin to get herself back under control. WTF? was the best she could come up with.

—⁓—

A few days later Meghan walked to Joe's front door. She'd driven by his house a thousand times, hoping to catch a glimpse of Shane. He hadn't answered or returned her calls.

She squared her shoulders and rang the doorbell. It was morning. She knew Shane was at school. Piper had told her sometimes she could catch him at home. Sometimes he'd swing back by his home after dropping off Shane. This had been her third attempt in as many days after seeing him in the shop that time.

Piper had been nice to her. Meghan had gone back to Lights Out the next day. The need to apologize was heavy on her heart for putting Piper in this spot with Joe. They'd talked for a while.

It seemed like she was forever apologizing for the choices she made in her life, part of the making amends process, of owning what she had done to herself and to others, digging through the rubble of her past.

God, help me to get through this. Allow me to let you guide me, to surrender to your will here. Only you know how hard this is for me, but with you by my side, we can get through this. This was always her prayer when she was determined to go forward, remembering to give it over to Him, always, when it became too much for her. He who'd been there for her when no one else had, who'd seen her at her lowest point, the point where she'd given up, and who had taken over. It was a good thing because she couldn't have helped herself. She was so glad that he was with her today.

She rang the doorbell again and then turned to leave, giving up for now. It opened, and there stood Joe, her big brother, who'd tried to help her, not knowing that it was beyond his power to do so.

"Can I come in?" she asked, calmer than she'd expected of herself; she had surrendered this over to God.

"Sure," he said.

She blew out a huge breath and followed him in. He remained standing by the door.

"Do you mind if I sit?" she asked.

"No, I don't mind," he said, watching her walk over to his couch.

"This is a lovely home," she said. "You've done really well for yourself. I'm not surprised by that, either. I knew you would. You were always determined that way."

"So what can I do for you?" he asked.

"I wanted to say I'm sorry first. One of the steps is to make amends for wrongs and hurt you've done to others. So I'm here today to try and make amends, Joe, to tell you how sorry I am for the hurt that I've caused you in the past. I'm sorry," she said, looking at him. He hadn't moved. "I also wanted to thank you for taking care of Shane for me both times."

"Where did you go?" he asked.

"Not anywhere good," she said, watching him but not seeing any signs of forgiveness. "But I'm better now. I wanted you to know that. I've been sober and clean for the last eighteen months. I'm living in Austin. I met and married a wonderful man, Aaron. He is fifteen years sober. He's a minister of a small church here in town, over near Eleventh Street, east of town. He's also a part-time counselor, giving back to others like us."

"I'm glad for you," he said. She could see that he meant it.

"I would like to see Shane," she said and watched him close up. She continued anyway. This was too important. "I understand your need to protect him, and I'm willing to work with you on this, to give you as much time as you need to get used to the idea of me, of having me around in your life and in his. To show you that I mean it this time." She took a deep breath and found his eyes again.

"I'm not looking to take Shane from you. I wish more than anything to have a chance to be his mother again, but I don't want to hurt him any more than I have," she said. "I would like you to consider allowing me to see him. I know you have temporary custody. Thank you for that. I'm hoping to prove to you that I am ready to be here, to be present in his life. That takes time, I know. I just want the chance to get to know him again, for you and him to see that I mean this."

He was silent and still standing.

"I'll think about it," he said, walking over to the front door. "I've got to get to work, but I have your number. I'll be in touch."

"Sure," she said, standing up and moving toward the door, too, touching his arm lightly.

"Thank you so much for the care you've given my son," she said, walking through the door that he now held open for her.

"Call me?" she said.

"I will," he replied, and watched as she turned and walked to her car, an older model sedan. She gave a tentative wave and he nodded. He watched as she pulled away from the curb.

───※───

Joe walked back into his home and sat down on the couch, reviewing what had just transpired, what she'd just said. She'd looked better than he recalled. She hadn't ever really looked completely free of alcohol when she lived with him. After they'd left their parents and after she'd run away from the first foster home she'd been assigned to, he rarely saw her sober, even after she moved with Shane to Austin to live with him the first time. She'd never really quit, just hid it or tried to hide it.

Seeing her always reminded him of his past. He'd worked hard to put that period behind him. It hadn't gone anywhere, but he thought of it less. Seeing Meghan again forced him to make the trek backward now to the old home on Edgewood Terrace, with his parents, fighting or finding his mother laid out on the floor drunk when he and Meghan would come home from school.

It shot through him, the feelings of fear that he'd failed his parents before he was old enough to learn that it hadn't been his fault. It shouldn't have been his responsibility at age ten to assume the role of the parent. But before then he'd felt the weight of them all, making sure he and Meghan were dressed, clothed, washed, fed, and homework done when it could get done.

He let it all come back and let it move him, remembering them being taken from their home, separated from his sister. He'd assumed the fault for that, too. He'd let his sister down again—the reason he'd tried so hard to help her and Shane.

He'd learned the hard way to depend on himself, only himself, alone. God, he hated it at first, but learned that it was only him he could really count on, until he moved to a new home. He was lucky to have found a set of parents who treated him like he was theirs, that had helped to heal some of his wounds.

And even then he hadn't expected to find someone for him, but Amy had come along. She was hurt in her own way, and he'd thought he could help her. Another let-down and another hurt. He plowed into school, first undergraduate and then on to graduate school. The latter he'd completed while raising Shane. In spite of it all, life had worked out for him, scars and all.

He wanted different for Shane. Shane he would protect, he would fight for. He rubbed his eyes and sighed.

He hadn't talked to Piper since the Meghan incident a few days ago. He avoided her calls, but he missed her. He was still angry at her, however irrational that anger was. She'd talked to his sister without his knowledge. She didn't know, his rational self tried to argue, but he wasn't listening to that part. He needed time to figure out what he wanted, if anything more, from her.

So maybe now was a good time to put a little distance between them. He knew her sisters would be leaving her soon. She'd told him that.

He would find a sitter for Shane. They only had another month and a half in school. He could swing that even if he couldn't find a sitter for the last month. He could probably fall back on his neighbor, Mrs. Lewis. She would help temporarily, and then Shane could return to Reye's for the summer.

Piper loved him, he knew that. She hadn't said it, but you didn't do the things she did for him unless you were in love. All the more reason he needed to back away, at least for a while. He didn't want to hurt her more than he had. Sure, Joe, he said to himself, but let it go. When had he become a coward? he asked himself. He didn't have an answer to that question. He needed time to sort everything out.

—⁓—

First week of April

Piper read through Joe's text, and later his e-mail. Again. She'd read it fifty times if she'd read it once since he sent it to her on Monday, their normal meeting time. He was going to spend some time working out his issues with Shane and Meghan...blah, blah, blah...He would take care of picking up Shane from here on out. Thank you, I'll be in touch. Okay...He couldn't have told her that in person? He couldn't work it out with her around? He'd even stopped coming to the shop.

Her feelings ran the gamut from anger to sadness, but anger predominated. She'd started for the door with every intention of driving over and demanding... what? That he love her? She ended up turning around. If she had to ask...

She was deeply hurt. The most painful time was at night before she fell asleep. She'd known the potential for that from the get-go, known exactly what Joe had or hadn't offered. He never lied to her about that, and there was no use pretending that he had.

There was also sadness for him, and that had surprised her. Meghan hadn't shared anything with her about their childhood, but she imagined it had to have been some tough junk for him to have created the wall he had around his heart. Joe and his sister's lives didn't sound like they'd been easy.

She had her dad, and although he may have been absent emotionally, she'd always felt safe and loved, taken care of by the women he'd chosen. Plus she had her Nanny and grandfather, who loved her beyond all reason.

Lastly, she'd felt more than a little awed by his ability to get beyond his beginnings and make a life for himself and for his nephew. He didn't drink, he worked hard, raised a kid that wasn't his—a stand-up guy altogether. Her stomach churned. She missed him.

The girls had moved into their parents' apartment a week ago. As soon as her dad returned he'd wanted them with him. He drove them to and from school now, the biggest surprise of them all. She'd just about had her fill of surprises.

It was quiet in her home now. No music, no barking from McKenzie and Pepper, nothing but silence. She didn't have much to do at the shops, either. She wouldn't fire those college kids who needed the money just because she now had time on her hands.

Chapter 19

Joe needed to talk to someone. He had just left his attorney. He headed to Reye's, hoping she'd be there. It was after lunch, two hours before school was out, so she would be free of children. He pulled up to her center, and her truck was parked outside. He walked over to the front door and knocked.

"Hey," she said, opening the door a few minutes later.

"Hey," he replied, stepping in. "Got a moment?"

"Always for you," she said.

"I just came back from the attorney's office," he said.

"Oh," she replied, her face turning serious. "Have a seat," she said, moving to the couch. He followed, sitting down beside her. "So what did he say?"

"Nothing. I don't have anything to worry about. The court views my sister's abandonment of Shane as a break in the mother-child relationship, which would overrule any tendency they might have had to rule in the mother's favor.

"Under these circumstances, the court typically decides custody based on what it finds is in the best interest of the child. And since Shane is with me, making good grades, happy, involved in outside activities, it would be highly unlikely that they'd give custody to her."

"That's a load off," Reye said.

"Yes, it is, but he also strongly suggested that I consider allowing Meghan to visit Shane—supervised, of course. It was his experience from numerous years at this, blah, blah, blah…that children seldom get beyond the loss of a parent, and if I could, I should try to help repair their relationship, or at least not impede it. I should give her some time to prove herself either way."

"Have you talked to Shane?"

"No."

"Are you going to?"

"At some point, yes," he replied.

"Give it some time," Reye said, reaching for his hand, holding on to it tightly.

—◦◦◦—

First week of May

Piper sat in her office waiting for her dad to show up. They were going to talk though the preliminary plans for adding some additional shops. She didn't have much else to do. Might as well put her time into creating something. If it couldn't be a family, maybe her business could be her empire, her new family. It was an inadequate substitution, in her humble opinion. It sure wouldn't feel like Joe did, with his body next to hers. Couldn't call her Renee in that way of his or listen to her as she rambled on in her usual way. Couldn't make her laugh, or tease her, but she couldn't have everything.

Where was Joe, anyway? It had been almost a month now. He hadn't called—not once—to check in with her. She was having an angry moment again. He'd just disappeared. Hadn't called to see how she was after the girls had gone. Hadn't they been friends? Guess not. She apparently had just been only Renee, the woman he'd wanted from the start.

She'd called quite a bit at first. He hadn't answered, the coward. She'd gotten herself under control and stopped. Okay, she called one other time, to talk; her emotions had taken control of her body. She hadn't been able to keep herself from dialing the number. He was busy at work. His voiced rushed. He'd found a sitter for Shane, school was almost out, so Shane would be heading back to Reye's. He said he hadn't called her, hadn't wanted to bother her now that the girls were gone.

That was so nice of him. Guess he'd decided to move on. All signs pointed that way, however abrupt his decision had been. She should move on, too.

Joe had left Shane with a sitter for the evening and was now in his car driving toward Meghan and her husband's home. He had called earlier in the week and agreed to have dinner with them tonight. Although he hadn't dreaded this meeting, he hadn't looked forward to it, either. He didn't want to go alone. Piper would go with you. Where had that thought come from? Who was he kidding? He'd thought of her often and he'd missed her plenty. Piper lived in his brain, swam around in his waking thoughts, simmered just under his skin while her counterpart, Renee, hounded his dreams.

Meghan and Shane were all he could take in emotionally. He wanted to resolve it alone, as he'd always done things, but this evening he found himself turning around and driving back to her shop, taking a chance that she'd be there. He parked and walked in.

"Is Piper here?" he asked.

"Nope. Not today," an employee—one of her usual clueless student workers—said.

"Thanks," he said. He turned around and walked back to his car, and then found himself heading toward her home, not willing to relinquish the idea of asking her to come with him. He parked in front of her home and walked to the front door and knocked, while checking his watch. He was met with silence. No barking of dogs. They were gone and so were the girls, he remembered. He'd been so wrapped up in himself, he'd forgotten.

"Hey," he said, when she opened the door. Surprise registered on her face first, quickly followed by hurt. She didn't say anything.

"I'm heading over to see my sister—my first time—and to meet her husband," he said. Then he stopped and looked around, clearly uncomfortable. "To...talk about Shane," he said, his eyes dead on hers now. "Would you come with me? I'm in need of a friend. I know it's short notice." It looked like it was killing him to ask her.

"I'll come. Just give me a second," she said, walking up the stairs. He stepped inside the door, closing it behind him, looking around at her home. He smiled. Music was playing. Piper and her music, another constant.

It took her less than ten minutes and they were on their way.

"Thanks," he said.

"You're welcome," she said, but didn't say much else.

"How have you been?" he asked.

"Fine."

"How are your sisters?"

"Fine."

"I'm sorry."

She shrugged her shoulders and continued to stare out the window. "How's Shane?" she asked.

"Good. He's been to your dad's apartment. He and Taylor are truly inseparable."

"So I've heard," she said. Her smile was weak, and she was back to looking out the window. "Does your sister live far from here?"

"No, we're almost there."

She nodded and looked out the window again. He was quiet the remainder of the trip. Ten minutes later Joe parked alongside the curb before a small, neat home. They were in one of the older neighborhoods located east of town, where homes were made from wood and sat on pier and beam, not concrete foundations like the newer models. It was painted white, trimmed in a pretty forest green. There were flowers around the front porch, which had been painted a light grey.

Piper got out and met Joe as he walked around the front of the car. They both made their way to the front door. Joe knocked. He was tense. Piper could tell from the stiffness of his posture.

The door opened. It was answered by a tall, on-the-skinny-side black guy. She was surprised. Her eyes darted to Joe. He was just as surprised as she was.

"You must be Joe," he said, sticking out his hand. "I'm Aaron. Married to your sister. She's in the shower. Spent too much time in the kitchen making sure dinner was just the way she wanted. I've learned to get out of her way," he said, smiling and stepping back to allow them entry.

"This is Piper," Joe said.

"Nice to meet you, Piper," Aaron said, extending his hand to hers.

"Nice to meet you, too," she said.

"You two have a seat and I'll go let Meghan know you're here," he said, pointing toward what must be the living room while he walked away.

They both sat on the couch, looking around. It was nice and clean in here, not fancy—chair, sofa, rug on the floor. Several portraits hung on the wall.

"Your sister's married?" she asked, turning to look at Joe, whose mind was a million miles away. She reached for his hand and squeezed it, not knowing if that would help. He squeezed back.

A few minutes later, Aaron and Meghan entered.

"I'm so glad Joe brought you with him," she said, reaching for Piper's hands.

"Me too," Piper replied.

"Are you two ready for dinner?" she asked.

"Yes," Joe and Piper answered in unison.

—⁓—

Dinner had been uneventful. Aaron, Piper, and Meghan had done most of the talking with the occasional input from Joe, who had chosen to play the closed-off role. They returned to the living room again after dinner for coffee. Piper had inhaled her slice of cake—lemon and light—one of her favorites.

"So, I've met with my attorney," Joe said, cutting into the chit-chat, getting to the reason for their dinner. He was about as subtle as a bull in a china closet, and all idle talk ceased.

"Okay," Meghan said, startled and wary. Her husband looked at Piper and gave her a reassuring smile.

"What is it that you want, Meghan?" he asked.

"As I explained to you at your home, I would like to get to visit and get to know my son," she said, working to get her anxiety under control.

"For…" Joe asked, not nice anymore. Not that he'd been nice to begin with, but he'd been somewhat cordial. Now he was the police interrogating a suspect.

"There is no reason to be hostile," Aaron said, more calm than Piper would have been under the circumstances.

"I'm not hostile. I want you to know that I will protect Shane from ever getting hurt or abandoned again."

Meghan put her hand on her husband's shoulder, a calming gesture. "I understand, Joe. I haven't spoken to a lawyer yet. I wanted to see if we couldn't come up with a resolution before we went to court. I don't have a lot of money to fight you, Joe, and I don't want to fight, anyway. I would like to meet Shane. We could start out slow and get to know each other. Hopefully over time I would prove to you and him that I am stable. Could we try that, Joe?" she asked.

"I'll think about it," he said, his face hard. "I agreed to meet with you today so that you would understand that I intend to protect Shane at all costs."

"I know that, Joe, more than anyone else. I know what you've done for Shane, what you will continue to do for him. I'm thankful for that protective streak. I know what you did for me as a child, the stepping in when our parents were too drunk to see straight. I know, Joe. I was there, too."

"I never said you weren't."

"Yes, but you're angry at me still. Angry at whoever. You've always been angry. You've got to let that go," she said.

"I'm not angry. Just looking out for Shane's best interests," he said.

"Our mother is still living, did you know that? Did you know that she is sober, has been for the last four years? She said she'd tried to call you, that you don't answer her calls or her letters. Is that true?" Meghan asked.

"This isn't about me or our mother, and I'm not the one who drank," he said, his anger showing now.

He and Meghan were alone in the room as far as Piper and Aaron were concerned.

"I dealt with our lives the best way I could, Joe. I've made mistakes. I've learned from them, learned to forgive those who weren't at strong as I was. Can you say that? You can't even forgive your own mother. You have to let go of that anger, Joe, before you can move on. You didn't drink, but you closed yourself off, except for Shane. Who else have you loved besides Amy, who had too many holes for you to plug?"

Who the hell is Amy? Piper wondered.

Joe looked away. "I didn't come here for this."

"Why did you come?" Meghan asked.

"To see what you wanted from Shane, to determine if you were going to fight for custody. To see if you were different, so that I could prepare if necessary," he said, looking at his sister, his eyes hard.

"I'm sorry, Joe, for hurting you, for hurting Shane, for hurting myself. I am living better, one day at a time," she said, looking away, getting herself under control, and then turning back to face him.

"I am asking to see my son. I'm asking for a chance to get to know him again, to prove that I deserve to be in his life. I've had my problems, but I have changed.

307

I would like a chance to love him again," she said. "But I'm not going to fight you on this, Joe. I'm not. It's up to you. I will not drag Shane through that. Not for me. But if you could look at the possibility of allowing me back into his life, I'd appreciate it."

Joe was silent, head down. "I don't know." He sounded tired now. "I don't want him to be hurt, not like me. I don't want that for him," he said, looking into his sister's eyes, his pain showing through now. "I'll think about it. That's all I can give you," he said.

"I appreciate that," she said, reaching for his hand.

"I'd better get Piper home," he said. Piper stood and followed Joe to the door.

"Sure. Thank you for coming," Meghan said as she and Aaron stood, following them to the door. They watched them walk to their car.

—⁓—

A glimpse into Joe's childhood was far more than Piper expected. She glanced over, taking in a silent Joe, eyes on the road in front of him, lost in thought, driving her home. She glanced over at him a few minutes later. Yep, same expression, stoic and quiet. He hadn't said a word to her since they'd left Meghan's. Joe, true to form, was holding all things in that really mattered, taking care of things alone as much as he could.

"Want to talk about it?"

"Nope," he said, continuing to stare out the front window.

They were in her neighborhood now, coming up to her street. A few minutes later he pulled into her drive. He sat for a second, the sound of her door closing bringing him back from his thoughts. He got out and followed her to the front door. He waited while she opened it. Then she turned to him.

"Want to come in?" she asked.

He nodded and followed her in. He walked up behind her, placing his arms around her waist, his head leaning into the curve of her shoulder. He didn't say a word. He just stood there, holding her.

"It doesn't seem like it now, but it will be okay," she said, her hand clasping his at her waist. He didn't respond except to turn her to face him. He looked into her eyes, bent his head and kissed her, touching her lips, slowly and softly.

She kissed him back. They remained like that, locked together, for a while. He pulled back, took her hand, and set off up the stairs to her room, pulling her behind him down the hall.

He reached her bedroom, walked them inside, and closed the door. He turned and kissed her again, mouth smooth and needy. His earlier gentleness was replaced by demand. He unzipped her dress, letting it fall to the floor. He quickly removed her bra and pulled her underwear down, and then slipped out of his own clothes.

He was so serious and sad. She smiled. He returned it, but his smile was so far from the full ones she'd seen the old Joe wear. He climbed into her bed and rolled on top of her.

He kissed her softly again, and then with an urgency she was hard-pressed to keep up with. He pushed her thighs open, his hand going under her arms, and pushed her upward on the bed. She used her heels to push further upward, too, to assist him, hoping to help, to soothe him somehow. He entered her with some force, drawing a moan from her, her legs going around his body to anchor her as he pulled out and thrust back in, again and again and again.

His hands found hers and he gripped her wrists, one in each hand. He held them above her head while he continued his onslaught on her body. His thrusts came hard and fast, sometimes nearly rocking her off the bed. His eyes were closed, and he was beginning to sweat. They both were, but he didn't stop. He was lost in his own mind, while she held on for the ride.

She lost track of time and just gave over her body to him as he still moved in her. He tilted her hips upward and she moaned, his hips driving into her, the force pulling her over, and he felt her start to come. He felt so right inside her, and always had, from the beginning.

It felt like home to him. He pushed harder into her, a few minutes away from coming himself. Oh, God. She felt incredible. He bent to kiss her, his mouth taking in her moans and pleas as he held her hands above her head and pushed one last time, as hard as he could. She screamed his name. He let go and came with her, closing his eyes at the pleasure that coursed through his veins, still pumping his hips, not wanting it to end.

His grip on her wrists loosened and he opened his eyes to find hers open and looking back at him. He bent to kiss her, softly.

"I love you, Joe," she said.

"This might not turn out like you want," he said. "I have lots of baggage."

"Is that a warning?"

"More like a fact," he said, quietly.

She looked at him, taking her hand and running it along his face to cup his cheek in her palm.

"I'll take my chances," she said, and he stared back; that unreadable Joe she loved so much was back again. He bent his head, taking her lips softly with his. She opened her eyes and watched as he lowered his head again, sweeping her along with him again. God, she loved this man.

Later on that night he watched her sleep, thinking back to Meghan and her husband. Shane meant more to him than he had known, and the thought of having to lose him hurt more than he could bear. He couldn't voice that yet. Having Meghan bring up their past was more than he could take, and the possibility of Shane enduring her yet again was more than he wanted to think about. He took a deep breath, letting it go into Piper's curly hair.

"It'll work out," he heard her say. He chuckled.

"Thought you were asleep," he said, pulling out of her embrace, rolling onto his back, and tucking his arm underneath her head.

"I don't know," he said, closing his eyes as his hand roamed over her body, no particular destination in mind, just finding comfort in having her here. He closed his eyes, letting go of Shane for a minute. He fell asleep.

He woke up later than he intended. Piper was still sprawled out asleep, tired from his second or third use of her body. He had wanted to hold her, to lose himself in her again, and she allowed him that. She loved him.

Was it love he felt for her? It was something. He missed her these last few weeks, and realized how much he'd come to rely on her, how much she gave to him. Was that love? It was the closest he'd come to it in a long time. He needed to talk to her. He would, but not now. After it was settled, he promised himself.

—⁓—

A little later Piper woke up, alone. Joe was gone, and it was cool in the spot where he'd been. He left her a note: "Thanks for coming with me."

"No problem," she replied into her soundless room. She hoped she'd helped him. She loved him, as scary as that was—especially now—and hoped it would turn out okay for him, for her, for them.

Chapter 20

End of May

Joe sat in front of the TV. Two weeks had passed since he and Piper had met with Meghan and her husband. He'd given some thought to Meghan's words, and had spent the last two weeks in too much thought about his mom and his life—past, present, and future. He hadn't spoken to his mom in so long. He couldn't even remember the last time they'd talked. His mother was now sober. What to do with that, along with what to do with Meghan? She was different. Having time away to think and reconsider, he'd been able to recognize the changes in her. This Meghan was different. But did that mean she would remain that way? Only time would tell.

He checked his watch. It was 10 p.m. This weekend was free, with the exception of Shane going over to Taylor's dad's apartment tomorrow. That reminded him that he hadn't called Piper, either. He hadn't seen her in two weeks. He'd sent her a text thanking her for coming with him. Not his best move, but neither was the note he'd left behind. He looked up to find Shane standing in the doorway.

"What's up, dude?" he asked.

"Don't forget tomorrow. I'm going over to Taylor's apartment."

"Hadn't forgotten," he said.

"Are you okay? You seem worried lately. You miss Piper, don't you?"

He smiled. "I do, but that's not entirely it. I've been meaning to talk to you about something," he said, watching as Shane walked over to the couch and sat down next to him.

"Your mom is living here now," he said and watched as Shane sat up, suddenly alert.

"Where?" he asked.

"She has a home, is married, actually, and more importantly, she's not sick anymore."

"She's an alcoholic, Joe."

"I know, dude. Wasn't sure how much you knew. You were young."

"I knew."

"She wants to see you again," he said.

"To live with? I thought you had custody of me."

"I do, and it can remain that way. But I would have to go to back to court if she doesn't agree."

"How is she?" he asked.

"The best I've seen her since she was a little girl," he said, and he meant it.

"What does she want?"

"For now, she wants nothing more than the opportunity to see you again, to get to know you…for you to get to know her."

"What do you think?"

"I think it's up to you, dude. What do you think?"

"I would like to see her. I mean when she wasn't drunk or sick, she was fun, happy, played with me. I miss her," he said, looking over at Joe. "I would like to see her again," he said, his voice sure.

"Okay," he said.

"When? Tomorrow?" Shane asked. Joe sat back, surprised by the hopefulness underneath his nephew's question.

"I'll have to call her first, but I'm sure that could be arranged," he said, pulling Shane in to his chest. "I'll always be here for you. You know that, right? Always. And if you meet your mom again and don't want to see her anymore, I'll be there, too," he said, wanting to make sure Shane understood he had an out.

"I know," he said.

"So are you headed to bed or do you want to watch a movie with me?" he asked.

"Movie."

"Okay, you grab one and we'll watch whatever you pick," he said, releasing Shane, who stood up and went to his room in search of one of his old favorites. They'd seen them all at least ten times. Joe could probably recite half of the lines in his sleep.

So he'd call Meghan tomorrow and take Shane over after he got back from Taylor's. Seeing his mother again had been tugging at his mind, too. Maybe he'd see about that, too, he thought as Shane put the DVD into the player.

"Popcorn?" Shane asked, heading toward the kitchen.

"Yes, and bring a beer back with you," Joe added.

"Sure," he replied. Joe heard him in the kitchen, rooting around, followed by sounds of popcorn popping. A few minutes later Shane returned and he and Joe sat back, a bowl filled with popcorn between them, beer for Joe, soda for Shane. And they did what they'd done for the last two years—enjoyed each other's company.

—⁓—

Joe drove toward Reye's, knowing it was Saturday and that he was taking a chance that she might be working. He avoided going to their home. He and Stephen weren't dear friends, hadn't ever been. They came close to blows once, and Joe knew Stephen only tolerated him because he and Reye were friends. Because of that, he tried to keep his distance.

He had time. He'd just dropped off Shane at Taylor's. He and Shane would visit Meghan later. He'd called her as he'd told Shane he would and heard the excitement and hope in her voice when he'd asked if it was okay to bring Shane by.

He pulled up to Home Away From Home. Reye's truck was parked outside. He parked behind it and walked to the door, which stood open behind the screen door. He knocked and went in.

"Reye," he called out. No answer. He heard banging from the back so he walked in the direction of the sound, the kitchen. No Reye. Only Stephen's legs extended outward, upper torso under the sink. Joe squatted down next to him and hit him on his legs to get his attention.

Stephen slid out and pulled the earphones from his ears. He looked at Joe.

"It's just me here, dude," he said.

"What are you working on?" Joe asked.

"Reye did something to the drain. Was trying to repair it before she could," he said and smiled.

"She didn't think you could repair it, huh?" Joe said, and laughed. Stephen chuckled. Reye was a good handywoman.

"How's Shane?"

"Fine," he said. "Reye told you that my sister's back?"

"Yep," Stephen said, standing up, walking to the refrigerator. "Want a beer?"

"Sure," Joe said, standing, accepting a beer from Stephen.

"Had to bring my own. Been here most of the day, working on Reye's to-do list," Stephen said.

Joe nodded.

"So how's the sister thing working?" Stephen asked, resting his back against the refrigerator door.

"I'm taking Shane over for a visit this evening. First time he's seen her since she left."

Stephen nodded and took a swig of his beer.

"How's that woman you're seeing? Piper, right?"

"Piper it is, although I haven't seen her in a while."

Stephen nodded.

"So, you and Reye, the right decision for you?" Joe asked.

"Absolutely."

"You didn't always know that."

"You're right, but I found out in enough time not to completely blow it."

"Is there a message in there?" Joe asked.

"Only if you want there to be."

"I like her, may even love her, but I'm not sure it would last. If I would last. If I'm capable. It's not her that I doubt."

Stephen was silent and Joe continued. "I found out my mother is sober. She wasn't the last time I saw her," he said, eyes on Stephen. "I've only seen one, maybe two marriages worth anything. My foster family's, and yours. I don't know if I could, but if I've got a shot with anyone, it's with her."

Stephen remained quiet at that declaration.

"So what do you think?" Joe asked.

"It's your call. Talk to her. Let her know how you feel, see what follows. That's all the advice I can give," he said. They were both quiet as they finished off their beers.

"It would be nice, though, for me," Stephen said, and Joe looked up, eyes questioning.

"Now that you love someone, you'll leave Reye alone."

"I was never your competition," Joe said.

"I know that. I wasn't sure you always did," Stephen said, and smiled. Joe laughed, and set his empty bottle on the counter.

"Tell Reye hello for me," he said, reaching to shake Stephen's hand.

"I will," Stephen said, watching as Joe left through the front door.

"So, dude. I called your mother this morning and she would like to see you today. You still up for it?" Joe asked, looking at Shane, who sat in the passenger seat. Joe had just picked him up from Taylor's.

"Been ready, born ready, stay ready," he said, smiling.

"Well then, here goes," he said and smiled back.

Joe parked in the drive and he and Shane made their way to the front door. It opened before they had a chance to knock. Meghan stood there, not sure what to do, and Shane walked to her and hugged her.

"Hey, Mom," he said, holding on tightly to her waist.

"Hey, Shane," she said, her arms going around his shoulders, pulling him in tightly to her. Aaron stood behind her, looking at them and then moving on to Joe. He smiled.

"Hey, I made some cookies, want to try a few?" she asked, looking down into her son's face. Both of them were suddenly a little teary.

"Sure."

"Come with me," she said, and she and Shane walked toward the back of the house where the kitchen was located.

"Want to give them some time to themselves?" Aaron asked.

"That works," Joe responded, and followed Aaron into the family room. It was quiet in here.

"I didn't have much of an opportunity to talk to you the first time you were here," Aaron said, taking a seat on the couch.

"No, you didn't," Joe said, taking a seat next to him. "I believe Meghan said you were a preacher."

"That's right. Been one for the last five years. I'm fifteen years sober. Grew up here. My family was poor, but Dad worked hard and we were fed. I always had the penchant for pushing the envelope. What would happen if? Funny trait to have as a kid, not so much as an adult," he said, chuckling. "I always wanted stuff, and didn't want to work that long road for it, either. I didn't want my dad's life; he played by the rules and had nothing to show for it. I wanted it quick. So I went into outdoor pharmaceutical sales. Drugs, on the corner. Life didn't work out quite like I planned. I started using, was lost for many years, until I reached a point where it was death on one side or surrender on the other. I chose to surrender. There were dark days in there, too. Anyway, found the ministry a useful place for a sinner, trying to show the God I'd found to others," he said, lost in thought for a second. "I met your sister. We became friends and then more later."

"How long have you been married?" Joe asked.

"Almost a year," Aaron answered.

"Your sister is an amazing woman," he said, sitting back, a smile on his face. "She is loving, kind, compassionate, and an unlikely match for me. But we've visited the same places. She understands my need to counsel, to preach, to help, and I get her hurt, her guilt at not being able to fix her family, her guilt for hurting you, her need to be loved. We all have that."

"She was always this sweet kid. She looked up to me, followed me around all the time," he said, smiling at the memory. "A nuisance, she was."

Aaron waited until Joe's eyes returned to his. "Got to let go of all that anger or it'll kill you. It'll keep the light of what God has promised for you from coming in. Trust me, I speak from experience," he added. Neither spoke for a while.

"On a less serious note, thanks for bringing Shane over. It means the world to Meghan, and she meant what she said. She wants to prove that she can be a good mother. Prove it to herself, to Shane, and to you. She loves and admires you. Talked about all you'd done for her, wanted to move here to be near you."

Joe looked up, surprised.

"Hey, you two," Meghan said, interrupting them. "We were looking for you. Come on in to the kitchen and eat some of my homemade cookies." A smiling Shane stood next to her.

"I was telling Shane about the cookies you tried to make. Remember, Joe?" she said, and he looked up.

"I do," he said, smiling at that long-forgotten memory.

"They were awful. Shane, your uncle was an awful cook," Meghan said, smiling.

"What? He still is," Shane said.

"What!" Joe said, standing, along with Aaron, and following Meghan and Shane into the kitchen. The four of them spent another hour or two talking and getting to know each other, remembering some of the good times Joe and Meghan had shared together growing up. When it was time to leave, Meghan and Aaron walked them to the door. Aaron and Shane walked through first, leaving Joe and his sister alone.

"Thanks, Joe, for bringing him. You don't know how much it means to me, how much you mean to me," Meghan said. "I missed you, having you in my corner. I didn't call you during rehab because I didn't want to disappoint you again. I needed to prove to myself that I could do this."

"Aaron seems like a really nice guy," Joe said.

"He is. Wants to be a father someday," she said, looking up at him. "How about you, Joe? What do you want?"

He shrugged.

"Piper is a great woman. She loves you."

"Marriage working for you?" he asked, his favorite question nowadays.

"It is. I know it's not for everyone, and not everyone wants it, but Aaron loves me within an inch of my life. It's so comforting to know someone has your back."

"So maybe you and me could work this out. Start out slow, see how things play out with Shane? Let the court stuff alone for a while. Just see if we can figure it out ourselves," he said.

"I'd like to try," she said.

"Me, too," he said, and she moved close to him, her arms going around his waist, her head in his chest. He hugged her back, a part of him easing a little, relaxing.

"One more thing," she said.

"What?"

"I think you should consider going to see Mom."

"Maybe," he said, and laughed when she squeezed him. She'd done that when she was younger, too. He laughed, and so did she, both remembering.

———

"I'm going to talk to her," Reye said when Stephen's eyes opened later on that night. He turned to look at the clock. It was midnight.

"What are you doing up?" he asked, stretching his arms over his head, running his hand through his hair.

"Thinking about the conversation you had with Joe. I'm going by Lights Out tomorrow to talk to her."

"Think that's a good idea?"

"If I leave it up to him, Joe might not ever get married. He loves her. He's just too stubborn and too scared to try," she said, laying on her stomach now, her head resting on her arms, looking at Stephen, remembering when they almost hadn't worked out.

"I don't want him to ruin the one good thing besides Shane he has in his life. I owe him that, for almost punching you, for supporting me, for being a good guy, being a friend. God knows if women leave it up to you guys, you'll fuck it up," she said.

"Is that so?" Stephen said, pushing her over onto her back, his hands at her breasts as his leg parted hers.

"Fuck it up, huh?" he said, kissing her neck. "I like fucking it up." She laughed, but closed her eyes and let his hands work their magic.

———

Reye walked up to the counter, taking stock of Piper. It was nice to find another woman almost her height.

"Hi. Welcome to Lights Out Coffee. What can I get for you this morning?" Piper asked, a smile on her face.

"I'll have a white chocolate mocha."

"Sure," she said, pulling out a cup from her stack, writing the name of Reye's drink on it.

"Do you have time to talk?" Reye asked.

"Me?" Piper asked, surprised at this request, looking over the woman who she didn't know standing before her.

"My name is Reye Stuart. I've known Joe and Shane for a while, and wanted to talk to you about them. I'm hoping I could help, maybe offer some insights into Joe," she said.

That had Piper's attention. "Let me finish with the customers here and I'll join you in a minute."

"Thanks," Reye said, moving down to wait for her drink. Piper worked through the customers in her line, glancing often at Reye as she waited for her drink order and then moved to the booth near the front window.

"Estelle, can you handle the counter for a minute?"

"I've got it. Go on," Estelle said.

Piper grabbed a juice from the refrigerator in the kitchen and went over to join Reye.

"I know this is strange. You don't know me, but I felt like I needed to speak to you on Joe's behalf. He's a really good guy," Reye said, getting to the point.

"Okay," she said.

"Joe and my husband belonged to the same soccer team and the same fraternity. They played intramurals throughout the university. Anyway, he didn't like me at first, and went out of his way to let me know that. It was mutual. I worked at the East River Community Center while completing my degree in education. I wanted to be a teacher. That's how I met Shane."

Piper nodded, listening.

"Shane was this quiet, shy kid who was struggling in school. I'd struggled in school, too, so I felt a kinship. I was always united with the underdogs, the overlooked. Anyway, to make a long story short, I found out that Joe was Shane's uncle. The same Joe I didn't much care for. I found out that his mother, Joe's sister, had alcohol problems. I'd never met her, but Joe was in school at the time, and he rearranged his life to accommodate Shane. And that was enough for me. We joined forces to make sure Shane stayed on track, and he has blossomed into this great, confident kid. Joe was responsible for that, and he became my ally when I was having trouble with Stephen, my husband," she said.

Piper was quiet, listening.

"I'm telling you this to say that Joe was once a very angry young man. His past, I imagine, wasn't the best. He's never talked about it with me, even after we became good friends. He took care of Shane, took him in, finished school, and did what was necessary to see that Shane had a good start. He's a good guy. Give him time to work through whatever he has to work through. I know it's none of my business, but I don't think he ever had much support in his life, not from what I've seen. I know he appreciates that about you, the sense that you are committed to family as much as he is.

"I'm happy he's met you," Reye continued, staring at Piper. "He's a rare one, Joe. So much so that I felt compelled to come by to encourage you. I didn't want him to run you off."

"Thank you," Piper said. "I have no idea what he's struggling with most times, and he hasn't talked to me about it, not with what's inside," she said, looking off, tears quickly forming in her eyes. "I can't help if he won't talk to me."

"Yeah, you can. You can be there for him in the way he is for those he cares about. Give him some time," she said, reaching for Piper's hand.

"It doesn't seem like I'm going to be able to let him go yet. Couldn't if I wanted to. You know how that is, I bet."

"I do."

"Thanks for coming to talk. It helps."

"You're welcome. My home is not far from here. Here's a card. My cell number's on there, too, in case you ever need to talk. Men can be tough customers, so I understand the need to vent," she said with a smile.

Piper smiled back and squeezed her hand.

Chapter 21

Joe sat, looking at Lights Out. It was almost two months since he'd talked to Piper. He, Shane, and Meghan had been busy. A lot had happened since that dinner with Piper. They were talking. It was easier now. They had talked a lot, covered a lot of ground from the old days to now. There had been a lot of ground to cover. He was going to talk to his mom. Meghan, like a dog with a bone, pushed him to do this, to talk to her, to forgive her, said that it would do more for him than he knew.

So he was leaving for Dallas as soon as he'd finished talking to Piper. That is, if she still wanted to talk to him. Joe walked up to the doors of Lights Out Coffee. He could see her standing at the counter, talking, smiling. He missed her. He entered. It wasn't crowded this morning. He saw Estelle blending drinks and Piper next to her, her smile in place, back to teasing her customers. He walked to stand in front of her.

"Hey," he said. He felt a relaxation not just of his body, but of his inner self, when he saw her. He could tell he'd caught her by surprise.

"Hi," she said, her smile falling away.

"Can I talk to you for a second, privately?" he asked.

"Why should I?" she asked, and heard Estelle grunt. She sighed, rolled her eyes, and changed her response. "Sure," she said, looking over at Estelle, who smiled. "You okay alone for a while?"

"Please," Estelle replied, one hand on her hip.

"In my office?" she turned back to Joe, eyes not so friendly anymore.

He followed her down the hall, taking in the sway of her hips. I missed her, he thought again.

She entered her office, walked over to the small couch in front of her desk, and took a seat. He sat down next to her.

"So," she said.

"I'm sorry," he said, getting to the heart of it, "for not calling, for not talking. It's been difficult. I wanted, needed, to sort some of it out alone."

She nodded.

"How have you been?" he asked.

"Fine."

It was quiet for a second between them as they looked over each other. Not much had changed with Joe. He still could warm her blood, and she still loved him.

"So," she said.

"So I've taken a couple of weeks off. Going to visit my mother."

"That's good. You never talk about her, but you don't talk about yourself much," she said. He was quiet at that.

"When are you leaving?"

"Now," he said.

"Where does she live?"

"Dallas. That's my home. I'd like to see her, then visit my foster father."

She nodded, not knowing what to say to that, either. She hadn't known about the foster family, not until that dinner.

"Shane's okay?"

"Yep. He's going to spend some time with his mother and Aaron."

"That's good, too. Glad it's working out for Shane and for you," she said.

It was quiet for a minute more.

"So," she said, looking down at her hands.

"So," he said, reaching for her hand. "I don't know what to do about us," he said, his eyes fixed on hers. "I've missed you. That I know. You mean a lot to me. I think I love you, and that's more than I've allowed myself to feel for anyone in a long while. I don't know what that means for me, though, if it's enough to commit to the long haul with you. And you want that, don't you? Marriage?"

She nodded.

"I don't want to hurt you," he said.

"It's okay," she said, stroking his hand, deciding to be honest, too. She knew she was taking a big chance. But she took those chances, and had with him from the beginning.

"I'm pretty tough. I've been making the best of things for a long time, so I'll be okay no matter whether you decide, to come back or not. I'm not going anywhere. I'll be here if you want to come back. But if you don't, then I can work with that, too."

He was quiet. He hadn't expected her to say that. He was now at a loss for words.

"I love you, Joe. You know that, right?" she said. He nodded. "Even if you don't decide to come back, that won't change, and I hope I'll find someone who will want to be here with me, to have a family with me. But I can't not love you. It wasn't a choice for me. It just is."

"Why?"

"Hell if I know," she said, laughing a little. "You're a tough nut to crack, that's for sure, and as guarded as they come…but you're also the best father a kid could have, the best man a woman could want. You can love, Joe, even though you're unaware of it, better than you think," she said, as he stared into her eyes, quiet. He looked down into his lap.

"Well, you better get going," she said, standing up, waiting until he caught her eyes and stood, too.

"Good luck in Dallas," she said.

He leaned forward and kissed her softly on her mouth.

"Thanks," he said, pulling back and leaving her office.

—⁓—

Joe didn't know what he'd expected, but it hadn't been this vibrant older woman, blonde hair tied back in a ribbon-wrapped ponytail, digging in the dirt in her back yard.

He'd gone to the front door, read the sign that said "Out in back" and walked around to find this woman, bent over, digging in the dirt.

"Mom," he said, surprised that that word had come from his mouth. It was one he hadn't used in too many years to count, a word he'd stopped using because he didn't believe she deserved it. In his youthful anger he had taken to calling her by her first name, Carol.

Where had that come from today? What was with this emotional stuff? He'd been in turmoil since Meghan reappeared, revisiting places he hadn't been in years. And now he stood here calling a woman he'd hadn't seen in a decade "Mom."

She looked up, stunned. She stood, not moving toward him, unsure. He could read that in her eyes, too.

"Joseph," she said. "Oh, my, I'd given up hope of ever seeing you again." She moved closer to him, removing her work gloves. "Look at you. You're such a handsome man. Oh, Joseph, thank you for coming. You've talked to your sister, another blessing." She looked around, took a breath, and clasped her hands tightly together, her attempt to calm herself.

"Do you have time to visit?" she asked.

"Yes," he said, and watched as she headed for the table on the patio.

"Please sit down. Let me get us something to drink. Are you hungry?" she asked, looking around.

She dotted her eye with a tissue from a box sitting on an iron hutch, mixed in with plants, books, and gardening tools. It matched the wrought iron table that sat in the middle of the patio.

"Have a seat, I'll be right back," she said.

He sat down in one of the chairs surrounding the table.

About five minutes later she returned with a tray, a pitcher of lemonade, and two glasses. She poured for them both, hands shaking a little as she handed a glass over to him.

"Your sister tells me that you have done a wonderful job with Shane. She is so grateful for you. We all are," she said, her eyes moving away from his and out toward her yard, which was filled with flowers. A chime rang as a breeze blew.

"I'm sorry," she said, turning back to face him. "Sorry for my part in making you responsible for us — your dad and me — responsible for our decisions," she said. He was quiet.

"It wasn't all bad. I do remember a few good times," he said, remembering what Aaron had said and deciding to let all that go, let the past stay in the past.

"Thank you," she said, tears running down her face. Joe reached for tissues and handed them to her. She laughed a little and wiped her eyes. "So Meghan tells me you have a girlfriend?" she asked and he smiled.

"If she will put up with me, I hope so," he said. Another decision made.

"She'll be lucky to have you."

"We'll see. I'll bring her by the next time I'm in town," he said.

"Oh, Joe, that would be wonderful."

"So you work out here much?" he asked. "It's beautiful."

"Yes, it's a new hobby of mine," she said, and they spent the next few hours talking, getting to know each other again, a small step in his resolution to move forward unencumbered by his past.

—⁂—

Joe walked away from the home where he'd spent the last few years of high school. He'd spent some time with his foster dad, helping both of his parents around their homes, talking giving way to laughter for both. He would come more often, and he hoped to bring Piper.

He thanked his foster father for providing him with a place that had given him a ray of hope that life could be different from its beginning. It had saved him in some ways. He walked over to his car, put it in gear, and drove away, heading back to Austin.

Maybe Piper was right from the beginning. You get what you get in life. You can make the most of it or not she'd told him, on more than one occasion. She had chosen to make the best of her life and so had he, in his own way. He now knew that he was capable of finding love and happiness.

Shane, Piper, Reye, Meghan, and maybe even his mother were now a part of his life. Should he waste this opportunity? Meghan had tried to reach out to him and he'd refused in his unwillingness to forgive. They were trying just like him, each in their own way. So, yes, he would forgive. He would let go of all that anger, accept the part of his earlier life that had shaped him; for good, as it turned out. He wanted to be happy. It was past time. He punched in Meghan's number.

"Hey, it's Joe. Just checking in on you and Shane," he said.

"He's fine. We are all fine," she said, and he listened as she shared the events of their days, of what they'd done together, and he could hear the thankfulness and love in her voice. He knew unequivocally that this was the right path for them.

"Mom told me you stopped by, stayed the week. Thank you, Joe," she said. "It means a lot to her; more than she or I could say."

"It means something to me, too," he said.

"So how long before you're home?" she asked.

"I'm on my way now, but I was going to stop by Piper's first," he said.

"It's about time," Meghan said, laughing

"I know. Finally. I know," he said, chuckling. And it was true. "I'll stop by tomorrow."

"We'll be here."

"Tell Shane hello for me, will you?"

"Of course I will. See you soon," she said.

—⁓—

He pulled into Piper's drive that night. It was late, almost eleven. He used his key to unlock the front door. The night light was on in the entry near the steps. He turned to disengage the alarm system and then reset it, pleased that she hadn't changed the code, taking it as a good sign. He paused and listened for signs that he'd awakened her.

He looked around at the clean clutter that was Piper Renee Knight and kicked off his shoes and started up the stairs, following the hall that led to her room. Another night light lit his way. The door was closed and he softly grabbed the door knob, turning it slowly, opening to find her on her side — t-shirt on, covers at her feet, arms stretched over her head, hair full and wild around her head.

He stood there for a second just taking her in, surprised at the stutter of his heart at seeing her again. He'd missed her more than he could say. His hands moved to his waist, and he grabbed the bottom of his t-shirt and pulled it over his head. Then he unbuttoned and unzipped his jeans and slid them from his body. His boxers were next. He crept softly to the bed and slipped into it, sliding over until his front aligned with her back, his arm going to her waist. He moved her hair away from her neck and kissed her there.

"Missed me, huh?" she whispered without turning around. She would know the feel of his body against hers anywhere.

"Sorry it's taken me so long to get here," he said.

"What took so long?"

"Wanted to make sure that this was where I wanted to be, that I could be here."

"And are you sure?"

"Yes," he said and sighed into her ear. "I went to see my mother, and then to the foster family that meant so much to me."

"Did that help?"

"Yes. I told you that we were raised by two parents who were alcoholics."

He was quiet as Renee lay on the pillow of his arm.

"They didn't start out that way. They were social drinkers, or that's what I thought. That's when I'd see them drinking. What did I know? My mother was good before then, took care of us until then, stayed at home with us, until my dad lost his job, and his area of expertise wasn't needed anymore. He had no transferable skills, and there were no more jobs, just lots of drinking. I had to learn to be the parent for both of them, for Meagan, and for me. At age ten, a kid shouldn't have to be an adult."

Renee took his hand and stroked it softly.

"I remember this one time, when I was eleven. Meagan had some program at school. My mom tried to drive us there. She drank more than I thought before we left and we got lost. We drove for hours before she stopped in some park. She went to sleep behind the wheel and remained that way, wouldn't wake up. Meagan went to sleep, but I couldn't. I stayed up most of the night, watching and scared. After she slept it off, she woke up, knew immediately where we were, and drove us home. I've never felt more helpless than I did that night."

Piper listened as he talked, all of his anger and resentment pouring out. Sometimes he was emotional but he'd continued to talk, telling her his life story. She'd allowed herself hope when she heard him enter, and now was so grateful to have him back, her love, sharing his hurts, a tough one for any man, but he trusted her with it, and she would not let him down.

"It's okay. Shane's going to be in the city. You can be in his life, and watch to make sure he's safe. Plus Aaron seems like a stable and good guy," she said.

"I know, but I've taken care of him it seems like forever. He's become my kid, too. Mine to protect against the world, like I wished someone had done for me," he said, his breath caught and he stopped talking for a minute.

"But she's changed, Meghan has. I can see that now, just as I have. I'm learning, not quite there yet, but learning to let go, to trust in others. Being with you and your crew and Shane were some of the happiest times for me—made the idea of home and family seem possible. I want that again, and I want it with you—a family, a partner," he said, moving her hair from her face as she turned to face him.

"I love you," he said, staring at her, the steel grey of his eyes intense, pleading a little, moisture present on his eyelashes.

"As well you should," she said, pushing him over onto his back, coming to sit on top of him. She watched him for a second, smiling, and bent down to kiss him, softly. "I love you, too, but you know that. I'm glad you came back because I've got something for you," she said, mischief in her eyes, before bending over the side of the bed and pulling out a large pink book.

"What's that?" he asked, lifting his head from the pillow to get a better look.

"You'll see." She bent over the bed once again, pulling out some pink rope this time. She'd picked them up at this place across town, along with some other goodies she planned on saving for later.

She set the book down on his chest. The correct page was already marked, and it fell open to the place she wanted.

"Put your hands in front, together," she said, demonstrating, hers arms bent at the elbow and touching from elbow to wrist. He followed her instructions and she began wrapping the rope according to the picture she saw before her, her head moving back and forth between the pages and his arms, her bottom lip caught between her teeth as she attempted to tie him according to the instructions. He held his arms in front of his chest, elbows together, wrists together just as she asked, watched her concentrating on her task.

He smiled. Coming back to her was so the right decision. His life, married to her, stretched out before him.

"I love you," he said again.

"I know," she said.

She reached for his hands, now tied to perfection, lifted them over his head, pulled them up to the top rung of her bed, and looped the cord around the top rod.

"Should we tie your feet, too, you think?" she asked him, serious in her question. He laughed again, it moving his chest up and down in turn moving her up and down. But he was laughing now, grey eyes filled with humor, staring back at her though lashes sprinkled with a few lingering tears. She laughed, too, happy that he was back with her.

She looked over at him, hands tied to the bed, wondering why she hadn't done this sooner. She took off her t-shirt and underwear and stood nude before him.

"Want the boots?" she asked. He gave her a wolfish grin, and she went into her closet. She came back out with pink, trimmed in rhinestone, leather boots on.

He barked out a laugh as she walked over to the bed. She joined in with his laughter until tears were present in both their eyes.

When their laughter had died down, she bent over and pulled out two additional ties, and proceeded to tie first one foot and then the other to the base of the bed, her hair covering her face as she intently bound his feet. When she was done, she looked up to find him still smiling, eyes dry and clear. He was wearing his I'm-game-for-this face.

She walked over to the bed and straddled him. She leaned over to kiss him softly, taking her time, moving up to kiss his nose and his eyes. "I love you," she said, serious now.

"I know," he said, staring back at her, serious as she'd ever seen him. "Thank you for hanging in there with me, for giving me space. I love you, Piper Renee Knight."

"Let's see if you still do after I've finished with you." She moved her mouth back to his for a kiss that was so potent, it elicited a groan from him. He started laughing again. She laughed as he pretended to try to break free. She knew he was faking, knew he wanted this. She moved her hips, rubbing over him before sliding downward taking him in to her body. She started to move, putting everything she owned into showing him that she loved him.

His eyes rolled back in his head a time or two, but he held on. Thirty minutes later, sated, used, he sighed as she collapsed on top of his body, her hair all over the place, both of them sucking in air.

"I'm going to pay you back for that," he said between breaths. "Just give me a couple of minutes." They laid still for a while, till their breathing slowed.

She released first one foot and then the other, and then leaned over, her arms outstretched, as she reached to untie his hands. She moved off the bed, removed her boots, and returned to her position back on top.

"You know what they say about payback, don't you?" she said, smiling down at him.

"No, what do they say?"

"I was hoping you could show me what a bitch she could be," she said before kissing him again. He growled, and taking her hands in his, flipped her over onto her back.

Laughter mixed in with sighs, a multitude of moans, and a few screams, but when it was over, they were right where they needed to be: in each other's arms.

About the Author

Ruthie Robinson resides in Austin, Texas with her husband and two teenage children. She holds a bachelor's degree in economics from Clark College and a master's degree in economics from the University of Texas in Austin (Go Longhorns!). She worked for more than a decade in the banking industry before turner her love of writing into a second career.

Ruthie enjoys being a mom, gardening, traveling, and reading.

2011 Mass Market Titles

January

From This Moment
Sean Young
ISBN-13: 978-1-58571-383-7
ISBN-10: 1-58571-383-X
$6.99

Nihon Nights
Trisha/Monica Haddad
ISBN-13: 978-1-58571-382-0
ISBN-10: 1-58571-382-1
$6.99

February

The Davis Years
Nicole Green
ISBN-13: 978-1-58571-390-5
ISBN-10: 1-58571-390-2
$6.99

Allegro
Adora Bennett
ISBN-13: 978-158571-391-2
ISBN-10: 1-58571-391-0
$6.99

March

Lies in Disguise
Bernice Layton
ISBN-13: 978-1-58571-392-9
ISBN-10: 1-58571-392-9
$6.99

Steady
Ruthie Robinson
ISBN-13: 978-1-58571-393-6
ISBN-10: 1-58571-393-7
$6.99

April

The Right Maneuver
LaShell Stratton-Childers
ISBN-13: 978-1-58571-394-3
ISBN-10: 1-58571-394-5
$6.99

Riding the Corporate Ladder
Keith Walker
ISBN-13: 978-1-58571-395-0
ISBN-10: 1-58571-395-3
$6.99

May

Separate Dreams
Joan Early
ISBN-13: 978-1-58571-434-6
ISBN-10: 1-58571-434-8
$6.99

I Take This Woman
Chamein Canton
ISBN-13: 978-1-58571-435-3
ISBN-10: 1-58571-435-6
$6.99

June

Inside Out
Grayson Cole
ISBN-13: 978-1-58571-437-7
ISBN-10: 1-58571-437-2
$6.99

344

2011 Mass Market Titles (continued)

July

The Other Side of the
Mountain
Janice Angelique
ISBN-13: 978-1-58571-442-1
ISBN-10: 1-58571-442-9
$6.99

Holding Her Breath
Nicole Green
ISBN-13: 978-1-58571-439-1
ISBN-10: 1-58571-439-9
$6.99

August

The Sea of Aaron
Kymberly Hunt
ISBN-13: 978-1-58571-440-7
ISBN-10: 1-58571-440-2
$6.99

The Finley Sisters' Oath of
Romance
Keith Thomas Walker
ISBN-13: 978-1-58571-441-4
ISBN-10: 1-58571-441-0
$6.99

September

Except on Sunday
Regena Bryant
ISBN-13: 978-1-58571-443-8
ISBN-10: 1-58571-443-7
$6.99

Light's Out
Ruthie Robinson
ISBN-13: 978-1-58571-445-2
ISBN-10: 1-58571-445-3
$6.99

October

The Heart Knows
Renee Wynn
ISBN-13: 978-1-58571-444-5
ISBN-10: 1-58571-444-5
$6.99

Best Friends; Better Lovers
Celya Bowers
ISBN-13: 978-1-58571-455-1
ISBN-10: 1-58571-455-0
$6.99

November

Caress
Grayson Cole
ISBN-13: 978-1-58571-454-4
ISBN-10: 1-58571-454-2
$6.99

A Love Built to Last
L. S. Childers
ISBN-13: 978-1-58571-448-3
ISBN-10: 1-58571-448-8
$6.99

December

Fractured
Wendy Byrne
ISBN-13: 978-1-58571-449-0
ISBN-10: 1-58571-449-6
$6.99

Everything in Between
Crystal Hubbard
ISBN-13: 978-1-58571-396-7
ISBN-10: 1-58571-396-1
$6.99

Other Genesis Press, Inc. Titles

Other Genesis Press, Inc. Titles (continued)

Other Genesis Press, Inc. Titles (continued)

Other Genesis Press, Inc. Titles (continued)

Other Genesis Press, Inc. Titles (continued)

Mae's Promise	Melody Walcott	$8.95
Magnolia Sunset	Giselle Carmichael	$8.95
Many Shades of Gray	Dyanne Davis	$6.99
Matters of Life and Death	Lesego Malepe, Ph.D.	$15.95
Meant to Be	Jeanne Sumerix	$8.95
Midnight Clear	Leslie Esdaile	$10.95
(Anthology)	Gwynne Forster	
	Carmen Green	
	Monica Jackson	
Midnight Magic	Gwynne Forster	$8.95
Midnight Peril	Vicki Andrews	$10.95
Misconceptions	Pamela Leigh Starr	$9.95
Mixed Reality	Chamein Canton	$6.99
Moments of Clarity	Michele Cameron	$6.99
Montgomery's Children	Richard Perry	$14.95
Mr. Fix-It	Crystal Hubbard	$6.99
My Buffalo Soldier	Barbara B.K. Reeves	$8.95
Naked Soul	Gwynne Forster	$8.95
Never Say Never	Michele Cameron	$6.99
Next to Last Chance	Louisa Dixon	$24.95
No Apologies	Seressia Glass	$8.95
No Commitment Required	Seressia Glass	$8.95
No Regrets	Mildred E. Riley	$8.95
Not His Type	Chamein Canton	$6.99
Not Quite Right	Tammy Williams	$6.99
Nowhere to Run	Gay G. Gunn	$10.95
O Bed! O Breakfast!	Rob Kuehnle	$14.95
Oak Bluffs	Joan Early	$6.99
Object of His Desire	A.C. Arthur	$8.95
Office Policy	A.C. Arthur	$9.95
Once in a Blue Moon	Dorianne Cole	$9.95
One Day at a Time	Bella McFarland	$8.95
One of These Days	Michele Sudler	$9.95
Outside Chance	Louisa Dixon	$24.95
Passion	T.T. Henderson	$10.95
Passion's Blood	Cherif Fortin	$22.95
Passion's Furies	AlTonya Washington	$6.99
Passion's Journey	Wanda Y. Thomas	$8.95
Past Promises	Jahmel West	$8.95
Path of Fire	T.T. Henderson	$8.95

Other Genesis Press, Inc. Titles (continued)

Other Genesis Press, Inc. Titles (continued)

Other Genesis Press, Inc. Titles (continued)

Things Forbidden	Maryam Diaab	$6.99
This Life Isn't Perfect Holla	Sandra Foy	$6.99
Three Doors Down	Michele Sudler	$6.99
Three Wishes	Seressia Glass	$8.95
Ties That Bind	Kathleen Suzanne	$8.95
Tiger Woods	Libby Hughes	$5.95
Time Is of the Essence	Angie Daniels	$9.95
Timeless Devotion	Bella McFarland	$9.95
Tomorrow's Promise	Leslie Esdaile	$8.95
Truly Inseparable	Wanda Y. Thomas	$8.95
Two Sides to Every Story	Dyanne Davis	$9.95
Unbeweavable	Katrina Spencer	$6.99
Unbreak My Heart	Dar Tomlinson	$8.95
Unclear and Present Danger	Michele Cameron	$6.99
Uncommon Prayer	Kenneth Swanson	$9.95
Unconditional	A.C. Arthur	$9.95
Unconditional Love	Alicia Wiggins	$8.95
Undying Love	Renee Alexis	$6.99
Until Death Do Us Part	Susan Paul	$8.95
Vows of Passion	Bella McFarland	$9.95
Waiting for Mr. Darcy	Chamein Canton	$6.99
Waiting in the Shadows	Michele Sudler	$6.99
Wayward Dreams	Gail McFarland	$6.99
Wedding Gown	Dyanne Davis	$8.95
What's Under Benjamin's Bed	Sandra Schaffer	$8.95
When a Man Loves a Woman	LaConnie Taylor-Jones	$6.99
When Dreams Float	Dorothy Elizabeth Love	$8.95
When I'm With You	LaConnie Taylor-Jones	$6.99
When Lightning Strikes	Michele Cameron	$6.99
Where I Want to Be	Maryam Diaab	$6.99
Whispers in the Night	Dorothy Elizabeth Love	$8.95
Whispers in the Sand	LaFlorya Gauthier	$10.95
Who's That Lady?	Andrea Jackson	$9.95
Wild Ravens	AlTonya Washington	$9.95
Yesterday Is Gone	Beverly Clark	$10.95
Yesterday's Dreams, Tomorrow's Promises	Reon Laudat	$8.95
Your Precious Love	Sinclair LeBeau	$8.95

Order Form

Mail to: Genesis Press, Inc.
P.O. Box 101
Columbus, MS 39703

Name _____
Address _____
City/State _____ Zip _____
Telephone _____ .

Ship to (if different from above)
Name _____
Address _____
City/State _____ Zip _____
Telephone _____

Credit Card Information
Credit Card # _____ ☐ Visa ☐ Mastercard
Expiration Date (mm/yy) _____ ☐ AmEx ☐ Discover

Qty.	Author	Title	Price	Total

Use this order form, or call 1-888-INDIGO-1	Total for books _____
	Shipping and handling: $5 first two books, $1 each additional book
	Total S & H _____
	Total amount enclosed _____
	Mississippi residents add 7% sales tax

Visit www.genesis-press.com for latest releases and excerpts.